The Esther Diamond Series:

LAURA RESNICK

ABRACADAVER

An Esther Diamond Novel

DAW BOOKS, INC.

DONALD A. WOLLHEIM, FOUNDER

375 Hudson Street, New York, NY 10014

ELIZABETH R. WOLLHEIM
SHEILA E. GILBERT
PUBLISHERS

www.dawbooks.com

First Printing, December 2014

1 2 3 4 5 6 7 8 9

This book is dedicated to the memory of my
grandmother,
Gertrude Diamond Resnick,
and to her mother, who came to America,
Esther Diamond

1

I don't have anything against the dead—not as long as they *stay* dead.

It's when they get reanimated that I become hostile. Also scared, creeped out, and nauseated, as well as violent if the occasion calls for it—which it usually does when you're being confronted by a frisky corpse.

In the normal course of events, obviously, the deceased *do* stay that way. But mystical Evil loves to mess with the mundane, and there are any number of dark forces that can make death less decisive than you'd think.

So when I got a phone call from an undertaker telling me that the departed had *departed*—as in, got out of the coffin and walked away—I didn't dismiss this news as drunken delusion or a dumb prank. I know that the unbelievable can happen because I've seen it with my own eyes.

Besides, John Chen wasn't a drunk or a prankster. He was a serious, credible person—as well as a graduate student at NYU pursuing a doctoral degree in biochemistry. So I didn't doubt his strange story when I heard it. John also worked part-time at his family's funeral home in Chinatown, which is how he came into contact with corpses, animated or otherwise.

I had met John via his side job, a temporary gig doing hair and make-up for *ABC*, an indie film set in his neighborhood and written, produced, and directed by his old school friend, Ted Yee. I had been cast as an insensitive uptown white girl whom the ABC (American Born Chinese) hero of the film dates for a while before realizing that his soul mate is actually a hardworking young woman who's lately immigrated from China.

Unfortunately, Ted Yee told me earlier today that he was calling a halt to the film. I mean that this was unfortunate for *me*, not for audiences who would now be spared the prospect of suffering through Ted's clumsy, cliché-ridden, low-budget melodrama. I'd had a difficult winter so far, and Ted's film was the only real work that had come my way since November. By "real work," I mean acting—that's my profession. When I'm not acting, I'm doing whatever work I can find that will pay the rent—which, even in a rent-controlled apartment like mine, is extortionate in New York City.

So to make ends meet after the Off-Broadway show I was in this past autumn finished its limited run around Thanksgiving, I had taken a job as Dreidel, Santa's singing-and-dancing Jewish elf, at Fenster & Co., the famous Manhattan department store that was probably destined to go bankrupt soon, what with mismanagement, truck hijackings, attempted murder, and the recent conjuring of a solstice demon that wanted to eat Manhattan. I have had more demeaning and humiliating jobs than being a retail elf, but not many.

After Christmas (and also after whole portions of Fenster's had been destroyed in confrontations between Good and Evil, as well as between criminals and the NYPD), I returned to my usual between-roles job of waiting tables at Bella Stella, a tourist trap and mob hangout in Little Italy. I liked my job there as a singing waitress, and the owner, Stella Butera, was a fair employer. But she was also allegedly laundering money for the Gambello crime family. So the cops raided the restaurant on New Year's Eve, closed the place down, and arrested a number of the people present—including me. (In my case, the charges were dropped. The other arrestees were now awaiting trial.)

After that fiasco, I was unemployed and couldn't find another job. I was down to my last few dollars in the world by the time I got cast in Ted Yee's low-budget Chinatown film, and I was *very* glad to have income and acting work again, even if the script was lame and the pay was modest.

But now that Ted had decided to quit the film and

shut down production, I was out of work once again and already worrying about how to pay my rent.

I knew that Ted was a dabbler, prone to embracing new artistic interests with great enthusiasm and then dropping them before long. So although I was disappointed by this turn of events, I wasn't exactly surprised. And to be fair, even a completely committed and disciplined writer/director/producer might well throw in the towel on this project, after everything that had happened.

Ted's first backer had died. So he found another backer—and that one died, too. Then he learned that his manipulative mother and controlling sister were responsible for those deaths, as well as for the nasty mishaps which had befallen other people involved in the film. In a nutshell, they were murderously meddling because they feared Ted's project would embarrass the family; and, in any case, filmmaking wasn't what they wanted Ted to do with his life. His sister Susan's obsession with preventing him from making *ABC* had even led her to attempt to murder an NYPD detective and try to shoot John Chen for helping Ted with the movie.

As a direct result of recently getting to know Ted's dreadful family, I made a solemn vow to be more patient with my own. They have their faults, God knows, but they don't inflict deadly curses on my colleagues. They are also safely distant from me, all residing in the Midwest, which makes patience a little easier.

But Ted, the poor fool, lived with his family—well, until now. Barely an hour ago, his sister had been arrested in the act of trying to murder John Chen in front of witnesses, so she seemed unlikely to return home for 20-to-life. And I had a feeling that Ted and his mother would soon be parting company, too. Lily Yee's mystical crimes couldn't be proven under the limitations of mundane law, but she had confessed them to Ted, and her inflicting such damage on his friends and colleagues in order to control his life seemed to be (understandably) the last straw for him.

Those dangerous and deadly curses were why I was in Chinatown now, making my way through the frigid, icy, and densely crowded streets while firecrackers exploded noisily and drumbeats echoed all around me. It was the first day of the Chinese New Year, the day of the firecracker festival and the lion dance. Having discovered that Ted's family members were responsible for the mysterious mayhem menacing Chinatown, I had come here today (in the company of my friend Max, an expert in such matters) to stop them—on what happened to be one of the most crowded days of the year in these narrow, bustling streets.

The rhythmic pounding of drums and cymbals were the traditional accompaniment to the colorful, athletic lion dancers who were still roaming the neighborhood, though it was late afternoon now. Each time I saw one of these creatures bobbing, bounding, and leaping around gracefully, it was easy to forget that the giant lion was a two-man puppet (one man was the head, and one was the body) rather than an enchanted four-legged beast. Each lion's massive, dragon-like head was decorated with fur, fringe, and sparkly designs, and they all batted their long eyelashes coquettishly at the various spectators and passersby.

Snow, ice, and slush covered the streets, along with confetti from the celebrations today. Hours into the festivities, people were still following the many roaming lion dancers around Chinatown, watching them engage in the ritual of collecting red envelopes of "lucky money" from shopkeepers in exchange for their dance, then "chewing" up fresh green heads of cabbage and "spitting" the mangled leaves onto people as a blessing, to ensure an abundant New Year.

We passed a cheerfully regurgitating red lion, and I brushed limp bits of cabbage out of my hair without slowing my pace, navigating my way through the thick crowd of laughing, smiling people. It was overcast now, the gunmetal-gray sky threatening to drop more sleet and snow on the city. The light faded quickly at this time of year, and I sensed darkness encroaching already.

"You missed some." Lucky, my companion, brushed at my wind-snarled brown hair to remove a few stray bits of leafy greens.

"Aren't your hands cold?" I asked, realizing for the first time that he wasn't wearing gloves.

"Freezing," he admitted.

"Here, I'll take Nelli." I was sensibly dressed for being outside in late January. But Alberto "Lucky Bastard" Battistuzzi had rushed out of the Chen family's funeral home on short notice today, after being alerted that John's life was in danger. "Give me the leash, Lucky."

The old hit man handed over the dog without protest and stuffed his hands into his pockets, shivering a little. Lucky had earned his nickname by surviving two separate attempts on his life because—both times—the gun that was pointed at him with deadly intent had jammed. (In fact, I had witnessed a third such incident the previous year, when a ruthless killer stuck a gun in Lucky's face, pulled the trigger—and nothing happened. He really *was* lucky.) A semi-retired hitter for the Gambello family, he was a valued advisor to the *capo di famiglia*, Victor Gambello, aka the Shy Don.

In the strange twists and turns of fate that so often characterize life, Lucky was also my trusted friend.

And in a relationship that originated with the previous generation, Lucky was a silent partner in the Chens' funeral business, as well as a close friend to the family. John called him "Uncle Lucky," and there was very little that the normally law-abiding Chens wouldn't do to protect him. Lucky, whose own relationship with the law was habitually adversarial, was equally loyal to them. So when I had phoned him earlier to warn him that John was in danger, he had risked his life and liberty without hesitation in a headlong rush to help save the young man.

He had also brought Nelli with him. A mystical canine familiar who had entered this dimension to confront Evil (with a capital E), Nelli had happened to be with Lucky when today's crisis arose, but she actually lived with our friend Dr. Maximillian Zadok. Now that John was safe, Lucky and I had left the scene, taking Nelli with us, and we were looking for Max.

A mage who worked for the Magnum Collegium, an ancient and secretive worldwide organization about which I knew virtually nothing (except that they were dangerously inept at vetting their own apprentices— but I digress), Max was the biggest expert on Evil in the tri-state area, and quite possibly in this whole hemisphere. While Lucky and I had dealt with the mundane evil of Susan Yee trying to shoot John on Doyers Street, Max was dismantling and disenchanting the secret workshop where Susan and her mother had concocted the curses they'd been inflicting on Ted's colleagues. It was located in the cellar of Yee & Sons Trading Company, the family business that Lily had long wanted her son to take over—and which Ted consistently said with fervent loathing he would *never* take over.

We reached Canal Street, and Nelli flinched mightily when a bright orange-gold lion suddenly leapt in front of us. Since Nelli was the size of a small pony, her involuntary yank on her leash jerked me off balance and I stumbled into Lucky.

He grunted as he caught me, then set me back on my feet as he said, "Maybe I should hang onto her, after all."

My gloved hand tightened around the pink leather leash. "No, I've got her." I gave a little tug and admonished Nelli to calm down.

She composed herself and wagged her tail hesitantly at the lion, which turned away from us and danced gracefully down the street, followed by clashing cymbals, pounding drums, and a crowd of spectators.

"Does she seem jumpy to you?" I asked Lucky, frowning down at Nelli's head—which came up to my solar plexus.

"Maybe." The old wiseguy shrugged. "Or maybe we're just feeling jumpy around her. After what happened back there . . ."

I knew he didn't mean John nearly getting shot. Or Susan's screaming violence when thwarted in her attempt to murder John. Or even the spectacle of the lion costume John had been wearing suddenly roaring fire at Susan when she pointed her gun at me—something I must remember to tell Max about later.

He was talking about what Nelli had done back there on Doyers Street. The reason we had left so suddenly. The reason we were looking for Max now.

As we waited on the corner for the light to change, I

contemplated our canine companion. "She only flinched when that lion startled her just now," I said quietly. "Like her usual self. She didn't snarl or attack."

"Of course not," said Lucky. "Our favorite familiar has got focus. There was a reason for what she done back there. Gotta be. We just don't know yet what it is."

The dangerous nature of Nelli's mission in this dimension meant she could be unpredictable—sometimes terrifyingly so. But she was essentially an affable, gentle dog, the sort who could safely be left alone with toddlers and kittens (though the kittens might bully her). So her sudden burst of aggression a little while ago had been as surprising as it was worrying.

It was that incident which had sent us tearing off to find Max. We didn't understand what had happened, but we had alarming suspicions about what it might signify.

Nelli shivered a little, and I realized she was cold. Her short fur wasn't sufficient protection at this time of year in New York, and she usually wore a winter vest when she came outside. (Actually, she had half a dozen seasonal vests. Max tended to spoil her.) Her massive head was long and square jawed, framed by two floppy, overlong ears. The fur on her paws and face was silky brown, and the rest of her well-muscled physique was covered by smooth, tan fur. Her eyes and face were very expressive (though, to be candid, they rarely expressed intelligence), and her mystical nature ensured she had some unusual abilities, as well as some unexpected vulnerabilities (such as an allergic reaction to vampires).

The dog shivered again, and I patted her head. "Poor Nelli. We'll be inside soon."

Yee & Sons Trading Company was less than two blocks away. I didn't relish returning to the store, given my various recent experiences there, but it was where I had left Max earlier today. Without any way to check his location now (he didn't have a cell phone), I figured that was the logical place to look for him, since it would probably take him some time to destroy and purify the workshop of such talented dark sorceresses as Lily and Susan.

As I continued petting Nelli, she wriggled a little, pleased with the attention, and then gave me a convivial head butt. As I staggered back a step, Lucky said, "See? She's actin' completely normal. Like it never happened."

That was a relief. We didn't have a maddened mystical familiar on our hands who outweighed me. Nonetheless . . . "I'm really worried," I said. "Scared. What if—"

"No, let's not spectorate," Lucky interrupted.

"I think you mean speculate," I said. Like a lot of wiseguys, he tended to mangle the language.

"This ain't our area of expertise, so we don't wanna run away with our imaginations. Let's wait until we tell Max what we saw, and we'll hear what he thinks."

I nodded and tried to push my fears out of my mind. *Lopez* . . .

I didn't really know what I thought Nelli's odd behavior today suggested. I just knew that, because of it, I was afraid that Lopez was in danger at this very moment. At *every* moment, in fact, until we knew what was going on.

Lopez was also, I suspected, thinking about breaking up with me again. His exasperated comments a little while ago had indicated as much.

The light on Canal Street changed, and I tromped across the slushy boulevard with Nelli, Lucky, and a gazillion other people while a chill wind whipped at my cheeks and hair.

We were going to have to talk (again) about last night. Lopez knew what I had done. I knew better than to hope he'd just drop the subject. And I certainly knew better than to hope he'd believe me the next time I explained that the *reason* I had broken into his car to steal his gourmet fortune cookie was because it contained a mystical curse that would cause his death as soon as the cookie was cracked. (Susan wanted Lopez dead because, as a favor to me, he was helping Ted with location permits for the film.) After stealing the deadly treat, I had taken it to Max to be neutralized.

No part of this explanation would be helped by the fact that my on-again, off-again boyfriend (mostly off-again) was a confirmed skeptic who clung resolutely to his steadfast belief in mundane phenomena and conventional explanations. (Well, to be fair, most people clung to that. I had clung to it, too, until it was no longer possible.)

He was also a detective in the New York Police Department's Organized Crime Control Bureau. Thanks to his job skills, he had easily found out who the culprit was last night after finding his car window smashed in and only one thing (his cookie) missing from the vehicle. Detective Connor Lopez was also not at all happy that the car in question belonged to the police department; I gathered that meant the smash-and-grab involved additional paperwork, thus augmenting his overall exasperation with having a patently insane almost-girlfriend.

But he didn't intend to turn me in for what I had done. That much was clear . . . and it was another reason that he was so conflicted about me.

Lopez was a straight-arrow cop and an honorable man, so he felt guilty and full of self-reproach every time he gave me a pass—and he'd given me a few by now. In fact, he'd completely violated his deepest principles a few times for my sake, and his tension over this—which I understood and regretted—was something else that came between us. In addition to, you know, his conviction that I was demented.

I wondered what it said about him that despite thinking I was nuts, he kept coming back.

I also wondered how to convince him I *wasn't* demented—or even unstable. *Could* I convince him? Just how rigid was his stubbornly conventional worldview? Would it alter, or at least loosen up a little, if he saw some of the things I'd seen since becoming friends with Max and discovering what a deeply weird place the universe really is?

In any case, yes, Lopez and I were going to have to talk about last night. And it wasn't going to go well.

Brooding about a man you're obsessed with can be so absorbing that I didn't hear the approaching siren until Lucky said, "Come on, let's not get run over. Pick up the pace."

He put a hand under my elbow and hustled me along. I glanced over my shoulder and saw a fire truck coming this way. We trotted the rest of the way to the sidewalk, along with all the other pedestrians crossing the broad width of Canal Street, then pushed our way through the throng there, eager to avoid the icy spray from passing wheels as the truck sped through the slushy streets. The vehicle slowed down when it reached our corner and honked loudly as it turned down the street. Since the noise was earsplitting, Lucky and I paused a few seconds to let the truck get ahead of us, then went in the same direction.

A moment later, we heard another fire truck screeching in the distance. It, too, turned down this street. We were half a block from the Yee family's store.

"Oh, Lucky," I said with dread, quickening my pace. "Do you think—"

"Don't jump to conclusions," he replied, also walking faster. "It's a holiday. Firecrackers. Smoke. Lions with flammable fringe." We rounded the next corner. "We got no reason to assume—*Whoa.*"

We stopped in our tracks and stared at Yee's Trading Company. The building where I had left Max earlier today was now engulfed in flames.

2

Smoke poured out of the windows of the century-old building which had housed Yee & Sons Trading Company for decades. Fire roared upward through the roof and out the front door. Emergency services were still arriving. As I stood there, my mouth hanging open, an ambulance and two squad cars pulled up, their sirens wailing and lights flashing.

And then, without conscious thought—certainly without anything resembling a decision—I dropped Nelli's leash and ran toward the burning building, screaming, "Max! *MAX!*"

A policewoman dived out of a squad car and threw herself bodily against me. The momentum knocked us both sideways, so that we staggered against another police car that had just pulled up.

"No! Stay back!" she shouted.

Nelli was barking, distressed by my screaming and this altercation. I heard Lucky shouting, but I had no idea what he was saying.

I fought the policewoman, wailing Max's name as I tried to get free of her grasp. Another cop joined her in restraining me.

"You have to get back, miss!" he shouted into my face. "*Stop!*"

I barely saw or heard the two people wrestling with me. All I could see was the burning building that had swallowed my cherished friend. "Max!"

"Esther! *Esther!*"

The familiar voice penetrated the panicky roaring in my ears.

Panting and still fighting the two cops, I called, "*Max?*"

"Esther, I'm here! I'm right here!"

I looked around—and when I saw Max trotting toward me, I sagged with relief. The cops were shouting stern instructions into my face, but I ignored them.

"Max!" I flung myself at him, squeezing him tightly and giving a sob of relief.

"It's all right, my dear. I'm fine." He returned my hug and patted my back. "Everyone is fine. No one was hurt."

"*God*, you scared me." I put a hand over my pounding heart as I stumbled back a couple of steps to get a good look at him.

A short, slightly plump man who looked about seventy (though his true age was well over three centuries), Max had innocent blue eyes, fair skin, a neatly trimmed white beard, and slightly long white hair. He was usually tidily dressed, but he'd obviously had a narrow escape from the fire. From head to toe, Max was smeared with soot and ash. His elegant calf-length Russian coat would never recover from this incident, and his hat was singed and stank of burned fur.

"Thank God you got out okay!" Lucky, who was holding Nelli's leash now, put a hand on Max's shoulder and gave it an affectionate squeeze. *"Grazie a Dio!"*

"We all got out." As the police loudly urged us to step behind the barricade they were erecting, Max gestured over his shoulder. I looked across the narrow street, and I saw that Lily and Ted were both there, alive and well, though as smudged as Max. After a moment, Max added quietly, *"Grazie a Dio."*

Standing behind the police barricade now, I watched Ted and Lily arguing on the other side of the street. Two police officers approached them. I could tell from their gestures that the cops were urging them to get farther away from the burning building. Ted and Lily were too engrossed in their argument to pay any attention. The rest of the street was being evacuated, and the police were taking control of the scene quickly, despite the crowds and the chaos.

Between the festival, this fire, and Susan's attempt to kill John, this precinct was having quite a busy day.

I turned my gaze to the burning building, recalling the abundance of retail stock inside the confusing maze of the Yee family's store. There had been some lovely objects and art in there, as well as some mind-bogglingly expensive furniture and antiques. I mostly had negative memories of the place, but it seemed like a sad loss, even so.

Watching the building burn, I asked, "Max, what happened?"

He started to speak, coughed a little, and pulled a bottle of water out of his pocket. I supposed that first responders had given it to him right before we arrived. He took a few sips, then cleared his throat and began explaining.

"Lily and I went down to the cellar to destroy the workshop where she and her daughter made those curse-carrying fortune cookies." Max's English was excellent, but it was not his native language. He had a slight, elegant foreign accent, reflecting his origins in Central Europe centuries ago. "Lily asked Ted to stay upstairs and mind the store, but he followed us down to the cellar, full of questions, accusations, and recriminations. I do not think he can forgive his mother or sister for any of this."

"Go figure," I said.

Lily had inflicted bad luck, illness, and injuries on

Ted's associates, but she had not planned to kill anyone. Susan was the one who had raised the stakes by adding murder to the mix. And Lily, who had taught her dark secrets to her talented daughter, soon realized that she couldn't control her. But the two women didn't fall out until Susan decided to kill John Chen.

Lily had not prevented the other murders—nor the attempt on Lopez's life only yesterday—but she had drawn the line at letting Susan kill a fine young man who was a longtime family friend. Lily had destroyed the cursed cookie Susan was preparing for John, which was why Susan—by now reckless in her homicidal obsession—had resorted to the more mundane method of simply trying to shoot him. She got the gun from a local thug named Danny Teng, who had been loosely connected with *ABC*.

I shuddered when I thought of Danny, who'd been hanging around the film set lately, bullying Ted, eyeing me with lip-smacking lust, and making lewd comments. There was at least one benefit to production shutting down and costing me my job: I'd never have to see that dangerous creep again.

Max continued, "But although Susan had run mad, her intelligence did not desert her. She suspected Lily might have an attack of conscience and try to destroy the workshop."

"So she booby-trapped it?" Lucky guessed.

"Precisely." Max removed his singed hat and examined it with regret. "A mystical booby trap. Susan didn't have the necessary time or skill to conjure wards that could withstand an assault from her mother, who possesses power similar to her own. Instead, she tried to make the consequences of destroying the workshop too dangerous to risk."

He dropped his ruined hat into the ankle-deep slush at our feet and gazed up at the burning building. "It was quickly apparent to me there would be a cost for obliterating her dark ritual space. But I underestimated how destructive Susan could be. Even knowing about the murders, I still didn't anticipate that she was prepared to destroy her home and her late father's legacy—the shop has been in the Yee family for many years." Max shook his head. "So I proceeded. And by the time I realized the full extent of the danger, it was too late. The whole building burst into flames. As you see."

"You and Lily and Ted were lucky to get out alive," I said, feeling my chest constrict as I realized how close Max had come to death. He often said that fire was the weakest element of his power. His ability to shield himself and the Yees from that conflagration long enough for them to escape with their lives had probably been precarious.

Thinking of fire made me think of Lopez again. He'd been present during Susan's mad murder attempt today. I recalled the way that unexplained flames had suddenly poured from the mouth of John's lion costume (he was one of the athletic dancers who roamed the streets during the festival), blazing at Susan the moment after she turned her gun on *me* . . . I felt sure Lopez had done that, though he didn't know it.

"We were very lucky indeed," Max said, glancing to where Ted and Lily stood. "I shall not be taking any of life's pleasures for granted for some time to come, I assure you."

I watched the flames rise from the building and recalled other incendiary incidents involving Lopez, before today's fire-spewing lion costume had probably saved my life by distracting Susan.

When Lopez was trapped in an underground tunnel with a serial killer who was about to slay again, there was a sudden, fiery explosion that killed the murderer while leaving Lopez and the other people present (including me) unharmed. When a villain had tried to escape from Lopez by holding a gun to my head, he'd been foiled by a shower of fiery sparks that rained down on him from light fixtures on the ceiling. On an occasion when Lopez and I were having a particularly volatile evening, my bed had burst into flames—while we were on it together. And during a Vodou ritual last summer, he had been involuntarily possessed by a fire spirit. Lopez remembered nothing about that trance, during which he had played with flames and hot coals without incurring any injury (though I assumed he'd had to throw away the trousers he'd been wearing that night, which were not nearly as impervious to fire damage as his own flesh was).

When I had realized earlier today what Susan intended to do to John, I'd called in the cavalry—that is, I'd phoned Lopez, who arrived within minutes, accompanied by a reassuring number of police officers, to help stop her. And then an unexplained burst of fire saved my life at a moment when Lopez was scared to death for me—as he subsequently told me with more crankiness than affection.

Given the pattern that seemed so apparent to me, I didn't understand how Lopez could fail to realize—or at least start to suspect—that *he* was the common denominator in these fiery incidents. But Max, who hypothesized that he was exhibiting some form of pyrokinesis, didn't consider his obliviousness surprising.

If this was an ability Lopez had possessed since birth or early childhood, Max had told me, then the unconscious processes that created these events might feel so normal to him as to be unnoticeable. And since the incidents seemed to occur only in moments of extreme stress, then they might be too irregular for Lopez to perceive a pattern, let alone identify himself as the source of that pattern.

In other words, I shouldn't be puzzled by his obtuseness. Anyone as stubbornly prosaic as Lopez was bound to be dense about this sort of esoteric phenomenon.

And it wasn't a subject I could picture myself raising with him. Well, not unless our pending conversation about the misfortune cookie that I'd stolen from his car last night went a whole lot better than I was expecting it to go.

As I watched the Yee family's store burn, I wondered if anyone else in Lopez's life—anyone besides me and Max—had ever suspected that he possessed mystical power of which he was unaware.

"It looks like the building will have to be gutted," I murmured. "They won't be able to save anything, the way the fire is consuming the place."

"It had a fierce beginning," Max said, "and it spread with terrifying rapidity."

"But despite the brushes with death on this one, I guess it's all come out good, huh?" said Lucky. "Not even someone as smart as the Gambello family's lawyer could get Susan off the hook after what she did today. Attempted murder right in front of a bunch of cops? *Stupid* don't even begin to cover it." He shook his head at the unprofessional sloppiness of that.

"Susan has been taken into custody?" Max asked.

"Yes. And she seemed completely demented while they were arresting her," I said. "Max, do you think she's got the ability to free herself from behind bars?"

He shook his head. "Only if she's in a facility foolish enough to let her set up a private laboratory and have access to many unusual ingredients. I've seen no evidence that she's able to exercise power in other ways."

"Well, that's a relief. I want her to stay in prison." After all, besides Lopez, she had tried to kill me and John, too.

Lucky said, "And what with this whole building burning down, the evil mother can't get any second thoughts about rebuilding that basement workshop to do some more dark magic."

"True," Max said pensively, his gaze drifting toward Lily for a moment.

With her daughter in prison, her business destroyed, and her son presumably planning to distance himself from her, there might not be anything left in her life that Lily cared about enough to go to such lengths again.

Max had told me before that Evil often consumed itself with its own voracious appetite. Looking at Lily, I realized once again that he was right about that.

Assuming a deliberately more upbeat tone, Max noted, "Fortunately, despite inconvenience to the neighbors, no one in the area appears to have been injured due to this conflagration."

"And it looks like the fire department is managing to prevent it from spreading," I added, watching them work and impressed by their efficiency. "So I don't think anyone besides the Yees will lose any property, either."

I looked at Ted and his mother again. They were now being examined by paramedics—and still arguing. Lily looked sullen and tragic—and still beautiful. Ted looked furious—which wasn't surprising, though it was unusual. He was normally a very affable guy, though feckless, incompetent, and unreliable.

"I feel sorry for Ted, though," I said. "He's done nothing wrong, and he didn't know his mother and sister were doing wrong. Yet he's lost everything. Even the store. I know he didn't care about it, but it was also his home—and it must have been worth some money."

"It's bound to be insured," said Lucky. "So unless someone can prove this fire was caused by mystical arson—"

"Unlikely," Max said. "They will look for mundane causes and will never find any."

"Then there's probably gonna be a nice payout," Lucky said to me. "If he's got any brains at all, the kid will talk his mom into splitting it with him."

"Well, after what she did, he's certainly got the guilt leverage for that." And I thought that walking away from his toxic family and their past with a wad of money in his pocket, free to live on his own terms and forced to become self-reliant, might be a very positive outcome for Ted Yee.

At any rate, it was certainly a positive outcome for

anyone else involved in this whole fiasco whom his mother and sister would have willfully cursed with misfortune or death in order to sabotage Ted's ambitions.

A shiver passed through me as I again recalled finding that deadly cookie in Lopez's police car. He could have died at any moment. The second that fragile cookie began to crumble, he'd have been doomed . . .

I fervently hoped that Susan Yee would spend decades behind bars.

And I realized something as I watched her home burn in the wake of her mystical booby trap. "Lily and Ted don't know about Susan's arrest."

"The cops'll catch up to events soon and tell 'em," said Lucky.

"Yes, I guess you're right." I suspected they'd both be relieved by the news, though probably for different reasons. And since I wasn't eager to speak to the Yee family ever again, I was content to leave it up to the NYPD to tell them what had happened.

The NYPD . . .

I glanced at Nelli and recalled that there were pressing matters I needed to discuss with Max. But looking at him now, I realized this wasn't a good moment for that. He had just survived a deadly inferno after performing mystical tasks that were probably exhausting.

I said to Lucky, "We should take Max home. He needs a shower, a hot meal, and some rest."

"Oh, that sounds wonderful," Max said on a sigh.

I looked around at the scene, wondering if he'd get in trouble for leaving it without making a statement to the authorities. But no one was paying attention to us—and I thought that Lily and Ted were unlikely to mention Max to anyone as a witness, let alone explain his involvement. It was in their best interests to stick with a simple and mundane story about today's events; the building suddenly caught fire, they didn't know how or why, and it had spread fast.

I took Max's arm and we turned away from the blazing remains of Yee & Sons Trading Company. Followed by Lucky and Nelli, we headed back toward Canal Street. We could probably hail a cab there, despite how crowded it was around here today . . . but could we find a taxi that would let Nelli come with us? She was an inconveniently *large* animal.

I remembered that Max had recently found a pet transport service that he used when going places with Nelli that weren't within walking distance of his home in Greenwich Village. I was about to ask him for the phone number, or at least the name, when my cell phone rang, startling me.

As a cruelly cold wind swept down the street, I pulled off a glove and reached into my pocket, clumsily answering the phone without bothering to see who the caller was.

"Esther Diamond," I said wearily, realizing how

ready I was to get out of the cold. It had been a long, busy, and very fraught day—and now darkness was descending.

"Hi, it's me." In response to my blank silence, the caller added, "John."

"Oh! John." I smiled for a moment, then asked with concern, "How are you feeling?"

"Pretty freaked out."

"Well, yeah," I said sympathetically. "I can only imagine. It *must* be freaky to see someone you've known your whole life suddenly point a gun at you with murder in her eyes."

"It's John?" Lucky asked me. "How is he?"

"Freaked out," I said, putting my hand over the phone for a moment. "See if you can find a cab that'll take us."

Lucky grunted skeptically but started looking around.

"Oh . . . yeah, I guess I'm still pretty freaked out about Susan," John said, sounding distracted. "I don't even know why she was trying to kill me. Some cop was just here asking—"

"Cop?" I repeated alertly. "What cop?"

"—and, well, I don't think he believed me when I said I have no idea *why*. Except that she seemed pretty crazy all of a sudden."

"Was it Lopez?" I asked. "The detective I was talking to at the scene?"

Hearing that name, Lucky grumbled, "What's Wonder Boy up to now?"

He was a little irritated with Lopez, who'd broken open a big case against the Gambello crime family a few weeks ago and was keeping busy lately by arresting a bunch of Lucky's associates.

"I mean, *really* crazy," said John. "Susan was like a rabid animal or something today . . ." I could hear him draw in a sharp breath as a new thought occurred to him. "I wonder if Ted's all right? I mean . . . do we know if Susan targeted anyone else?"

That was a complicated subject, so I settled for saying that Ted was unhurt, and Susan hadn't shot at anyone else. I started to tell John about the fire that was consuming the store, but before I uttered more than a syllable, he interrupted me to say that he hadn't called to talk about Susan or Ted.

"No?" I said absently, pointing out an approaching cab to Lucky while deciding how to phrase the news about the fire.

"*Oh*," John said. "No, I'm sorry, I didn't call about that, either, Esther. Not right now."

Lucky tried to wave down the cab, but it roared right past us. Perhaps the driver had noticed our soot-covered friend and our pony-sized dog.

"What's not right now?" I asked.

"Our date."

I blinked. "Huh?"

"I mean, I *am* going to ask you out. Obviously. Like we talked about today."

We did? I blinked again. I had no memory of talking about it.

He continued, "Just not right now . . . Well, unless you *want* it to be right now?"

"Um . . ." I frowned, caught off guard.

John was asking me out on a date? And he thought we had talked about this?

I tried to remember what he'd said to me in the chaos after Susan was arrested. Something about thanking me, calling me, dinner . . .

Oh.

I realized, not for the first time, that I can be such an idiot sometimes.

I liked John. A lot, in fact. But I hadn't realized until just now, when John baldly used the word "date," that he had been showing interest in me—*that* kind of interest.

John was subtle and courteous about it (which was the kind of man he was), and that was one of the reasons I'd been oblivious until this moment.

But the main reason I hadn't noticed John flirting with me—which I now realized he had been doing lately—was because I was obsessed with Lopez. Or at least very preoccupied with him. And we were dating again. Or trying to date, anyhow . . . unless, after last night's smash-and-grab, we were already in another off-again phase? Either way, I was involved with him. Well, kind of involved. We had a relationship, anyhow, though we weren't *in* a relationship. Not yet, really. Or maybe we were, but we didn't—

Okay, stop.

I let my breath out in a rush and gave myself a mental kick. This was not the time to try to find the right word for whatever was between me and Lopez. So far, we had *never* found the right word for it, and it certainly wasn't going to happen now, standing in ankle-deep slush on a noisy street corner in Chinatown while Max and Lucky both looked at me with concern, no doubt wondering what John was saying that was making me go all tense and fidgety.

On my phone, John said, "I mean, I want to ask you out later, when my head is clear, instead of right now when I'm so freaked out."

Oh, no, I thought uncomfortably. John wanted to go out with me. What was I going to do? What should I say to him?

I'd had no problem recently turning down Danny Teng (multiple times), because he was a sleazy thug who made my skin crawl. But I hated the thought of rejecting John, who I really liked.

I was unprepared. How had I not seen this coming?

Come on, don't beat yourself up. There's been a lot of Evil and fear and deadly cookies ever since you met John. And you've been working long hours, too.

Plus, things had been so volatile with Lopez lately.

Oh, when are things not *volatile with him?*

"Esther," John prodded. "Is that okay?"

I really needed to focus here.

"Is John okay?" Lucky asked.

"I don't know," I replied.

"What's going on?" Lucky demanded.

"I'm sorry, I know I'm babbling," John said. "And not making much sense."

"No, it's okay," I said vaguely. "You're fine."

"Is something wrong?" Lucky asked, worried about his honorary nephew, who'd had a close brush with death today.

"Would you just look for a cab?" I said.

"A cab?" John repeated blankly.

"Not you," I said. "John, what's going on? Why did you call?"

He took a breath. "I really need you to bring your friend Dr. Zadok here."

"Where is 'here'?"

"Oh! Sorry. I'm at the funeral home."

I looked at Max, covered in soot and patently weary, as I asked John, "When do you want to see him?"

"Right now." When I didn't answer immediately, John said, "It's important, Esther."

"All right. We're still in Chinatown," I said a little reluctantly. "We can be there in a few minutes. But what's going on?"

"Well, um . . . This is going to sound weird."

"Uh-huh." I gestured at Lucky, trying to tell him we wouldn't need a ride, after all.

John cleared his throat. "One of the departed . . . I mean, a few minutes ago, one of our corpses just kind of . . ."

"Yes?"

". . . just kind of got out of its coffin and walked away."

3

Chen's Funeral Home was in a turn-of-the-century building in what had previously been Little Italy, a neighborhood which had shrunk to just a few short blocks over the decades while Chinatown had by now grown to encompass much of the old Lower East Side. The funeral business operated in an L-shaped structure with two entrances that were on different streets, their façades separated from each other by the other buildings on the two blocks; unless you knew what lay behind the public faces of the two well-established funeral parlors, you'd never guess they were one business.

One entrance was for Chen's. The other entrance, around the corner, was for Antonelli's Funeral Home. The distinctive, old-fashioned exteriors respectively looked Chinese and Italian. Antonelli's entrance was decorated with thick marble pillars, carved vines and flowers, plump angels, and trumpeting cherubim. Chen's was austere black and gold, with Chinese characters over the door. Lucky's uncle and John's grandfather had run one business with two separate clienteles for some forty years, processing the bodies for both funeral parlors in the middle, at the junction of the L-shaped building.

Decades after the founding of that successful partnership, the Chens ran both halves of the business now, and there were many Chinese funerals in Antonelli's, as well as in Chen's. The Chen family continued to use the European name and décor of the Antonelli section, though, since they also served a non-Chinese clientele. Lucky, who had inherited his share of the company from his uncle, was a silent partner who kept his name and his nose out of the Chens' reputable business. But given the high mortality rate in Lucky's own line of work, I assumed he referred plenty of customers to Antonelli's Funeral Home.

The Chinese side of the building, through which we entered the funeral home now, was decorated in elegantly somber shades of gold and red. There were several tapestries hanging on the walls, as well as some banners that displayed graceful Chinese calligraphy. During visitations, several tables here were typically draped in white linen and covered with traditional offerings of food, liquor, and brightly colored paper replicas of things the deceased had enjoyed in life and hoped to continue enjoying in death: cars, money, a boat, a house, and so on.

I had been here a number of times by now, so the setting was familiar to me. I could see that the Chens were starting to prepare for a wake, which wasn't surprising. They ran a successful, well-established business, and their facilities were in frequent use.

Besides, John had already told me there was a dead person in a coffin here today. Or, rather, a dead person who was *no longer* in his coffin . . .

"Alberto!" John's father, Nathan Chen, greeted Lucky with obvious relief. "John said you were all right, but I've been worried. He didn't know where you went after Susan was arrested—and I couldn't call you, because you left your phone here."

"Figures. I rushed out of here pretty fast after Esther warned me about Susan." Lucky added, "And we've been so busy since then, I didn't even notice it was missing."

Looking stunned by the day's events, Nathan said, "I always had a feeling something would go wrong with the Yee girl. So tense, so judgmental and bad-tempered. But trying to *kill John?*" He shook his head. "No, I never once imagined that. And I can't thank all of you enough for risking your lives to protect John today! He never suspected Susan had anything against him, so he'd have been an easy target if not for your bravery."

We assured him it was our pleasure, he thanked us several more times, and then we accepted the hot tea he offered us.

Nelli, who had spent time here with Lucky lately, greeted Nathan affectionately. He withstood this patiently, though he obviously wasn't a dog person.

Nathan Chen was not as tall as his sons, John and Sam (Sam was the elder brother, a full-time mortician who would one day take over the business), but he had the same trim build, good posture, and attractive features. He was a widower in his early sixties, with a pleasantly lined face and gray hair, and he had the gentle manners of someone accustomed to dealing sensitively with bereaved families.

There were many obvious differences between Lucky and Nathan, who was a law-abiding Chinese-American businessman and respected member of the community. But the two men had known each other all their lives, and despite how little they might have in common in terms of education, lifestyle, and career choices, they were bound by friendship and trust.

"Miss Diamond." Nathan nodded to me, then he turned to Max. "Dr. Zadok. I am grateful to you both for coming here on such short notice. John says you are knowledgeable in matters such as our . . . our . . . what happened here."

"Please call me Max."

"And call me Esther," I added.

Max started to ask, "What exactly *has* happ—"

"Esther! Uncle Lucky!" John entered the elegant reception hall via the door that led to the offices and workrooms—the portion of the building where the Chens prepared bodies for visitation and burial. That area of the mortuary was contemporary and utilitarian, in contrast to the elegant visitation rooms. "Dr. Zadok, I'm so glad you're here."

"Max," said the old mage. "I insist."

John was a tall, handsome, American-born Chinese man, a year or two younger than my twenty-seven years, with thick, shiny hair, broad shoulders, and an appealing smile. He was also bright, sensible, kind, and had a dry sense of humor. I enjoyed John's company— and wished I didn't feel so self-conscious now that I knew he wanted to date me.

What am I going to do about that?

The moment to nip this in the bud by signaling that I wasn't interested had already passed me by. I thought John was someone who would notice such signals, but since *I* was too dense to notice he was flirting with me, I hadn't sent them. So he had brought up the subject of asking me out, and my distracted cluelessness had evidently come across as reciprocal interest.

The fact that I liked John ensured that I felt terrible about that now. And the fact that I found him attractive and probably would have been interested in him if I had never met Lopez made me feel as if I had led him on—which guilt made me feel annoyed with John for being attracted to me in the first place. If he had just had the sense not to notice me, I thought grumpily, then I wouldn't now be stuck with feeling bad about accidentally letting him think I wanted to go out with him.

However, rather than gazing at me with fervent longing now, John was clearly stressed and distracted this evening—and no wonder. He'd nearly been murdered today, and he'd apparently also had a disturbingly weird experience here a little while ago.

Pouring the tea he had offered us, Nathan asked Lucky where he had gone after leaving the crime scene. Lucky caught my eye and then, keeping the story simple, said we'd gone looking for Max, from whom I had gotten separated. Still keeping it simple, Lucky also told John and Nathan about the fire we'd witnessed at Yee & Sons Trading Company. Father and son commented on the dark fate of the Yees, who only days ago had been a respected Chinatown family with a successful business, much like the Chens themselves.

We were all silent for a moment of somber reflection, though I doubted that John and Nathan were thinking the same things that I was thinking about the misfortunes of the Yee family.

Then Lucky said, "I know Sam's with his wife and kids today. Big holiday, and all that. So I guess this is everyone, huh? I think we should get down to business."

John let out a slow breath and nodded. "Yeah, we

should talk about this. If I can explain it without sounding crazier than Susan Yee sounded today. I have no idea what to think about what happened here a little while ago. Or what to do—if anything." He paused, seemed to give himself a mental shake, and said, "I'm going to make a concerted effort not to babble. I swear."

"That's perfectly all right, John. Something has obviously distressed you," said Max. "What has happened here?"

Nathan and John exchanged a look, and the father said to the son, "You tell them."

"Are you sure? You're the one who saw—"

"You start," Nathan said firmly.

"Okay." John collected his thoughts for a moment, then began, "After the police took my statement and said I could go home—I have to go down to the station and give another one, but they'll call me about that . . . Tomorrow maybe? I don't know." He paused. "Sorry, that was almost a babble."

"You're doing fine," Max said soothingly, well accustomed to the confusion and distress of normal people who encounter mystical phenomena—if that was indeed what had happened here. "Please continue."

"Um . . . I came back here, took a shower, tried to relax. But I was so wound up after what had happened."

"'Course you were," Lucky said gruffly. "Lookin' down the barrel of a gun held by that crazy girl."

"And where the hell did that fire come from?" John

wondered. "I didn't imagine it, did I? Susan dropped the gun because fire shot out of my mouth, right? Um, out of the mouth of the lion head I was wearing, I mean."

I thought we should probably move on, so I said, "It's been a really weird day all around. So, anyhow, you came back here, took a shower, and then . . ."

"Then John called me," said Nathan.

"That's right. I didn't want Dad to hear from the Chinatown grapevine about what had happened. That would scare him to death—especially since creative editing would ensure that by the time the story got to him, people would be saying I was dead or maimed or in a coma."

"John," his father admonished faintly.

Lucky said to Nathan, "So you dropped what you were doing and came here straight away."

Nathan nodded. "After I got here, we talked for a while, and then I thought maybe work would help John calm down and get his mind off what had happened. So I suggested he do Mr. Capuzzo's hair."

"Whose hair?" I asked.

"Capuzzo is a client whose wake will be held in Antonelli's this week," said John. "And I thought Dad was right when he said that focusing on some work might help me calm down."

I sincerely doubted that touching a corpse would help me recover from nearly having *become* one . . . but, then, I hadn't been raised in a family of morticians, whereas John had. And, after all, for all that I loved being onstage, I was well aware that the prospect of performing in front of an audience struck many people as terrifying rather than exciting or enjoyable. To each his own, it takes all kinds to make a world, and so on.

"So I did Mr. Capuzzo's hair. And it did calm me down a little. Then . . ." John frowned, looking distracted again.

"Then the detective showed up," Nathan reminded him.

"Oh, right, the cop." John nodded.

"Was he looking for me?" Lucky asked darkly.

"No, for *me*," said John.

"Was it Lopez?" I asked.

"Who?"

"Detective Lopez from the OCCB."

Years of friendship with Lucky apparently ensured that Nathan recognized the initials. "He did mention being from the Organized Crime Control Bureau, but his name wasn't . . ."

His voice trailed off as the door chimes tinkled softly. Nathan rose from his seat to greet the newcomer, and we all looked in the direction of the entrance hall to see who it was. I wondered with mingled tension and hope whether it would be another cop—one particular cop, of course—and I was both disappointed and repelled to see who it actually was.

Danny Teng appeared in the broad doorway of this reception room. He was *dai lo*—the leader—of the Red Daggers, a Chinatown gang that worked for the Five Brothers tong. He was violent, stupid, dangerous, and sexually aggressive enough to be menacing.

"Is Uncle Six here yet?" he asked the Chens, not even bothering to say hello.

"Not yet," said Nathan. "The police might release the body to us in a couple of days."

What's left of it, I thought.

Lucky exchanged a glance with me, and I could see he was thinking the same thing.

Uncle Six, aka Joe Ning, had taken a swan dive off a sixth-floor balcony, and it seemed certain he would have a closed-casket funeral. No matter how good the Chens were at their profession, they weren't miracle workers.

Joe Ning, head of the Five Brothers tong, had been murdered by Susan Yee because he'd financed Ted's film after the first backer died (also killed by Susan). But apart from me, Lucky, and Max, no one recognized the significance of the broken gourmet fortune cookie found near the spot where Uncle Six had slipped and fallen to his death. To the mundane world, Joe Ning's death appeared to be accidental—or possibly a suicide which his immediate family members, the only other people in his apartment that night, were determined to conceal. Because Ning was a kingpin in Chinatown's criminal underworld, I assumed the cops also considered murder a possibility—but death by cookie would never occur to them. And they would never believe Susan had killed him with a curse, not even if she confessed to it.

Looking at Danny now, I hoped for Ted's sake that there was never even a vague rumor about Susan's involvement in the tong boss's death. Danny was so amoral and bloodthirsty, he might retaliate against Ted if he ever suspected the ex-filmmaker's sister had whacked the old man. And with someone like Danny, retaliation would mean another funeral.

As *dai lo* of the Red Daggers, Danny had reputedly done a lot of special jobs for Uncle Six. In fact, Ning had assigned Danny to watch over his newest investment, Ted's film, which was why Danny had been hanging around the set of *ABC* lately. He was on the set when he got the news of Ning's death, and he'd been so enraged and out of control, I was afraid he'd lash out and hurt me or Ted. It was a relief when he stormed off to go commit mayhem somewhere else, and I had hoped never to see him again.

Not happy about seeing him now, I noticed he was swaying slightly, and I supposed he'd been drinking— as was often the case.

"When you get Uncle Six here," Danny said to Nathan, slurring his words a little, "you gonna do right by him, you hear me? You gonna make him look good."

"Yes, of course," Nathan said soothingly, with as much confidence as if Ning had died of a something much less messy than a very long, hard, fast fall onto a city street.

"Uncle Six deserves the *best*."

Danny, who was about my age, spoke English with a slight Chinese accent; his first language was Cantonese. His long hair was slicked back and tied in a ponytail, as usual, and he sported a little mustache and goatee that didn't suit him. He habitually wore blue jeans, boots decorated with silver studs and chains, and a black leather jacket. And he was almost certainly armed.

"Uncle Six *will* get the best," Nathan assured him.

"If he don't," Danny warned blearily, "then I'm gonna cut you."

John rose to his feet, openly angry about seeing his father threatened. Striding forward, he said tersely to Danny, "You need to leave. Right *now*."

Nathan turned his back on Danny (which I wasn't sure was wise) as he stepped into John's path, put his hands on his son's shoulders, and met his gaze. "John," he said quietly, "let me handle this."

John ignored his father's request. "Get out," he said to Danny—who started laughing.

I didn't like to intrude, but I rose to my feet, too, and placed a hand on John's arm. "Your dad's right," I said quietly. "Let him deal with this."

I had seen on a previous occasion that Nathan had an enviable ability to deal calmly with thugs like Danny and take some of the edge off their aggression. Probably because he was a respected elder in the community. Whereas a tall, muscular young man like John would just make Danny feel challenged—especially the way John was glaring at him right now, as if ready to throw down with him.

Nathan and I exchanged a glance, and I said more sharply, "John! Your father has this under control."

After another tense moment, John let his shoulders sag a little and he nodded his acquiescence. He was a smart man—and he respected his father.

In any case, Danny was no longer paying attention to him. He had noticed me. Oh, joy. "Esther . . . what are you doing here? And why are you dressed like that?"

Danny was used to seeing me in costume for Ted's film, where I'd played an airheaded uptown slut who never felt the cold. Not wanting to interact with him, I ignored the question.

Nathan turned back to Danny again, subtly stepping between us to shield me from the gangster's gaze, which I appreciated. I looked over my shoulder, surprised that Lucky hadn't intervened. He was still seated in his chair, leaning back, one hand stroking Nelli's head to keep her calm, since she had sensed the tension in the room and was uneasy . . . But the expression on Lucky's face was chilling as he stared hard at the drunken young thug who'd just threatened the Chens. I sometimes forgot that, although he always said it was strictly business, Lucky had killed people—including some very dangerous people. Looking at him right now, I was amazed it was something I was *ever* able to forget.

But Lucky had a cool head and excellent command of his temper. And, like John, he respected Nathan. So he let this scene play out without his interference. Which was very fortunate for Danny Teng, I suspected.

Nathan started walking toward the exit, his body language encouraging Danny to accompany him. "We will, of course, keep you informed of funeral arrangements. I know you were a valued associate in Uncle Six's life, and you will be involved in the rites of his death. He would have it no other way."

"Hmph. Fucking right." Despite his language, Danny sounded slightly mollified. But then he said with dark savagery, his voice floating back to us, "I'm gonna find who killed Uncle Six, and I'm going to blow him away, the bastard!"

Just to be on the safe side, I decided I'd call Ted and advise him to think seriously about getting out of town for a while.

I could hear Nathan's voice in the hallway, thanking Danny for his "visit" and bidding him a good evening.

When he returned to this room, he said in gentle admonishment to his son, "You need to exercise more patience, John. Consider the excellent example your uncle has just set."

Lucky grunted. John looked at the ceiling.

"What a dreadful young man," Max said. "I fear he will cause terrible grief someday, if he has not already done so."

"He's a stupid, vicious thug," John muttered.

"No argument there," I said. "But your father handled him very skillfully."

John scowled for a moment, then smiled ruefully and admitted, "He did." He met his father's eyes and shrugged. "Sorry."

"You've had a difficult day," replied Nathan, dismissing the subject.

"Which brings us back to the purpose of our visit," said Max. "Before that young, er, person interrupted your narrative, you had just finished working on the deceased Mr. Capuzzo's coiffure. And the gentleman was, I take it, quite dead?"

"*Quite* dead," John confirmed.

"Unquestionably," said Nathan. "I examined John's work after he was done, and I guarantee that the deceased was . . . well, *deceased*. No question whatsoever."

"What happened next?" I asked.

"I turned my back to put away some tools and refill some supplies that were running low. I was concentrat-

ing on these tasks for several minutes before I heard . . .
heard movement behind me."

I felt a chill. "No one else was in the room but you
and the dead guy—uh, you and the departed?"

"No one else. I didn't react at first—"

"You didn't?" I blurted. *I'd* certainly have reacted.

"The recently deceased aren't exactly silent," John
said to me.

"What does *that* mean?"

"Upon death," said Nathan, "body chemistry starts
changing, tissues begin breaking down, gases expand
and release . . . And noises can accompany some of these
processes. Occasionally there's even a little movement."

"Oh," I said faintly, realizing I'd probably be more
nervous on my future visits to this place. It had never
occurred to me that the corpses here might gurgle or
shift.

"But what the dead don't *ever* do," said John, "is get
up out of their coffins and walk away." He paused,
then added, "Well, until today."

"That was the movement you heard?" Max looked
to Nathan for confirmation.

"Yes. I realized after a moment that the sounds I was
hearing were too noisy and continuous to be normal,"
said Nathan. "I turned around to look, thinking perhaps there was a mouse or something in the room with
me." He looked at me, then at Max, then at Lucky.
"There wasn't."

"What *was* there?" Lucky asked, on the edge of his seat now.

"Yes, what?" I prodded.

Nathan met John's gaze, then said with obvious reluctance, "Mr. Capuzzo had gotten out of his coffin and was walking away from it, with his back to me. He was moving slowly and awkwardly. And . . . and . . ."

"And?" Lucky and I said in unison.

"And I screamed," said Nathan. "I've never screamed like that in my life. I think I just kept on screaming."

"You did," confirmed John. "Scared the shi—um, scared me to death. So I came running."

"While I was screaming, Mr. Capuzzo collapsed, fell down, and just lay there. Not moving."

"About five feet away from his coffin," added John. "It's where he was lying when I entered the room."

"Did you examine him?" Max asked.

"Well, not at that exact moment," John said. "We both, uh . . . needed a time-out. But after a few minutes, yeah, we looked him over."

"And?"

"And he was still dead," said John. "I'm a scientist. My father's an experienced mortician. We're sure. This guy has been dead for at least a day."

I glanced at the door leading to the working rooms of the mortuary. "Is he still here?"

"As far as I know," said John.

I repeated, "As far as you know?"

"We closed the door, I called you, and we haven't gone back in that room since."

"Understandable," said Max. "And probably wise. I would, of course, like to examine the body."

"Oh, yay," Lucky said gloomily. "I was hoping we'd get to visit this thing."

But Max liked to be thorough and methodical, so first he asked the Chens to tell their story again, and this time he kept stopping them to ask for more details or get clarification.

Upon reaching the climax of his tale again, Nathan said, "So I turned around and saw Mr. Capuzzo, with his back to me, walking away from his coffin. And I screamed."

"And I came running," said John.

"Where exactly were you at the time?" Max asked.

"When I heard Dad scream?" John looked around. "Actually, I think I was right about here."

"Doing what?"

"I was on my way to the office, coming back from the front door. I had just shown that cop out of the building."

"The cop!" I exclaimed, startling the others.

"Yeah, the cop who came here to ask me some questions about today," John replied. "The one who seemed skeptical when I said I didn't know why Susan wanted to shoot me."

"An OCCB detective, right?" I prodded, remembering what Nathan had said only a moment before Danny's unwelcome entrance.

Lucky sat bolt upright and met my gaze as the penny dropped. *"An OCCB detective."*

Nathan said soothingly, "He wasn't here for you, Alberto. He—"

"Who was he?" I demanded.

John shook his head. "Not the Latino cop you mentioned. This guy had an Irish name . . . He was a redhead . . . I don't remember—"

"Quinn," I said with dread. "Detective Andrew Quinn."

John looked surprised. "Hey, yeah, that was the name. Quinn. You know him?"

"Quinn." Lucky fell back against his seat as he looked darkly at Nelli. "Same guy."

"First Nelli," I said to Lucky. "Now *this.*"

"It can't just be coincidence," he said.

"What can't be coincidence?" John asked.

Max looked from Lucky, to Nelli, to me. "What is the significance of Detective Quinn?"

"It's why we left the scene of the shooting so suddenly today," I replied. "Why we came looking for you. We didn't understand exactly what it meant, but we were pretty sure it was a big deal."

"What was a big deal?" John asked, apparently realizing we weren't talking about Susan trying to kill him.

I looked at Nelli for a moment, then continued, "After Susan was arrested and things were calming down a little, Detective Quinn walked past Nelli and Lucky. That was all—just walked past them."

"Didn't come close to us," Lucky added. "Didn't even look in our direction."

"And Nelli went *berserk*," I said. "She tried to attack Quinn."

"What?" John looked at the dog, who panted cheerfully at him, then rolled over onto her back, asking to have her belly scratched. *"Nelli?"*

At the sound of her name, her tail wagged.

"God alone knows what would have happened if Lucky hadn't kept such a firm grip on her," I said. "She acted like she was prepared to rip out Quinn's heart."

"This Nelli?" Nathan asked.

The Chens knew her and were well aware of her gentle, friendly temperament (as well as her tendency to drool, shed, and chew on other people's belongings).

"How did Detective Quinn react?" Max asked with interest.

I shrugged. "Like any normal person would when a dog Nelli's size suddenly gets aggressive. He looked startled, gave her a wide berth, and kept on going where he was going—the other end of the street."

Lopez had chewed me out about Nelli's behavior, but Quinn had just put distance between himself and the dog, and then he ignored her after that.

"She couldn't take her eyes off the guy," said Lucky.

"Even after he was about fifty yards away from us, she just kept staring and growling . . . And the *look* in her eyes."

"And now this," I said. "Quinn shows up here for a few minutes, and next thing you know, Mr. Capuzzo's corpse tries to go walkabout."

"Hmm."

"Max, there's something really *wrong* about this guy," I said, feeling very worried now.

"Wait a minute," said John. "You think that just because Max's dog doesn't like him—"

"She ain't just a dog," said Lucky. "Nelli is a mystical familiar who entered this dimension to confront Evil."

"O . . . kay," said John.

Nathan wisely said nothing.

Lucky continued, "The only other times I ever seen her behave that way, she *was* confronting Evil."

"Hm," said Max.

"Have you ever had a corpse hop out of its coffin here before?" I asked the Chens.

"No, of course not." John paused, then asked his father, "Um, have we?"

"Of course not!"

"And then it happens for the first time only a few minutes after Quinn comes here—Quinn, who Nelli thinks is evil!" I looked at Lucky again, "No, that's not just coincidence."

"So there's a weird . . . or maybe 'evil' cop in the NYPD?" John mused. "Not to sound cynical, but that's not exactly unprecedented."

"John," Nathan admonished.

"What?"

"There's more to it than that," I said with a terrible, cold dread.

"What is it, my dear?" Max asked with concern, recognizing my distress.

"Quinn is Lopez's new partner," I said. "They're together every day. In dangerous situations. With loaded weapons. Lopez probably trusts him. Probably *has to* trust him."

"Ah." Max nodded gravely. "I understand."

"If I'm right and Quinn is evil, then Lopez . . ." I tried to keep my voice steady. "Then Lopez is in danger." I looked at Nelli and added, "Very serious danger."

4

"So that's Mr. Capuzzo?" I looked down at the corpse in the Chens' workroom.

The body lay on its stomach in an ungainly sprawl, neck in an awkward position so that the face was looking up. I was glad the eyes and mouth were closed. I think I'd have had nightmares if the face were frozen in a rictus of screaming horror. For example.

"Yep," said John. "That's him."

Although I'm not overly squeamish, I would rather not have joined the others in examining the corpse. But it had been generally assumed that I would do so, and I didn't want to seem like I couldn't hold up my end.

"His hair looks good," said Lucky, who was holding Nelli's leash.

"Thanks," said John. "I tried some new product—"

"Let's not talk about his hair," I said. "Let's talk

about the fact that he's lying about five feet away from his coffin."

It appeared that Mr. Capuzzo had been all ready for his viewing, right before he got up and tried to leave. He was dressed in a nice suit, hair and makeup finished, expensive coffin wide open. Add a bunch of floral arrangements, and it would be a classy wake.

"How did he die?" asked Max.

"Heart failure," said Nathan.

The deceased looked like he'd been well into his eighties. He was a short, trim, well-groomed man—though the grooming was the Chens' handiwork, of course. He might have been a slob in life, for all I knew.

"Where exactly was he when you first saw him in motion?" Max asked Nathan.

"He was just finishing his, um, exit from the coffin." With an expression that indicated how uncomfortable he was doing this, Nathan demonstrated what he had seen, showing us how Capuzzo had braced himself on the edge of the coffin while lowering his feet to the floor. Then John's father took several slow, awkward steps the way that the dead man had done. He said to Max, "He moved . . . strangely. I didn't for a moment suppose he was alive. I couldn't see his face, but even from behind, he didn't . . . didn't *look* alive. Even though he was in motion. I know that doesn't make any sense, but—"

"Oh, it does," Max assured him. "Reanimated bodies do not resemble the living. Well, not in my experience."

John had indeed summoned the right person to help with this weird situation. Max knew what he was talking about, having encountered more than one sort of still-lively corpse over the course of his long and varied life.

Nathan said, "Then Mr. Capuzzo collapsed right there, as you see. John came through the door only a second or two later."

"And I saw Capuzzo lying here in a heap, and Dad staring at him and screaming," added John.

Looking a little bored, Nelli sat down.

"Hm," said Max. "Did the corpse make any sounds?"

"I don't know." Nathan paused, then said, "If it did, I don't think I would have heard it after I started screaming."

"Was there an odor or unusual smell?"

John shook his head. "I don't think so. But I was so confused by the scene—and then so freaked out by what Dad told me—I'm not sure I'd have noticed any odors."

"I don't recall any smells," said Nathan. "But I was even more shaken than John, so . . ." He shrugged and shook his head, indicating he couldn't answer with confidence.

"And I gather the electricity didn't fail? You weren't plunged into darkness?"

"No."

"Hm." Max walked around the corpse, studying it with a frown of concentration on his face.

"Just looks like a dead guy to me," said Lucky—and he certainly spoke from experience. "I don't want you to take this the wrong way, Nate, but we gotta ask the question. Are you *sure* about what you saw?"

Nathan didn't take offense. This was evidently his first full-body contact with a mystical event (which was indeed what this seemed to be), and he was obviously well aware of how crazy his story sounded.

"Alberto," he said solemnly, "I swear on the memory of my wife, I saw exactly what I've told you I saw. I've spent most of my life working with the departed, and I'm not fanciful, let alone prone to hallucinations. I didn't imagine this. I've *never* imagined something like this. It really happened, just as I've described."

"Okay." Lucky nodded, accepting this. He trusted Nathan and, unlike his friend, he'd actually had a number of mystical encounters, so the story didn't sound as crazy to him as one might suppose. "So what do we think, Doc?"

"Reanimation doesn't seem to have damaged the corpse," Max said pensively. "Sometimes there can be . . . oh, a sort of internal combustion as mystical forces devour the dead organism. It can leave behind cooked flesh, charred remains, corpses that appear to have been partially cremated, melted organs—"

"But not in this case," I interrupted, not wanting to hear the whole list.

"No," Max agreed. "Nor does there appear to be any liquidation of the physical form."

"Liquidation?" John repeated.

"Let's not digress," I said, eager to avoid more revolting imagery.

"Esther is right. Let's proceed with what's here, rather than discussing what is not," said Max. "Will someone assist me in turning him over?"

I took Nelli's leash from Lucky and stepped back as he and John dealt with Mr. Capuzzo. They did it efficiently and without hesitation, both being accustomed, in their separate ways, to handling dead bodies.

Now that the deceased was lying on his back . . . he still just looked like an elderly man who'd been well prepared for his upcoming wake.

Looking more alert now, Nelli rose to her feet and approached the corpse. Lucky let go of her leash as she lowered her head and began sniffing Mr. Capuzzo with focused interest.

"Nelli is examining the body for traces of mystical influence," Max explained.

I saw a somewhat dubious glance pass between the Chens.

After about a minute of sniffing, Nelli seemed to lose interest—and then she whined a little and licked Mr. Capuzzo's ear.

"Oh, Nelli, *don't*," I blurted. "No!"

She paused, looked at me, then gave the ear another slurp with her long pink tongue. Revolted, I picked up her leash and tugged on it, urging her to leave the body and come to me. After she did, I told her to lie down. Nelli remained standing.

"Did she learn anything, Doc?" Lucky asked.

"Apparently not." Nelli was looking around the room now, cheerful and relaxed. "Her reaction indicates she can detect no lingering traces of whatever animated this body."

"Well . . . good," said John.

"Now what?" asked Nathan.

After a moment of gazing down at the dead man, Max got down on his knees beside the corpse. "I wonder if . . ."

I looked away when he prized open one of Capuzzo's eyes and leaned close to peer into it.

"Do you need a penlight?" John asked.

"Ah, yes. That would be most useful."

John found one and handed it to him. Lucky and the Chens watched attentively while Max spent the next few minutes examining the corpse by looking into various orifices and tapping on various bones.

I mostly tried to look elsewhere.

When it came to examining a corpse, I was prepared to lend moral support but not to lend a hand. Protecting New York from Evil is Max's job, so he has to be able to stomach tasks like the one he was engaged in now. But for me, this kind of thing is just . . . let's call it volunteer work.

I don't help Max confront Evil because I'm nobler than the average person (though I'm flattered that Max thinks I am). I mostly do it because it's a matter of common sense and self-preservation to stand up and *do* something when someone's trying to summon a demon that will eat half of Manhattan (where I live and work), or kill a bunch of New Yorkers (of whom I happen to be one) to appease dark forces, or commit human sacrifice with innocent bystanders (such as me, my friends, or my potential employers) to gain riches and power.

Yes, I've seen things.

And now there was *this* situation, where I was afraid that Quinn, the gun-toting person with whom my mostly off-again boyfriend spent all his working hours, was mystically dangerous—a phrase which, based on what I'd encountered since meeting Max, rarely meant "might cause someone a migraine" and very often meant "will terrorize people and take lives."

The possibility that Quinn was animating the dead for some nefarious purpose filled me with dread. We had previously encountered someone who was raising zombies, and that was a *very* dangerous situation—and a ruthless, deadly foe. I was extremely worried about the prospect of Lopez spending his time with someone like that.

A wave of cold washed through me as I suddenly recalled something Quinn had said to me recently about Lopez.

"I swear, there are days he's so hard to live with, I'm not sure it's a good idea for me to be carrying a loaded gun."

He'd been complaining to me of Lopez's prolonged bad mood, caused mostly by problems between us. At the time, I assumed Quinn was being facetious. Now I found myself wondering if the comment was, instead, an indication of how lightly he viewed the prospect of killing his partner.

Between my fears about Nelli's powerfully negative reaction to Quinn and my anxiety about Nathan's description of the reanimated corpse that Max was currently examining right in front of me, I was feeling a little overwrought—so I almost jumped out of my skin when my cell phone rang.

"That's mine," I said a little breathlessly, feeling my heart pound.

I fumbled in my purse for my phone. In my agitation, I was all butterfingers, and it flew out of my hand and skittered across the floor to hit Mr. Capuzzo in the head. I gasped and put my hand over my mouth as the phone slid into the cradle of his neck.

The men all looked at me. So did Nelli.

"Are you okay?" John asked.

"Fine," I lied. "Fine. I'm sorry."

I didn't know why I was apologizing. It wasn't my

fault that I was the only person in the room who wasn't comfortable around dead bodies.

John picked up my still-ringing phone and handed it to me. "Here you go."

"No! I don't want it *now*."

They all looked at me again.

I took a steadying breath and said, "It *touched* him." I realized I didn't sound as calm as I'd intended.

The phone stopped ringing as the call went to voice-mail.

John looked uncertainly at Lucky, as if expecting him to know what to say.

Fortunately, Lucky did know. "The lady don't want to handle a phone that just touched a dead body. Can you . . . sterilize it or something?"

"Oh! Of course. Sure," said John. "Right away."

John went over to a worktable and found some cotton pads and alcohol which he used to wipe down my phone. While he was doing that, Max rose to his feet, assisted by a hand from Lucky.

"I find absolutely nothing unusual or untoward about this body. Which, if I may say so," he added politely to Nathan, "will make a most decorous presentation at the wake."

"If he stays in his coffin," John muttered.

After a glance at me, Lucky said, "Maybe we should put him back in there now."

"All right." John handed me my phone, which now

smelled of rubbing alcohol. "You take the legs, Uncle Lucky."

While they returned the departed to his casket, Max asked Nathan, "What can you tell me about Mr. Capuzzo in life?"

"Let's see . . . He was raised in Little Italy and knew Lucky's uncle, who brought my father into the business. His widow says it's why he wanted his wake to be here." Watching his son settle Capuzzo into his coffin, Nathan said, "John, the suit needs—"

"I know." John straightened one sleeve of the suit, then the other. "I've got it."

Nathan nodded and returned his attention to Max. "We handled his brother's funeral two years ago. It's a fairly large family, so I assume we'll have many of the same mourners this time. None of them live in Little Italy anymore." Not many of the old families still did. Little Italy, once a big swathe of lower Manhattan, was now just a few blocks of shops and restaurants. "They're scattered around the tri-state area these days."

"You met Mr. Capuzzo when handling his brother's funeral?" Max asked. "What sort of man was he?"

"We only exchanged a few words," said Nathan. "He seemed quiet and polite."

John stepped away from the casket, and Nathan turned his attention to Mr. Capuzzo, whom he fussed over until he was satisfied with his appearance.

While he worked, he continued, "They're a respectable family. Mr. Capuzzo owned several shoe stores. His widow is a very courteous lady, even in her sorrow. And their eldest daughter, who has been making the arrangements with us, has been easy to work with." He added, "You can tell a lot about a family by the way they behave in their time of bereavement, and the Capuzzos seem like good people."

"Have they made any unusual requests? Or given you any strange restrictions?"

"No, nothing."

"Why are you focusing on Capuzzo?" I asked impatiently, wondering if Lopez was keeping company with a mystical time bomb. "This is about Quinn. It has to be! He's the guy who made Nelli go ballistic today. The guy who was leaving this funeral home just as the corpse got frisky."

John snorted a little with laughter. Nathan looked pained by my phrasing.

Lucky said, "I think the doc is trying to find a connection between Capuzzo and Quinn. Am I right?"

Max nodded. "Or between Mr. Capuzzo and whatever attracted Detective Quinn to this mortuary today."

"*I* attracted him," said John.

We all looked at him.

"Do we all remember the *shooting* today?" John prodded.

"Why did he want to question you about that?" I challenged, thinking it had just been a pretext.

"Because he's a cop."

"This isn't his case. The Fifth Precinct is in charge of Susan's arrest. Quinn is in OCCB. So why did *he* come here to question you? Why not a detective from the Fifth?"

"I don't know. Because he was there? He witnessed what happened . . . And maybe he thinks it's connected to his case."

"What case?"

"Besides asking why Susan wanted me dead, he asked me a lot of questions about Joe Ning."

"Ah." Lucky nodded. "Chinatown underworld boss."

"Organized crime," John said to me. "Organized Crime Control Bureau. See?"

"So you're sayin' he came here because of his perfectly legitimate business interests." Lucky added, "In a manner of speaking."

"Seemed like it at the time," said John. "Before the dead started dancing."

"John," admonished his father.

"And now?" I prodded.

John thought about it. "Honestly . . . it still seems like it. He was very . . . cop-like. You know. Asked a bunch of rapid-fire questions about the shooting, Susan, me. Then he suddenly switched to asking about Joe Ning—which caught me off guard and kind of confused me. Then he switched back to asking about Susan, which caught me off guard again."

"I know the feeling," I said gloomily. At his least romantic and most inquisitive, Lopez had used the same technique on me a few times. "What did you tell him?"

"That I've known Susan since I was a kid and thought we got along fine. We weren't ever *close*, but it never once occurred to me she might try to—"

"No, I mean about Joe Ning."

"Oh." John shrugged. "Big man in Chinatown. Big funeral. It'll probably have to be closed casket. Not much else." John shook his head. "I don't *know* much else. I met Uncle Six a few times, but it's not as if we ever hung out together. I only know what everyone in the neighborhood knows, or what's in the news."

"Police!" his father said suddenly. "*That's* what's in the news."

"Pardon?" said Max.

"I saw the story on local TV today, in passing," said Nathan. "Uncle Six—"

"I'm sorry to interrupt," I said, "but could we talk about this somewhere else?"

I seemed to be the only one who minded that we were still in the same room with a dead body.

"Oh. Of course," said Nathan. "Forgive me, Esther. Let's go into the office."

"Good idea," said Lucky. "Esther's an actress. She's very sensitive."

I didn't think it was *sensitive* to want to finish our

conference in a room without a corpse, but since I was getting my way, I didn't argue.

To my relief, we left the workroom, crossed the hall, and entered an office with the usual administrative trappings and equipment—desks, computers, phones, paperwork, filing cabinets, and so on. I had been in this room several times before, and I found it reassuringly prosaic right now.

Nathan took a seat at his desk. John stayed on his feet, leaning against the other desk. Lucky, Max, and I all sat down. I was feeling the exertions of the day by now, so I was sure they both must be very tired, since they were each older than I—Lucky by at least thirty-five years, and Max by more than three hundred years. (He accidentally consumed a life-prolonging elixir as a young man in the seventeenth century, thinking it was remedy for his fever. It was this whole big thing. I think the lesson is: don't drink anything brewed for you by an alchemist in the early stages of dementia. Anyhow, Max wasn't immortal, but he had spent centuries aging at an unusually slow rate.)

Since I was the one who had interrupted him, I prompted Nathan to continue now. "You were saying something about today's news?"

"Yes. Uncle Six's lawyer is blaming the police for his death."

I lifted my brows in surprise. "Well, *that's* a theory I

didn't see coming. He thinks the cops pushed Joe Ning off that balcony?"

"No, the attorney claims the police drove him to suicide."

I frowned. "How?"

I didn't know much about Chinatown underworld bosses, but I assumed they were tough and resilient. Not the sort to dive off the sixth floor of a downtown building just because the cops had them on the ropes.

"I didn't get any details," Nathan replied. "I only saw the story in passing."

John folded his arms across his chest. "But Detective Quinn coming here and asking me questions about Uncle Six would suggest that OCCB is investigating him."

"What kind of questions did Quinn ask you? What did he want to know?" I asked John.

"Since I scarcely knew Uncle Six, it wound up being pretty general. And he had some questions I couldn't even take a guess at."

"Such as?"

"Did Uncle Six seem stressed or depressed lately? Was he anxious or afraid of something? Who stood to gain from his death?" John shrugged. "Quinn might as well have asked me questions about hockey or knitting."

"Anything else?"

"Well, he wanted to know why Uncle Six was financing Ted's film."

"And since you've worked on the movie," Lucky said doubtfully, "he thinks you're a connection between Uncle Six and Susan Yee?"

"I don't see how," John replied. "If there's a connection between Susan and Joe Ning, it's not me, it's Ted."

That was, in fact, the connection which had gotten Uncle Six killed by a cursed fortune cookie, but I decided not to digress. Nathan and John had both been skeptical about that theory the last time we met, and the matter was resolved now, after all.

"Then I assume the police will talk to Ted, since it was his film." I added uncertainly, "Unless a defense attorney keeps him away from cops because his sister is being charged with attempted murder."

"Why *did* Susan try to kill me?" John wondered. "What did I ever do to her?"

I figured he and Ted would talk about it, since they were friends, and I didn't want to expose anything Ted would prefer not to reveal. So I kept it brief. "It was the film, John. Susan didn't want Ted to complete it. She heard you talking to Ted about your plan for finding more backers. And she knew that, unlike Ted, you're an organized, capable person with follow-through, so if you were involved, it would actually get done . . ." I shook my head. "And she went off the rails. Decided to kill you in order to—"

"To bring a halt to Ted's film?" Nathan blurted in shocked outrage.

"Seriously?" John looked stunned.

"That—that—that *lunatic* girl!" Nathan sputtered. "Trying to take John's life for something so . . . so . . ."

He couldn't find the words. Which was understandable.

"Poor Ted," John said pensively. It seemed typical of John to think about how his friend must feel now, despite what had nearly happened to *him* today. "And poor Lily."

Lucky, Max, and I exchanged a look, wondering what to say. I guess we decided to say nothing, since we all remained silent.

Nathan paused in his sputtering. "Yes . . ." he said slowly. "Poor Lily. Husband dead. Wretched daughter going to prison. Business burned down. And Ted . . . well, he's not a *bad* son, I suppose, but . . ."

"He's no murderer," I said. "That puts him a lot higher than Susan on the merit chart."

We talked for a little while about today's events as Nathan wrestled with the realization that he'd nearly lost his son over such a trivial matter as Susan being embarrassed by Ted's film. I thought it was ironic that she was so angry that Ted was doing business with people like Joe Ning and Danny Teng, since that fastidiousness had not prevented her from going to Danny when she wanted to get her hands on a gun.

I wondered if the police would be able to charge him for that. The gun had been used in an attempted murder, after all.

Cheered by the thought of Danny Teng potentially going to prison (a place I suspected he'd been before), I decided to get off the gloomy subject of the Yee family.

"Is there anything else that Quinn asked you about?" I said to John. "Did he, for example, ask if you had any corpses here today? Did he see Mr. Capuzzo?"

"Or touch him?" Max asked.

"No, we stayed in the reception area, and Uncle Six was the only cold body we talked about."

"So that was it? Nothing more?"

John thought back. "Oh, he also asked me about Paul Ning—Joe's brother. But that was another dead end. I know Paul's reputation, and I saw him around Chinatown once in a while, but I never met him," said John. "And based on what I've heard about him, that seems to be the only way to get along with him—just never meet him."

"Hm." Paul Ning was in prison for murder. Lopez had been the arresting officer. He and Quinn had recently been rebuilding Lopez's original case because Joe Ning had hired an expensive lawyer to get the conviction overturned and free Paul—a man who no one but Joe, his older brother, seemed to think should be free again. Now that the powerful Uncle Six was dead, it was assumed that the effort to free Paul was also dead. I said doubtfully, "I suppose Quinn could have come here to tie up some loose ends . . ."

"Strictly business?" Lucky shook his head. "Maybe,

but I don't buy it. Not yet. This guy who Nelli thinks is dangerous shows up here, and a corpse starts walking? We gotta follow up on this."

"Yes," I agreed firmly. "We must."

"I know you're worried about your boyfriend. But me, I'm thinking about how much damage an evil cop can do. 'Cause even when they *ain't* evil, they're a whole lotta tr—"

"Boyfriend?" John repeated sharply, looking at me.

I returned his gaze and felt so awkward I couldn't think of what to say.

Lucky glanced at John's face—and started back-pedaling. "More like her *ex*-boyfriend. Or maybe not even that. Just some bum who didn't deserve her. But she still cares about h . . . cares what *happens* to . . . Um, just because things didn't work out between them, it don't mean she wants to see him get whacked by something evil."

"Close enough," I said. "Stop talking now."

"No problem," said the old mobster.

5

John turned his gaze from Lucky to me. And unlike *some* people, he chose his words carefully. "The cop you're concerned about—Quinn's partner—is the guy you've been seeing?"

I suppose "seeing" was vague enough to be accurate, so I said, "Yes."

"Are you still . . . I mean, is it over?"

"Um . . ." I had no idea what the answer was to that.

He asked, "Do you still want . . . um . . . do you—"

"John," his father admonished. "Is this any of our business?"

Apparently recalling that we weren't alone, John cleared his throat and changed the subject. "So the question is, what do we do about our . . . your . . . the suspicion that Detective Quinn is dangerous?"

"The same thing we must do about Mr. Capuzzo," said Max.

"Bury him as soon as possible?" I guessed dubiously.

"No, find out everything we can about him," Max replied. "Between Nelli's reaction to the detective's presence at the crime scene today, and the detective's subsequent presence here today when Mr. Capuzzo was reanimated by an as-yet-unidentified influence, there is currently only one thing we can state with certainty."

I guessed again. "There's something very strange about one or both of them?"

"Correct!" Max beamed at me, his favorite student. "Therefore, our first task is to learn as much as we can about both men, so that we can ascertain—"

"—exactly *what* is strange about one or both of them," I concluded.

"Precisely!" He paused, then said, "You've met Detective Quinn, Esther. Did you notice anything about him? What sort of man does he seem to be?"

"He seems like . . ." I shrugged. "A regular guy."

Detective Andrew Quinn looked like he was in his late thirties. Average height, average build, average features. The most noticeable thing about him was probably his red hair. His face was lightly freckled and a little careworn, like he'd known his share of trouble in life. He was a bit of a smart aleck and perhaps a little crass, but he seemed serious about his work and, on the whole . . .

"Just a regular guy," I said again.

"That was my impression, too," said John. "He was deep into cop mode when he came here, so I wouldn't say he was *friendly,* but he seemed reasonable, professional . . . ordinary. I don't think it would have occurred to me in a million years that he might have something to do with Mr. Capuzzo getting, uh, reanimated. Not until you guys brought it up. There was nothing . . . weird about Detective Quinn. He didn't give off a 'vibe' or anything like that."

I nodded in agreement. "He's only been partnered with Lopez for a few weeks, and I've only spoken with him once." He had urged me to sleep with Lopez (again), which Quinn figured would put the guy in a better mood and make him easier to work with. "It would be a wild exaggeration to say we hit it off, but he was pretty easy to talk to, and I can't think of anything about him that seemed 'off' or odd. Not even in retrospect."

"His reaction to Nelli today seemed pretty normal, too," Lucky added.

"That's right," I said. "He just acted like a guy avoiding a vicious dog. Not like some evil entity who felt *exposed* by Nelli's keen animal instincts."

"Still, if he *is* strange . . . evil . . . whatever," said Lucky, "he'd be good at covering, right?"

"True," I said. "If he weren't good at it, then he'd have been exposed before now."

"Yeah, for one thing, your boyfr—uh, Detective Lopez would notice quick if Quinn ever seemed, y'know . . . *wrong*."

"Lopez?" John looked at me again. "That's his name?"

"The guy is smart. He don't miss much," said Lucky. "I'm not Wonder Boy's biggest fan, but—"

"Because of Esther?" John asked.

Lucky scowled. "Because Lopez is the cause of these unconscionable intrusions of privacy that are hurtin' the perfectly legitimate business interests of Victor Gambello and a bunch of our associates."

"Oh!" John said in surprise. "He's in charge of the investigation into, um . . . that?"

The Chens never mentioned Lucky's criminal life. It was a feat of considerable tact, given that Lucky had been deeply involved in Gambello business for decades and was famous—or notorious—in certain circles.

"No, I think his lieutenant is in charge of the case," I said. "And it's a big investigation, involving a bunch of detectives. But Lopez is the one who found some key evidence, and he's been making a lot of the recent arrests."

"Is Detective Lopez . . ." Nathan glanced anxiously at Lucky. "Is he still making arrests? I mean—should you leave town for a while, Alberto?"

"It's okay, Dad," said John. "A cop at the scene of the shooting today told Uncle Lucky he's in the clear."

Nathan looked relieved. He asked Lucky, "This is definite? You're sure?"

The Chens had been worried about Lucky during the OCCB's recent sweep through the Gambello family. Lucky had been worried, too, in fact, and he'd been hiding out here in the funeral home before finally learning earlier today that the cops weren't looking for him.

"Definite," said Lucky. "Detective Lopez and I kinda bumped into each other today, and to give him credit, he told me fair and square, they got no evidence against me."

"*That* was Lopez?" John said to me. "That cop who told us that?"

"Yes."

"Oh." John looked bemused for moment, then shrugged. "He didn't seem . . . Well, I guess after Uncle Lucky told me about the guy who didn't treat you right, I pictured this cop walking around with *jerk* stamped on his forehead. But that detective seemed like an okay guy."

"He is an okay guy," I said. "We just . . . never mind."

"And he seemed like he was on top of things, too," said John. "Good at his job, I mean."

"He is good at his . . . Can we talk about something else?"

"How about we return to my point," said Lucky, "which is that Detective Lopez would notice if there was something weird about Quinn. I don't mean that Quinn's *not* weird. I just mean, if Lopez don't see it—even after spending every day with the guy for a few weeks—then we sure ain't gonna see it just from meeting him once or twice."

"Yes, you're right," said Max, who'd had a frown of concentration on his face while the rest of us had been talking. "Another police interview or a social encounter is likely to be insufficient exposure for our purposes. Especially if Detective Quinn is a skilled dissembler, as we suspect may be the case. It would be advantageous if we could monitor him for a protracted period."

"You mean, spy on him?" I asked doubtfully. "Follow him?"

"Don't you think a detective would notice something like that?" said John.

"Especially if he also has mystical power?" I added.

"Mystical . . . Oh, you mean if he's someone who can animate a corpse, for example?" said John.

Nathan said faintly, "Between John nearly being killed and then Mr. Capuzzo . . . Well, this is turning out to be one of the worst days of my life."

"Hang in there, Nate," said Lucky. "We're on it."

"It'll be okay, Dad," said John. "I'm fine, Susan's in jail, and Dr. Zadok—I mean, Max—knows about stuff like our—our . . . stuff like this."

"We need to get in this cop's life and dig deeper," Lucky said to Max.

"Yes, we shall have to find a way," Max agreed.

Lucky said hesitantly to me, "It seemed today like you're on speaking terms with Lopez again. Am I right?"

"Yes . . ." Well, for the moment, though it might not last. I met Lucky's gaze and realized why he was asking. "*Oh.* You want me to pepper Lopez with questions about Quinn."

Max said gently, "If it wouldn't be too awkward for you, Esther, it could be useful. Detective Quinn's professional partner—a person who spends a lot of time in our quarry's company—is our most likely source of information until we can think of something more inventive."

Thinking of my smash-and-grab last night to steal Lopez's deadly fortune cookie, I said, "I'm not so sure Lopez will be forthcoming, but I'll figure out something." If Quinn was a danger to Lopez, then I was going to find out, one way or another, whether Lopez was speaking to me or not.

"And I will pursue inquiries about Mr. Capuzzo," said Max.

"Where will you start?" Nathan asked—a little anxiously, I thought.

"The widow," Max replied. "I shall visit her under the guise of discussing the details of her late husband's upcoming wake."

"Oh." Nathan looked sad for a moment. I supposed he was thinking wistfully about the large Capuzzo family who had some money and were easy to work with. And also thinking about how they might abandon their sentimental attachment to this funeral home after meeting Max.

"I'll go with you, Doc," said Lucky.

"Oh?" Now Nathan looked alarmed. "Are you sure that's a good idea, Alberto? The Capuzzos might recognize your name."

"Hmm. Good point." Lucky nodded. But Nathan's relief was short-lived. "I'll use a fake name. Do you think I should wear a disguise?"

"No," I said quickly, recalling Lucky's brief masquerade as Sugarplum, one of Santa's elves, when we were investigating the mystical mayhem at Fenster & Co. during the holidays. I had seldom seen anything more tragic than Lucky in that disguise, and I shunned anything that might keep the memory alive—such as another disguise.

"Yeah, you're right, kid," he said. "My face ain't famous."

"Actually, it is," I said, "but only in very specific venues."

Nathan cleared his throat. John looked at Nelli, who lay snoozing quietly on the floor at Max's feet.

Lucky said, "So a phony name is all I need to go undercover with the doc."

"Oh, good," Nathan said in a thin voice, his expression strained.

Well, he had wanted our help. He had no one to blame but himself.

"So we're goin' to pump the widow for info about Capuzzo, while posing as associates of Antonelli's Funeral Home."

"It's a fine plan," Nathan said wanly.

Lucky looked at me. "And you'll pump Lopez about Quinn."

I nodded, feeling a little wan myself.

Max said to the Chens, "Be sure to notify us if anything else alarming occurs."

"We will," said John. "I have to admit, I'm looking forward to getting Mr. Capuzzo out of here."

I rose to my feet. "Well, it's been a long day for all of us."

"It's a New Year I'll certainly never forget," said Nathan, also rising.

As we all left the office and headed toward the building exit, John took my elbow and guided me out of earshot of the three older men, who were chatting about the fire at Yee & Sons, Max's sooty appearance, and the fact that Nelli was probably hungry by now.

"It *has* been a long day," John said to me in a low voice, "but I'm kind of keyed up. I don't suppose you'd like to go somewhere and . . . just talk for a while? We could get a drink or something to eat . . ."

Since I had a shrewd suspicion that he wanted to talk about me and Lopez—or maybe about me and him—I was relieved to have a good excuse for declining. "I'm sorry, John, I can't. Max has had an exhausting day, including being caught in that fire at the Yees' store. He's older than he looks, and I think he's running on fumes by now. I want to get him home, get a hot meal into him, and take Nelli for her late walk so that he doesn't have to."

"Right. Of course." John nodded, obviously understanding my concern. "He does look pretty worn out. Okay, well, maybe next time?"

"Sure." I pulled out my phone as I said over my shoulder, "Max? What's the name of that pet transport service you use? I really don't think we'll get a taxi."

Looking at the face of my phone, I realized I hadn't checked my messages yet.

"Oh, don't call a service," said Nathan. "John will give you a lift in the hearse."

"Absolutely," said John.

"How thoughtful," Max said with a tired smile.

"Oh." I put my phone back in my pocket. "Thanks."

Max lived in a roomy but spartan apartment above his perfectly legitimate business interest, Zadok's Rare & Used Books, which was in an old townhouse on a narrow street in the West Village.

The bookstore had a small, fiercely loyal customer

base, and it got some foot traffic from curious pass-ersby. But the shop was primarily an inconspicuous home base for Max's demanding role as the Magnum Collegium's local representative, responsible for pro-tecting New York and its inhabitants from Evil.

His laboratory, where strange and magical things happened, was in the cellar below the store. Among other things, it was down there that he had conjured Nelli last year. Max's mystical familiar had entered this dimension as a large, furry, enthusiastic champion in the perpetual confrontation against Evil—and had scared me to death at the time, before I realized she wasn't some voracious hellhound intent on ripping out our throats.

Looking at her now, I reflected—not for the first time—that she'd be a more convenient comrade if she could speak, or write, or at least mime. If only she could *tell* us why she had reacted so hysterically to en-countering Quinn. Was it something about the way he smelled? Or the way he moved? Was there an evil light glowing in his eyes that the rest of us couldn't see? Did other dogs react negatively to him, or was the trigger-ing factor something that only a mystical being could sense? I suspected it was the latter, since Quinn's life would be awfully inconvenient if every canine who saw him went as crazy as Nelli did today.

I had initially hoped Nelli had made a mistake—perhaps confused Quinn with someone or something else and was reacting on the basis of misidentification. But after what had happened at the funeral home as soon as Quinn visited the place . . . No, it was no mistake. I felt certain of that. Nelli had definitely sensed something dangerous about him.

But *what?*

"I wish Nelli could talk," I said to Max in frustration.

"If she could talk, then she might not be able to detect dangerous entities or contribute powers to our work which I lack," he said placidly. "A mystical familiar possesses gifts which are not available to other types of beings. Just as you and I possess the gift of speech, which is not available to an individual of Nelli's nature."

"Hmph."

"This soup is delicious," said Max. "Exactly what I needed."

"It is good," I agreed, and I ate some more of mine.

John had dropped us off here a little while ago, along with Nelli (who fit comfortably in the roomy back of the hearse), and was now on his way to Queens to drop off Lucky. A widower with a daughter who lived out of state, Lucky had sold the family home and bought a small condo in Forest Hills, not far from where Victor Gambello, the Shy Don, had an impressive house with a large, well-manicured yard. (I had seen it a couple of times on TV, in the background behind journalists reporting on Gambello indictments or deaths.)

I had gone to the local deli to pick up some hot soup and sandwiches while Max showered and changed, and then he joined me in the bookstore for this quiet, companionable meal. The night was bitterly cold, but we were cozy and warm now, relaxing in a pair of comfortable old easy chairs next to the bookstore's little gas fireplace.

The shop had well-worn hardwood floors, a broad-beamed ceiling, and dusky rose walls. It contained a rabbit warren of tall bookcases stuffed with a wide variety of books about the occult printed in more than a dozen languages. The stock ranged from recent paperbacks to old, rare, and very expensive leather-bound tomes. There was also a small refreshments station which Max kept stocked with coffee, tea, and cookies for his customers, and a large, attractive old walnut table with books, papers, and various paraphernalia on it. Along the far wall of the shop there was an extremely large wooden cupboard that happened to be possessed; although the cupboard was prone to alarming displays of smoke, noise, shrieks, and agitated rattling, it had been silent and dormant lately—which was a relief, since Nelli barked furiously when it acted up. I'd had enough drama for one day.

There was a stairwell at the back of the shop. One staircase descended to the laboratory. The other led up to Max's apartment on the second floor—and to Hieronymus's rooms on the third floor. The evil apprentice was long gone, but I still thought of those rooms as his—and not in a happy way.

I didn't regret what we had done to that homicidally maniacal creep, not for a moment; but it nonetheless haunted me at times. Dissolution, which was his fate, was not the same thing as death, but it was a lot like it—so *much* like it that the difference seemed pretty trifling to me. I hadn't dissolved him, so to speak, but I had certainly helped. And I'd do it again, too . . . But that didn't mean it was something I could ever tell Lopez about.

They say that secrets are bad for a relationship. While I stared into the glowing flames of the gas fire, feeling pleasantly full, I reflected that the truth could be bad for it, too. I wished Lopez hadn't found out that I was the one who smashed in his car window and stole his fortune cookie. At the time, I had felt too panic-stricken by the sight of that deadly confection to realize—or care—how conspicuous my behavior was.

Oh, well. It couldn't be helped. He knew, and I'd just have to deal with that. Given the same set of circumstances, after all, I'd do exactly the same thing again. The cookie had to be removed and neutralized—and *immediately*, too. Lopez would have died very soon (perhaps only moments) after that fragile, murderous thing sustained any damage—such as being broken open, as fortune cookies usually were.

When Max finished eating, I insisted he go straight

up to bed while I took Nelli for her walk. It was a bitterly cold night and the sidewalks were a mess—slushy,
icy, and filthy. While Nelli, now dressed in a mauve
vest lined with faux fur, took her time about sniffing
every revolting object lying on the street, I decided I
might as well take advantage of the relative privacy out
here to phone Lopez and get our argument over with.
Then I'd ask him about Quinn.

I wasn't sure whether I was relieved or disappointed
when all I got was his voicemail. I left a message asking
him to call me back. "I really want to talk to you," I
said. "So call even if it's late, okay?"

After I got back to the store, I removed Nelli's vest
and sent her upstairs to bed, too, in Max's apartment.
Remembering that I still hadn't checked my messages—
and there had been a call while I was at the funeral
home—I decided to warm up for a few minutes before
going home. I turned on the electric kettle to make myself a cup of hot tea, then I sat down and looked at my
phone.

There was only one message, and it was from Thack,
my agent. I supposed he'd found out *ABC* had been
shut down and called to discuss it with me. I hoped he
could make sure I at least got paid through the end of
the week. I wondered briefly when Ted had found time
today to contact Thack, but I was suddenly so depressed by the thought of the lost income that I didn't
follow that train of thought.

It had been a bad winter for me, and I had no financial cushion. I was going to have to start looking for work first thing tomorrow, something that would keep money coming in until I got another acting job. Waitress, retail clerk, office temp . . . I'd have to find something, and soon, or I wouldn't be able to get through the coming month.

To my surprise, though, Thack's message was not a condolence call about *ABC*. He obviously didn't even know the project had closed down. His message said he needed my filming schedule right away, because *D30* wanted me back on set for an unspecified number of days, to reprise my role as Jilly C-Note.

I was so happy, I jumped out of my chair and cheered. Then I looked guiltily at the ceiling for a moment, but I didn't really think I'd been loud enough to disturb Max.

The Dirty Thirty, known affectionately to fans as *D30*, was a cult hit on cable television and the most controversial show in a group of prestigious New York-based police dramas all produced by the same company. Their flagship program was *Crime and Punishment* (aka *C&P*), and their other big successes were *Criminal Motive* (the "brainiest" of their shows) and *Street Unit* (aimed at "the young, hip, now generation," yet somehow not a disaster).

I had done a couple of bit parts for *C&P*, and then last summer, I got cast in a juicy role on *The Dirty Thirty*, playing Jilly C-Note (not her real name), a homeless bisexual junkie prostitute suspected of killing her pimp. (The violent death of her pimp was *why* Jilly was now homeless.)

D30 scripts were dark, gritty morality plays in which flawed characters had to decide between various bad alternatives and always seemed to wind up making the worst possible choice—even on those rare occasions when they had good intentions. In my episode, the morally bankrupt cops of the corrupt Thirtieth Precinct pressured my character over the murder of her pimp, even though they had no solid evidence against her, in order to pump her for information about other criminal activity in their precinct. They knew but didn't care (well, not enough to mend their ways) that forcing Jilly to inform on her acquaintances was likely to get her killed. One of the detectives, Jimmy Conway, also used Jilly for sex.

(Most cops, including Lopez, hated *D30* with a deep, bitter, and unbridled loathing.)

Detective Jimmy Conway, a lead character in the ensemble cast, was an edgy, tightly wound, emotionally decaying cop struggling with alcoholism and (since getting shot in the first year's season finale) post-traumatic stress disorder.

I wondered what sort of a basket case Conway would be now that he had been shot *again*.

Michael Nolan, the actor who played Conway, had suffered two heart attacks before we finished filming my episode. Doing some fast rewrites to explain Nolan's sudden absence from the show, the writers had pumped two more bullets into Conway and hospitalized him indefinitely.

Most of my scenes had been with him, so as a result of the rewrites to eliminate Nolan from the rest of that ill-fated episode, much of my role had been cut, too. Though I still received full pay, I was very disappointed, since it was a juicy script and an interesting character. The people at C&P Productions kept saying that I had been a pleasure to work with and they felt bad about cutting down my part so much as a result of circumstances. They told Thack they'd find something for me on one of their shows, to make it up to me, and they had auditioned me a couple of times since then, but nothing had come of it.

I had by now assumed I wouldn't be working for C&P in the foreseeable future. And I certainly hadn't expected to reprise my role as Jilly C-Note.

I wondered if this meant Michael Nolan was ready to go back to work. Although I hadn't seen the show (my budget didn't stretch to a cable TV subscription), I'd heard that since his heart attacks, Nolan had only appeared two or three times as Conway, always lying in a hospital bed, weak and barely verbal. But it had been more than five months since the actor was hospitalized, so he might be in much better shape by now than his character was.

Thrilled at the prospect of doing some well-written and well-paid TV work, and trying not to get my hopes too high ("an unspecified number of days" could mean as little as a half day of work), I started to return Thack's call—but then I looked at the time and decided to wait until tomorrow.

The best plan now, I realized, would be to head home before it got any later or colder, get a good night's sleep, and then call Thack first thing tomorrow. I turned off the kettle, turned out the lights, and closed up Max's shop. I walked toward the subway, floating on the hope that the lousy luck which had plagued me for the past couple of months was finally changing.

On the way home, I tried Lopez one more time. He still wasn't answering.

6

Thackeray Shackleton had reinvented himself upon moving to New York ten years ago by shedding his past as a Lithuanian-American vampire from Wisconsin, changing his name in tribute to two of his heroes (William Makepeace Thackeray and Sir Ernest Shackleton), and fully embracing his current incarnation as a cultured man-about-town and reputable theatrical agent. He was also a foodie who somehow managed to stay slim—which was just as well, because he had a fortune invested in his exquisitely tailored suits and casual wear.

As you'd expect of a well-dressed man who loved theater and watched his weight, Thack was gay. He was also a mostly non-practicing Catholic, an avid supporter of the New York Public Library, and a wine snob. None of which had anything to do with his being a hereditary vampire from a long line that extended (at least in theory) all the way back to the Lithuanian medieval warrior king, Gediminas.

I only learned about the vampirism a few months ago. It was, understandably, something that Thack kept very private. For one thing, publicizing his origins would attract precisely the sort of goth guys and vampire groupies whom Thack loathed, while simultaneously repelling the sort of erudite, socially conventional people he identified with. For another, claiming vampirism could easily call his credibility (and sanity) into question in our mundane and judgmental world. Finally, he was, by emphatic choice, largely disengaged from his vampire roots. Thack only drank a little blood during ritual ceremonies on the rare occasions when he visited his very traditional family back in Oshkosh.

Thack seemed a little defensive about turning his back on his heritage, but I understood. After all, I almost never attend synagogue unless I'm visiting my parents back in Madison.

The fact that Thack and I were both from Wisconsin was just coincidence. But it meant we had things in common—a strong work ethic, good manners . . . and a fervent desire not to go back to the region where we had learned those sterling values. Although we were both transplants, we had each sunk our roots deep in New York City and considered it our permanent home. Despite what it cost to live here.

The prospect of actually being able to afford that cost of living was among the reasons I was so happy about what Thack told me the following morning.

"I'm sorry to hear about *ABC*. And Ted Yee should have told *me*, not you—that bum!" Thack said over the phone. "It's my job to break news like that to you. I suppose he was utterly tactless?"

"Well, he'd had a run of bad lu—"

"Well, don't worry, Esther. His choosing not to finish the film has nothing to do with his obligations to you. I saw to that in your contract. If he's got any of his backer's money left, I'll squeeze it out of him."

That was a conversation I would leave to Thack and Ted, though I suspected there wouldn't be as much money left as Thack hoped.

"Anyhow, this turn of events works out well, in its way," he said, "because it would have been a shame if your contract for a low-budget, low-quality indie film that didn't pay well wound up interfering with a juicy guest spot on an award-winning television show with an obscenely elastic budget." He paused, then said, "Unless Ted Yee's facile, inarticulate persona was just a façade, and he was actually a brilliant writer and director? Oh, dear, *please* don't tell me *ABC* would have been the sleeper hit of the year or a standout sensation on the film festival circuit."

"No, it was pretty lame," I assured him.

"Just as well it folded, then," Thack said ruthlessly.

"I've had an availability check. *D-Thirty* would like to get you back on set in your previous role as Jenny Diver."

"Jilly C-Note."

"Close enough. You'll be scheduled for scattered days over a period of about three weeks, doing both studio and location shoots. It's a little vague at the moment because the scripts aren't finalized yet."

"Starting when?" I asked.

"Next week."

"And the scripts aren't final?" I asked in surprise. Sure, things changed at the last minute all the time with TV and film, but shooting schedules, sets, and locations were usually determined in advance, not at the last minute.

"Between you and me," said Thack, "I gather this is Michael Nolan's doing. He says he's ready to go back to work now. He doesn't want to wait until the new season starts filming."

"It sounds like Jimmy Conway is about to experience a miraculous recovery."

"Well, you know how competitive this business is," said Thack. "Nolan has been out for months. Other actors saw their chance. So did writers who don't like Nolan."

Nolan was not a likable guy. He was, however, a charismatic actor whose compelling performance as Jimmy Conway had done a lot to generate the fascination people had with this acclaimed show, which had not initially been expected to succeed (network television, the usual stomping ground of C&P programs, had refused to touch it because of the dark tone and raw subject matter).

Thack continued, "So other actors stepped into the spotlight, and their characters have flowed in to fill the void left by Jimmy Conway when he got shot—*again*. That guy must be the unluckiest cop in the whole city."

"But Michael Nolan still has clout," I guessed, "so when he recognized the danger, he decided he couldn't afford to wait until next season to reclaim the focus."

"That would be my guess," said Thack, "based on the tidbits my C&P contact has let drop."

It didn't surprise me. In addition to being rude, arrogant, and narcissistic, Nolan was also a workaholic. He had risked his health to keep working, and he'd paid a steep price for that. He had his first heart attack on the *D30* set while we were filming on location at night. The second heart attack a few days later—a day on which he tried to return to work—was so severe it nearly killed him. He'd been recuperating since then. Nolan no doubt *hated* being sidelined and would do whatever was necessary—after months of absence, during which time other actors' characters had been fascinating his fans—to rise again to the top of the talented *D30* heap.

"So," said Thack, "now there's a frantic last-minute

push to restructure the final episodes of the season in a way that inserts Detective Jimmy Conway back into the story arc. And that's where your character comes in."

"How?"

"I have no idea. And I don't think the producers have a very *clear* idea, since they didn't even know if you were available when I was contacted yesterday. In any case, they're not going to tell me anything about the script. And you'll have to sign a confidentiality agreement." He added with amusement, "They seem to be treating their unwritten season finale as a bigger secret than the location of the Holy Grail."

"I suppose it's a question of ratings."

"If anyone asks you, you are not to tell them your Chinatown film was canceled," Thack instructed. "Because when I call C&P, right after I get off the phone with you, I shall negotiate a fee commensurate with the stress and inconvenience of your having to rearrange your schedule on a cutting-edge, award-quality indie film in order to accommodate *D-Thirty*."

"Ah. This is an example of why you're the agent and I'm just the thespian."

"Another reason is that I get terrible stage fright." He added, "Keep your schedule open for the next few days. If you're filming next week, their wardrobe department will need to see you right away."

After we ended the call, I felt a burst of optimism and energy. My luck was finally turning around! The fee for this job would cover my bills for a while, I'd get to work on something a lot better than Ted's film (let alone waiting tables or doing filing and typing), and I'd get exposure on a respected national TV show.

It was all good.

Until Lopez called.

"Sorry I didn't call you back last night," he said. "I just got your message a few minutes ago. My phone died yesterday."

"When?" I wondered. It had been working fine before the shooting when I called him for help, and then I had seen him using it in the aftermath.

"A little while after my *car* died," he said wearily. "When Quinn and I were ready to leave the scene of the shooting, we found out we couldn't. The car wouldn't start."

"Oh." Car and phone dying on the same day. No wonder he didn't sound perky. "This was a police car?"

"Yeah—and it's the third one in a row we've had problems with." He added bitterly, "So much for providing the police force with reliable equipment so that we can protect and serve."

"Three cars in a row?" I could see how that would get wearing. Trying to see the bright side, I said, "But at least you don't have to pay for repairs, right? The cars belong to the department."

"And considering what we use them for—going to crime scenes, investigating murder and armed robbery, responding to emergency calls—you'd think the department would maintain the damn things. It's not as if I'm relying on their cars to cruise for chicks or go on a beer run."

"Did you just say 'cruise for chicks'?"

"But *no*, making sure we don't freeze to death in the middle of winter because the heater keeps breaking down, or installing a police radio that actually *works* so that we know what's going on in the city we're paid to protect . . . *That* is apparently too much to ask of NYPD support services in the twenty-first century."

"You've made this speech before, haven't you?" I guessed.

"Sorry," he said sheepishly. "I didn't mean to . . ." Over the phone, I heard his long sigh. "But this has been going on for weeks. I'm getting really fed up."

"And yet you conceal it so well."

Now I heard his soft snort of laughter. "Yeah, well . . . I guess yesterday was the straw that broke my back. I waited *forever* in the freezing cold for the tow truck—which I think set out for the Bowery by taking a shortcut through Patagonia or something. I was there for so long, in temperatures that could kill a Yeti, I thought I'd start collecting my pension before the truck finally arrived."

"The car was parked on the Bowery?" In the whirling collage of my memories of the shooting, I vaguely recalled that was the direction I saw Lopez coming from, though he was on foot when he appeared on Doyers Street to help prevent Susan from killing John.

"Well, not *parked* so much as just left sitting there," he said. "As you may remember, we arrived in kind of a rush. Which reminds me . . . Susan Yee intended to kill this guy John Chen because . . . she didn't want him to help her brother make the movie?"

"Yeah. Where'd you hear that?" I wondered if Quinn had known when he'd questioned John about it yesterday.

"Cops tell each other things."

"Oh, of course. You got it from the Fifth Precinct."

"I've heard a lot of really dumb, pointless, inane motives for murder," he said. "But I think Susan probably wins the grand prize with that one. I mean, why not just sabotage the financing or vandalize the equipment? She's a straight-A grad student, for God's sake. You'd think she could come up with a better plan than one that'll get her sent to prison for a long, long time."

"I think she had already tried sabotage and vandalism," I said carefully. "But Ted was more perseverant than she expected."

"So she decided to make the leap to murder," he said in disgust. "Jesus."

"Actually . . ." This might be the moment to raise the subject of the deadly fortune cookies.

He continued, "And trying to kill Chen in the middle of that crowd was even crazier. Come to think of it,

I'll bet her lawyer has a good shot at an insanity defense."

I chickened out. Instead, I tried to direct the conversation to a different problem. "What does Detective Quinn think about it?"

"Andy? I think he said, 'Crazy murdering bitch.' Which seems to be the majority view at the Fifth, too." He paused, then said in a different tone of voice, "I'm really glad you didn't get hurt. And I'm sorry that Ted's not finishing the film. I know you were glad to have the work."

"You talked to Ted?" I asked in surprise.

"No, that info came from my buddy in the department's film unit who was helping me get those location permits for Ted. He called Ted to get some details he needed, and Ted told him it was over, no permits needed." Lopez added, "Ted also told him about the fire. Did you know the Yees' whole store burned down yesterday?"

"Yes, I saw it," I said. "I was, uh, walking that way at the time."

"Fortunately, no one was hurt," he said. "It's too bad about the movie, though. From what Susan told the cops about her reasons for trying to kill John Chen, it sounds like there was a new plan to get more backers."

"Well, a *tentative* new plan." Trying to move the conversation back to Quinn, I said, "I stopped by the funeral home to see how John was after the shooting. He said Detective Quinn—um, Andy—had just been there."

"Yeah, he went there to get some details from the intended victim."

"But isn't the Fifth Precinct in charge of the case?"

"They are, but I thought we should follow up, too, since we'd been at the scene. And since Joe Ning's wake will be at Chen's, it also seemed like a chance to see if they know anything useful about his final days."

"But you didn't go?"

"Someone had to stay with the car," said Lopez. "I lost the coin toss."

"Ah."

"And then I wasn't able to reconnect with Andy until hours later, when I got to a landline." He started to sound exasperated again. "That cell was the second phone that's died on me this month!"

"You *are* having a run of bad luck." Not as bad as mine, but I could understand why he was aggravated.

"Don't even get me started," he muttered. "Now my computer at work has gone haywire, and IT can't figure out what's wrong with it. I think Andy screwed up something when he used it, but he claims I've got gremlins."

"*Anyhow,*" I said, "you found out your phone wasn't working while you were freezing to death in Chinatown, waiting eternally for a tow truck?"

"I swear, the Bowery must be the windiest street in

this hemisphere. And when I tried to call to ask where the damn truck was and found out I *couldn't* call . . . I got upset."

"Upset?"

"Okay, I acted out. Shouted and cursed and kicked things."

"Color me astonished." It wasn't hard to picture him blowing his stack at that point. Everyone has their moments.

"I scared some kids," he admitted guiltily. "That was unintentional, but their granny got mad. She hit me and called me bad names. I think she was speaking Fujianese, so I didn't know what she was saying. But I could tell from the kids' faces, they were *bad* words."

"You had a hard day."

"Yeah. Still I guess Ted Yee and John Chen both had a worse day than I did."

"What are you doing to your phones, anyhow, that they keep dying on you?"

"I'm not doing *anything* to them. They're just dying! Shoddy manufacturing or something."

I could tell from his tone that I was the umpteenth person to ask him that, so I dropped the subject. "Look, the reason I called you . . ."

When I didn't continue, he prodded, "Yes?"

"Well, we didn't finish talking about what happened the other night, did we?"

"The other night?"

"What I did the other night," I specified.

"What you did . . . Hmm. Remind me what you did the other night?"

"All right, I know you've had a bad week, but that's no reason to be mean," I admonished.

"Okay. You're right." There was a pause. "Well, do you want to start, or should I?"

"I'll go." I took a breath and forged ahead. "I panicked when I saw the cookie in your car, because those things are deadly. If you had cracked it open—if *anyone* had cracked it open—it would have killed you instantly."

There was a brief silence.

Then he said, "Killed me instantly?"

"Yes."

"How? Would death rays have burst out of it and turned me into ashes?"

"Don't be facetious. I'm trying to—"

"You're telling me that a cookie crumbling would have killed me, and you think *I'm* being facetious?"

"These deadly cookies are what killed Joe Ning and Benny Yee." Benny, an underworld figure of lower status than Ning, was Ted's uncle, and he had been the film's previous backer—until Susan killed him with a misfortune cookie. His death had been attributed to natural causes.

"I see. Benny Yee and Joe Ning were killed by cookies." Lopez's voice was deadpan. "That's your theory?"

"They were killed by mystical curses concealed in the cookies," I clarified.

"Did Max give you this idea?" he asked wearily.

"That's not important. I'm trying to tell you—"

"How many times do I have to ask you to stay away from him?"

I tried to keep my voice level and reasonable as I said, "He's one of the best men I've ever known. You have no idea how many people he has helped."

I could tell Lopez was trying to sound reasonable, too, when he said, "Look, I know you're very fond of him. And I know he's devoted to you. But, all things considered, I still don't think this is a good friendship for you."

"I'm not letting you pick my friends for me," I said firmly.

"Esther, he keeps putting these crazy ideas into your—"

"Will you stop blaming Max?" I said irritably. "Lucky is the one who—who . . . uh . . ."

"Lucky?" His voice was tense now. "Oh, that's great."

Well, the cat was out of the bag, so I might as well continue. "The death curses were originally Lucky's theory, not Max's," I said. "And he was right."

"Just *great*," Lopez said. "While I've got some fast-talking TV lawyer breathing down my neck and claiming I'm a corrupt cop just because Joe Ning fell off a slippery balcony, my girlfriend is chasing magical cookies with a famous Gambello killer. My week just can't *get* any better, can it?"

I sifted through that outburst, trying to decide which item to address first. I picked the part that was unfamiliar to me.

"What TV lawyer? Who's calling you corrupt? I don't . . ." Then I remembered what Nathan had said he'd seen on the news. "Oh, *wait*. That attorney who's claiming the cops drove Uncle Six to suicide—he's blaming *you*?"

"Yep," was the terse reply.

"Why?"

"Because he wants attention," Lopez said sourly. "He wants TV cameras focused on his face and microphones shoved under his nose. And because he thinks an NYPD cop trying to keep a killer in prison is an easy target."

"This is the same lawyer that Uncle Six hired to get his brother's conviction overturned?" I guessed.

"Yeah. But Joe's eldest son, who's head of the family now that the old man is dead, isn't dumb enough—thanks be to God—to throw away a fortune in legal fees trying to overturn a rock-solid case, if I do say so myself, in an attempt to get his rotten uncle back out on the streets so he can commit another murder," said Lopez. "Uncle Six's body—or what's left of it—wasn't even cold by the time the family terminated Goldman's services."

"Goldman?"

"Alan Goldman. The lawyer."

"Ohhh," I said in disappointment.

"What?"

"Nothing." I scowled. "I just hate it when the rich, sleazy lawyer is Jewish, you know?"

"Yeah, and I hate it when the drug-dealing thug is Hispanic," he replied. "But that's life, and nobody asks our opinion before they make those choices."

"I guess," I grumbled. "But why doesn't Goldman just move on to defending the next wealthy criminal?"

"Maybe he doesn't have another case lined up. Or not one that'll keep him in the spotlight right now."

"Oh, come on, the city must be full of dirty people with deep pockets who are in legal trouble," I said. "And it's not as if anyone's *paying* him to accuse you of driving Joe Ning to suicide. So why bother?"

"I think Goldman planned to position Paul Ning's case as a civil rights suit where he sought 'justice' for a hardworking family who'd been unfairly targeted because they're Chinese immigrants." Lopez blew out his breath. "Well, Joe Ning's fat fee isn't on the table anymore, but Goldman can still get plenty of media attention as a crusader trying to expose a corrupt department and a bent cop whose determination to keep Paul in prison drove a Chinatown community leader to suicide. Blah blah blah."

"But he can't prove—"

"He doesn't have to *prove* anything," Lopez said bitterly. "The media don't care about proof. They care about attention, just like Goldman. All he has to do, to get lots of mileage out of this, is keep insinuating and accusing." He added, "But since he's threatening to sue the department, maybe he thinks he can still get a fat fee out of this."

"Do you really think he'll go through with that threat?"

"I don't know. He probably doesn't know, either. Not yet. But threatening it gets him the kind of attention he wants."

Some of the questions Quinn had asked John made a little more sense now. Lopez and his partner wanted to know if Joe Ning had seemed distraught in his final days.

I knew Uncle Six had been murdered by Susan, but I couldn't prove it. Lopez seemed convinced it was an accident. And it would be easy for someone to claim that it was suicide.

"So if Joe Ning complained to anyone about the cops trying to keep his brother in prison," I said, "or if a few people thought he looked sad or stressed lately, then a fast-talking, telegenic lawyer who's eager to be seen as a crusader—"

"—could really run with that," Lopez said gloomily. "And maybe get somewhere."

"Is your job in danger because of this?" I asked with

concern. I didn't think that being a cop meant *everything* to him, but I knew it meant a hell of a lot.

"God, I hope not." Apparently not liking the way that sounded, he added in a sturdier tone, "It shouldn't be. I haven't gone anywhere near Joe Ning—or Paul, or anyone else in the family. I just followed procedure to make sure an old conviction was ready to stand up to scrutiny." After a moment, he muttered, "But that doesn't mean the media won't make a meal of this, with Goldman doing everything he can to encourage them."

"I'm sorry you're going through this."

"Joe Ning is turning out to be a thorn in my side even when he's dead," he said grumpily.

"And I'm sorry you had to do a lot of paperwork and maybe tell some lies because I smashed in the window of your police car. Your previous police car, I mean."

"That was the one where the radio kept going dead," he muttered.

"Look, I was worried about you," I said quietly. "So I did what I had to do."

"Break into my car and steal the death-ray cookie," he said. "That was what you had to do?"

"Yes."

"Okay, listen," he said, his tone changing. "Everything else aside . . . like your crazy cookie theory, your friendship with Max, your close association with a

Gambello killer, and a lot of really weird water that's flowed under the bridge ever since I met you . . ."

He'd called me his girlfriend a few minutes ago, but this sounded like the start of a breaking-up speech.

"*Everything* else aside," he said, "Esther, if you thought there was something deadly dangerous inside my car . . . why didn't you just call me?"

"Call you?"

"You know, on the *phone?*" he prodded. "You've got my number, and I was right in the neighborhood. Why didn't you call me and say, 'I'm worried about this thing in your car, and we should . . .' I don't know—drop it into an acid bath or something?"

It had never occurred to me to call him that night, since I knew he wouldn't believe me—and would certainly veto the idea of taking the cookie to Max to be neutralized, which was the only safe solution.

"The situation was urgent," I said. "You were in danger. I had to get rid of that thing—without arguing about it with *you* half the night."

"Did smashing in a car window really seem like a better plan than arguing with me?" he demanded.

"Well . . . yes," I admitted.

He sighed. "Okay, it's this. Right here. *This* is why I just can't figure out what to do."

"What to do?" I repeated.

"About you," he said. "About us."

My heart sank a little.

"I can't get on an even keel. I can't think straight anymore . . . I try to move forward, and I wind up moving in circles. Esther, I just can't . . . can't *do* this."

I could tell he was very serious now.

"Are you . . ." I cleared my throat. "Are you breaking up with me?"

7

When asking that question, I deliberately omitted the word *again*, since it would just add humiliation to my hurt.

"Breaking up with you?" he said. "Are we even together? I don't even know *that* much."

I didn't know, either. But whatever the right word was for what was between us, I had a feeling that it wasn't *together*.

We'd slept with each other, but only once. The closest we'd ever come to going on a date was when he bought me a chili dog in the park on a cold December night. Since we'd met—no, since he'd first broken up with me—months at a time passed without any contact between us. Recently, we'd gone several weeks without even being on speaking terms.

Sounding frustrated, he said, "I have no idea what's going on with us."

"A few minutes ago, you called me your girlfriend." As soon as the words were out of my mouth, I regretted them.

"I did?" He sounded puzzled.

Ouch. That hurt.

I decided not to pursue it. Instead I asked, "What exactly are you trying to say to me?"

"Good question." He was silent for a moment. "I think there is something I'm trying to say, I just don't know what. But, uh . . ."

"But?"

"I have the feeling that this isn't a phone conversation."

I frowned. "Yes, it is. We're on the phone."

"I mean, I think if we're going to talk about us—and it seems like that's something we need to do—we should do it in person."

Right. Where I could see him. So that losing him would hurt even more. Good plan.

Can you lose someone you're not even together with?

"Maybe you're right," I said. "Maybe this isn't a phone conversation."

"Esther, I . . ."

"What?"

By the time he finally spoke, I thought he'd changed his mind about saying something.

"I think about you all the time," he told me.

"Oh," I said, surprised and pleased. And now I felt a little better. This was what he could do to me, without even trying.

"But I . . . well, I tried to date you, and it didn't work," he said. "I tried to break up with you, and that didn't work, either. I tried to stay away, and I couldn't. I tried to get back together with you, and it was a mess."

That depressing summary, I realized, was an accurate account of our relationship.

"That's why this isn't a phone conversation," he said, sounding tired. "It's not nearly simple enough to talk about over the phone."

"No, it's really not," I agreed.

After a moment of silence, he asked hesitantly, "So are we done talking? For now, I mean?"

I was about to say yes, but then I remembered there was another subject we needed to cover. "There's one other thing."

"What?" he asked warily.

"What can you tell me about Detective Quinn?" I asked.

"Huh?" He sounded understandably surprised.

"Andy."

"Yeah, I know who you mean. Why are you asking about him?"

Inspiration struck me. "Is he single?"

"Yes," Lopez replied. "Well, divorced. Why?"

"I have a friend I was thinking he might like," I lied.

"You want to set up one of your friends with Andy?" he asked dubiously.

"Maybe," I said. "He seems like a decent guy. And he has a good job. But I only met him that one time. So I need to know more about him."

"Like what?"

I thought quickly. "Does he like animals?"

"Why is *that* what you want to know?"

"My friend is a dog lover."

"Well, we've never talked about it, so I don't know."

"Speaking of dogs," I said oh-so-casually, "I hope he wasn't too upset about Nelli's behavior to him yesterday?"

"You mean, was he upset that a dog the size of a minivan tried to go for his throat?" Lopez said. "Actually, he took it pretty well. Never even mentioned it. But now that you bring it up, Esther, you've got to talk to Max about that d—"

"Andy is divorced?" I interrupted. "Has he told you what happened?"

He paused for a moment, deciding whether to let me get away with changing the subject, then gave in. "Not really. Just that marriage is tough, especially when one partner is a cop, relationships turn sour, that kind of thing." After a moment, he added, "His first wife left him for another man, but he doesn't seem bitter about that. It sounds like the marriage had already run its course by then."

"*First* wife?" I prodded.

"Yeah, he was married twice. The second divorce—I think that one bothers him more."

"Bothers him in what way?"

"Still hurts."

I tried to think of what else to ask. "How about on the job? You're with him all day long. Is he good company?"

"He's okay. We get along."

Lopez's traditional male reticence about these topics was frustrating. Most women I knew, including me, could have riffed for at least ten minutes on any one of those questions. So could Thack, as well as quite a few actors and male cabaret artistes of my acquaintance. But Detective Lopez stuck to annoyingly brief answers as I continued poking and prodding. Since the two men had been working together for only a few weeks, he also just didn't know that much.

It sounded like Quinn had a checkered career in the department, but Lopez was vague about that—and it obviously hadn't been checkered *enough* to prevent Quinn from becoming a detective second grade and getting assigned to the OCCB. His personal life had a few problems ("like most people's" Lopez said), and his two divorces had played havoc with his finances (whereas unemployment was what tended to play havoc with mine). But there wasn't anything about him that sounded . . . well, *evil*.

"Is he Catholic?" I asked.

"Lapsed."

I phrased my next question carefully. "Is he into any New Age stuff?"

"Like what?"

"Unconventional beliefs or unorthodox practices?"

In the silence that followed, I realized I had over-played my hand.

"All right, now I have a question," he said. "What the hell are you doing?"

"Trying to learn more about Quinn."

"Why? For real, this time."

Oh, well, no point in playing dumb. It would just annoy him. "Because there's something strange about him."

Lopez snorted.

"*Really* strange," I said.

"Talk about the pot calling the kettle black."

"That's why Nelli reacted so badly when she—"

"You know what? I don't even want to hear it. Just don't tell me."

"I'm just saying—"

"*No*," he said. "I've had enough. Breaking into my car to steal a cookie is one thing, but this is a *person* you're talking about. And my partner."

"That's why I'm so con—"

"So whatever the hell has got you fixated on Andy now, let it go, Esther."

"But—"

"I *mean* it," he said. "Drop it, forget it, and move on. And leave Detective Quinn alone."

"If you'd just—"

"We're done here, Esther." Before ending the call, he added, "Oh, and do something about that neurotic dog of Max's before she mauls someone, would you?"

After that, I sat staring moodily at my phone for a while, working my way through anger, frustration, sadness, worry, and resignation.

In retrospect, I thought the entire conversation had gone worse than expected. Moreover, I didn't think I had learned anything useful about Quinn, but now Lopez would be defensive about his partner—and might even warn Quinn that I'd taken an interest in him, so to speak.

I felt like I had failed in every respect.

Plus, it sounded as if, even though Lopez had feelings for me, he was giving serious consideration to ending our . . . whatever was between us.

Which didn't change the fact that he was partnered with someone who I suspected of reanimating the dead. Someone who I feared might be very dangerous—and might be a menace to Lopez.

I had to learn more about Quinn. And Lopez certainly wouldn't help.

So I needed to find another way.

But no bright ideas were coming to me, and I wouldn't have a chance to talk to Max and Lucky before this evening. They were venturing out to the suburbs today to interview the bereaved Capuzzo family and find out what they could about the departed. We would meet at the bookstore this evening to compare notes and decide what to do next.

Meanwhile, I'd been so busy lately that I'd had no time to do laundry or clean the apartment. And since I didn't need to go look for a job today—long live *The Dirty Thirty!*—I decided to spend the day catching up on chores.

I lived in a rent-controlled apartment in the West Thirties. The High Line, a public park built on an elevated old freight rail line, now ran along the West Side, starting below Fourteenth Street and ending in the lower Thirties. Frenzied development followed closely behind the gradual construction of this park, and so the area had gotten more upmarket—as well as more expensive. My street, however, hadn't changed a bit yet, and it was almost as elegant as the floor of a public bathroom.

My apartment had the usual flaws of rent-controlled accommodation, being shabby, poorly maintained, and drafty. But I had a lot of space for a person of my modest income living in Manhattan—though it would be considered cramped by the standards of cities with more elbow room. The place was furnished with thrift shop finds, hand-me-downs, and items abandoned by roommates who'd fled New York after a year or two. Although I would have less financial strain if I got a roommate again, I enjoyed the privacy of having my own apartment, so I preferred working a little harder to cover the rent on my own.

All of my clothes were clean and so was most of my apartment by the time Thack called me back that afternoon. I had an appointment for a meeting at *D30*'s production offices to get a partial script, do a read-through with Michael Nolan and some other cast members, and talk about scheduling. I'd also need to go for costume fittings.

"The first thing that production will ask you to do tomorrow is sign the confidentiality agreement," said Thack. "You'll be in the final three episodes of the season, and they want to discuss the story arc with you—but not until after you guarantee you'll willingly die under torture rather than reveal their secret plot points."

"I'll probably have to simulate performing oral sex on Michael Nolan," I said, "so don't joke to me about torture."

I was also very happy with the fee Thack had negotiated. The money would keep the wolf from the door for a few months. And multiple episodes of *D30* would look good on my résumé and maybe generate some interest at auditions.

All right, yes, my love life was a mess and I was worried about an evil corpse reanimator lurking among us, but at least my career was coming up roses for a change.

There wasn't much in my kitchen besides rice, beans, pasta, and a discount tub of nonfat yogurt. Now that I was sure there was a brief spell of decent income in my immediate future, I went grocery shopping and indulged extravagantly in things like chicken, salmon, fresh vegetables, chocolate, and bran muffins. I also bought a modest bottle of wine, which I took with me to Zadok's Rare & Used Books that evening so that Max and Lucky could help me celebrate.

"Ah, yes!" Max said, when I told them my good news. "That was the drama where you played the, er, not entirely respectable young woman with whom one of the policemen is infatuated."

"Talk about art imitating life," said Lucky.

I ignored that. "Detective Conway isn't really infatuated with Jilly C-Note," I said. "He's just using her for convenient, um, gratification."

They had brought back some Italian carry-out, and we were sitting down to a casual dinner at the big walnut table. Nelli lay by the gas fire, gnawing contentedly on a large bone.

"He seemed infatuated to me," Max said as he put some lasagna on a plate and passed it to me. "There was, if I may so, a perceptible alchemy between your two characters."

I opened the bottle of wine and poured a glass for each of us, pleased that he had paid so much attention to the episode I was in. It wasn't as if Max was a television watcher, after all.

As we all started digging hungrily into the food on our plates, I asked them about the results of their expedition.

"We got squat," said Lucky.

"Our interviews and researches produced only a negative result—which I am inclined to think we can consider conclusive."

"Meaning?"

"Capuzzo's clean," said Lucky. "I mean, *really* clean. Good husband, good father, good neighbor, good employer, and a good Catholic. Never involved with anything mystical, occult-related, illegal, or even a little woo-woo."

"And no connection to Quinn?" I guessed.

"The last time Mr. Capuzzo engaged with a police officer, as far as anyone knows, was twenty-four years ago when he reported a burglary at one of his stores."

"Hm."

"Nate was right about the widow being a nice lady," said Lucky. "She sent some cannoli home with us."

"And she gave Nelli that lovely bone."

"You took Nelli with you?" That must have been a surprise for the Capuzzos.

"I wanted to see whether she would react to anyone

in the Capuzzo family the way she reacted to Detective Quinn," he said. "But she was perfectly relaxed in their household throughout our visit."

"So now we turn our full attention to the redheaded cop, I guess," said Lucky. "Did you squeeze any juice out of Lopez?"

I immediately banished the mental image that phrase evoked. "I got less than squat. I got squat's rejects."

I summarized what I had learned from Lopez and explained that I'd told the truth (or started to) when he demanded an explanation. I concluded, "I don't think any of the information I got tells us anything relevant. Lopez is no longer a source. And it's possible he'll alert Quinn to my suspicion."

"Ah, don't beat yourself up, kid. Lopez is a detective. He was bound to notice he was being interrogated."

"He was in a pretty bad mood to begin with, too," I said. "It turns out that he's the cop who that lawyer—the one Nathan saw in the news—is blaming for Uncle Six's 'suicide,' so that situation is causing him problems."

"Oh, really?" said Lucky. "Lopez is being investigated? Got some legal trouble? What a shame. My heart bleeds for him."

I ignored that, too, since Lucky's resentment was understandable. It could have been avoided altogether, of course, if he had not chosen a life of crime; but it was understandable.

I changed the subject. "Plus he's got gremlins, so he's pretty stressed out."

"He must be mistaken," Max said seriously. "Gremlins are a myth. There is no such thing in reality."

"I didn't mean real ones," I said with a smile. "It's a saying, Max. When your appliances and electronic devices keep breaking down, people say your stuff is infested with gremlins."

"Ah, I see!" He beamed. "That's rather clever."

"Any chance these gremlins will wipe his computer clean of anything to do with Victor Gambello?" Lucky asked grumpily.

"Well, his computer is one of the things that's stopped working," I said. "But I really doubt OCCB leaves all the evidence or records for a big case in one cop's computer, with no duplicates or backup anywhere else."

"Sometimes I really hate technology," Lucky grumbled.

"By now, I think Lopez probably hates it, too. He's on his third cell phone in one month—they just keep dying on him." I frowned. "I wonder if there should be a recall? Does—"

"Do I understand correctly that two separate cell phones have ceased functioning for Detective Lopez recently? As well as his computer?"

I nodded. "He's been having a run of bad luck. Oh, and then there are the cars."

"What about the cars?" asked Lucky.

So I told them.

"He *has* been having bad luck," Lucky said—with noticeable schadenfreude. "Tell me more. I'm enjoying this."

"It's Detective Quinn," Max murmured, staring at me.

We both looked at him.

"What's Quinn?" I asked.

"The malfunctioning of communications devices, the disruption of electrical equipment, the unexplained breakdowns in machinery . . ." Staring off into space as he considered these incidents, Max mused, "And there was also Nelli's reaction."

"What are you on to, Doc?" Lucky asked. "What are you thinking?"

"All of these things have occurred in the vicinity of Detective Quinn."

I hadn't thought of it that way, but now that Max mentioned it . . . "Well, yes. I guess. He's around Lopez a lot, so he'd be around any machines or devices that Lopez uses when he's working." I remembered something Lopez had said, and I added, "And he used Lopez's computer before it went haywire. Lopez told me he thought Quinn had done something to it—by accident."

"Where are you going with this, Max?" Lucky wondered.

"These incidents are signs of the demonic," he said.

"A car breaking down is a sign of the demonic?" I asked doubtfully.

"Not as an isolated incident, no. But as part of a repetitious pattern? *Yes*." He stroked his beard pensively. "Three cars, two phones, a computer . . ."

I gasped as I realized something else. "Lopez said all of these things had happened within the past few weeks!"

"Ah!" said Max.

"I get it!" Lucky slammed his hand down on the table. "They've been happening since Quinn became his partner!"

"And that's why Lopez, despite spending lots of time with him, hasn't noticed anything weird about Quinn! Because the weirdness isn't in Quinn's own behavior, it's in what's happening *around* him. And it would never occur to Lopez to associate Quinn with these incidents. The only reason he thinks Quinn may be the one who messed up his computer is that the guy used it one day. Apart from that—well, knowing Lopez, it's not a connection he would see, despite how observant he is." I added, "It's not a connection I would see, either, if you hadn't pointed it out, Max."

"So we're saying Quinn is a demon?" Lucky asked.

Max shook his head. "No, I think it more likely that

Quinn is being oppressed by a demon. Incidents such as the ones Esther has described are common in cases of demon oppression. That would also explain Nelli's reaction. She may not have been aggressive toward Quinn, but rather toward something that is enmeshed with him. An entity which is present wherever he is present, but not visible to us."

"But Nelli saw it," Lucky said, looking at the dog with admiration.

"Or sensed it," said Max.

"Good work!" Lucky said. "Good Nelli!"

Upon hearing her name, Nelli wagged her tail, but she did not pause in her enjoyment of her bone.

"Then this demon is what animated Mr. Capuzzo?" I guessed.

"I assume so," said Max.

"Why?"

"Yes, that is the question we must explore."

"Oh," I said, disappointed. "I thought you might already know."

"Well, certainly there are demons that take a strong interest in death, graveyards, tombs, mummies, corpses, human remains . . ."

I pushed my plate away, feeling my appetite wane.

"But reanimation of the dead is unusual."

"Was it just a prank?" I wondered. "It frightened people. Could that have been the goal?"

"Well done, Esther!" Max beamed at me. "Demons thrive on fear, so that is certainly a possibility."

"Then there are other possibilities, too," Lucky guessed.

"Yes. We shall have to investigate this more closely to narrow them down. So we still need what we needed before."

"More information about Quinn," I said gloomily.

"And more direct observation of him. There are a number of questions for which we need answers. Who or what is this demonic entity? How or why did it attach itself to Quinn? Is Quinn aware of it or not? And . . ."

"And?" Lucky prodded.

I think I knew the next question. "What does it want?"

"Correct," said Max. "And what will it do in order to get what it wants?"

Thinking of Lopez again, I said, "And who will it hurt?"

8

"I don't got time for you," I said. "I'm working. When you come around like this, you're costing me, detective. You understand what I'm saying? You're *costing* me."

"Yeah, whatever. We gotta talk."

"Oh, really?" I said with scathing contempt. "Is this another one of those talks where you unzip while I get on my knees and open wide?"

"No, it's the kind of talk where you tell me exactly what you did for Little Ricky last night."

"Got on my knees and opened wide," I lied, injecting bitterness into my voice.

"I don't mean that," Michael Nolan said, flipping to the next page of his script. "He used you to carry a sample of his merchandise into the Last Call Bar."

"I don't know what you're talking about."

"What was in it for you, Jilly? Did he pay you? Did you owe him a favor?" Nolan paused, and his voice changed as he said, "Or did he give you more junk? I keep telling you, that stuff's gonna kill you."

"You're barking up the wrong girl," I said firmly. "I got nothin' to do with—"

"Don't even go there, Jilly," he said. "We've got you on video."

"Doing what?" I challenged brashly. "Going down on Little Ricky? Oh, gosh, I'm *blushing*."

"No, we got you accepting illegal merchandise and carrying it into a place of business for a criminal transaction."

"Oh, bull—"

"Next time, don't conspire right outside a building that has a surveillance camera."

"I didn't conspire!"

"You're gonna tell me who you met with to turn over that sample . . ." Nolan paused, then broke character and said, "I don't like the wording here."

We were sitting around a rehearsal table at the C&P company's production offices. It wasn't a full-cast read-through, since most of the *D30* actors were currently filming on location, but a couple of regular cast members were here to read the scenes they would appear in with my character. Benoit, the director for this episode, was also here; he was French-Canadian, and it was pronounced Ben-WAH—as I'd learned after initially say-

ing it wrong. There was also Kathleen, who was the
writer/producer for this episode, and her assistant, as
well as the usual army of staff. Working on a C&P production was unbelievably luxurious compared to most
of my experiences. I suspected that if I wanted to blow
my nose, one of the production minions in the room
would anticipate this and pull the tissue from the box
for me.

". . . who you met with to turn over the sample . . ."
Nolan shook his head as he read the line again. "It's
clunky."

Kathleen nodded and typed a note into her laptop.
"You're right, I'll fix it."

"Let's continue," prompted Benoit, his French accent very slight.

"You're gonna tell me blah blah blah," said Nolan.
"Which will be fixed."

"Which will be fixed," agreed Benoit. He seemed
like a patient man, which is a good thing in a director.

We were reading a flashback scene in the upcoming
episode. Detective Jimmy Conway, still lying in his
hospital bed (where he'd been for so long that he
should probably think about making a down payment
on his room and hiring a decorator), was finally semi-
lucid, verbal, and trying to remember how he got shot
(again).

He'd been suffering from traumatic amnesia ever
since waking up a few episodes ago. "And that's not

just a dramatic device," Kathleen had assured me when explaining the story. "It's not unusual for someone who has suffered a traumatic accident to be unable to remember it or the events leading up to it. It's completely credible that Jimmy doesn't remember what happened for hours before the shooting."

"Okay," I'd said.

I didn't really care about the veracity. To be honest, I was just glad that Jimmy was having so many flashback memories that involved Jilly. I liked working.

I glanced at Nolan now and read my next line, after Conway insisted that Jilly was going to tell him who she met with. "I don't know what you're talking—"

"You're on *camera*, Jilly! We *got* you!" His voice was getting louder.

"You're full of it," I said. "Get lost."

Kathleen's assistant read the description of action here. "Jilly tries to walk away. Conway grabs her arm."

"Jimmy," said his partner, Detective Cal Donner, played by former underwear model Kihm Hazlett. "Come on."

Kathleen's assistant, whose name I couldn't remember, read, "Donner tries to restrain Conway, who shakes him off and gets rough with Jilly, who's trying to get away."

"Let go!" I said angrily. "This is police brutality."

"You're gonna tell me," Conway insisted. "Tell me!"

"Jimmy!" Detective Donner shouted. "Stop!"

As written, this is where the scene would cut away from the nighttime street corner where we exchanged these lines in the flashback sequence, and it would cut to Jimmy Conway's hospital room with disorienting swiftness, reflecting Jimmy's own confused state of mind.

Seated beside the bed, where Conway was still hooked up to some tubes, Donner said with concern, "Jimmy . . . that never happened."

"Huh?"

"There was no surveillance camera. We never had any video of Jilly C-Note."

"Are you sure? But . . . but what about the—"

"Jimmy . . ." Kihm shook his head and said, "I wasn't there. I never even saw you that night."

"What?" Nolan said in vague, distressed confusion.

"What you're remembering . . . it didn't happen."

It was the end of the scene. After a moment, Nolan said to Kathleen, "I think I need another line there."

"We're going to get a close-up as you realize what he's telling you," she replied, apparently recognizing that what he meant was that he wanted the final moment of the scene to focus on him, not on the other actor.

"Hmm," said Nolan. "That might be okay."

Kihm Hazlett's expression changed to a subtle, wry smile as he kept his gaze fixed on his script. He'd been working with Nolan for a while and knew him well. I suspected he had rather enjoyed the break from No-lan's daily company that the actor's two heart attacks had given him in recent months.

Kihm was a California blond who'd made a few embarrassingly bad straight-to-DVD movies after aging out of the underwear game. He'd fallen off the radar for a decade or so after that, then eventually reinvented himself as a capable middle-aged character actor. He'd auditioned for *The Dirty Thirty* when it was a controversial new project that the networks wouldn't touch, and the producers had cast him against type. Still a good-looking guy who kept in shape, he played perhaps the ugliest character on the show. While Jimmy Conway was corrupt, conflicted, and complex, Cal Donner was a bigot, a brute, and a mean bastard. He was also hardworking and loyal, though, so he got the job done, and he covered for Conway, who went off on drinking binges and sometimes fell down on the job because of his PTSD.

The police of the *actual* Thirtieth Precinct, which ran alongside the Hudson River from West 133rd Street up to West 155th Street, loathed this show's portrayal of their team so passionately that *D30* didn't even do location shoots there anymore. A TV production company needs the support of local law enforcement (or at least a grudging minimal level of cooperation), and this cast and crew got the sort of reception from the cops of the Three-Oh that I would get at Fenster & Co., where I had accidentally destroyed most of the fourth floor last month while confronting Evil.

Anyhow, although he was a workaholic and a loyal buddy, Detective Cal Donner wasn't exactly the sharpest knife in the drawer, so despite his going on a rampage to find his partner's shooter after Michael Nolan had his heart attacks, he still had no idea who'd shot Jimmy Conway . . . and it was a plotline that had faded from view after a few weeks, as other characters entered the spotlight with new storylines that eclipsed Nolan's absent character.

So now Conway was trying to remember the night he got shot, but his memories were unreliable—as in the scene we'd just read. As he continued trying, throughout the final three episodes of the season, it would be unclear whether he was having memories or hallucinations . . . but it would become increasingly apparent that he was obsessed with Jilly C-Note.

Donner, eventually believing that Conway's focus on Jilly meant she knew who the shooter was, would go after her in the next episode. Finding Jilly wouldn't be easy, and when he did . . . in predictable Donner fashion, he'd wind up beating her badly in his rage and frustration. Even Donner wasn't dumb enough to do that to someone who might hire a lawyer or file a complaint, but a streetwalker like Jilly wouldn't do either thing. She'd just yearn for revenge on every cop in the dirty Thirtieth Precinct, wishing she could make them pay for the things they'd done to her.

Meanwhile, it wouldn't be clear whether Conway remembered harassing Jilly over criminal matters the night he was shot, or whether he was just sexually obsessed with her and fabricating those memories in the confusion of his morphine withdrawal. (In addition to everything else, recovering from the shooting had turned Conway into a morphine addict. Really, I thought, it was amazing that any of these characters could even get through the day.)

I'm unlikely casting for a leading man's sexual obsession in a more mainstream style of American television show, since my looks aren't Hollywood gorgeous, but—as with casting the handsome, gentle-eyed Kihm Hazlett as a brute with an ugly soul—*D30* didn't make predictable casting choices.

I can play romantic leads onstage, and the camera lens doesn't crack when it focuses on my face—actually, I look okay on screen, since I have decent bone structure and good cheekbones. But I'm not the sort of actress who gets exploited for her beauty while young and then cast aside after she turns forty (and then subsequently seeks plastic surgery in an effort to prolong her career as a babe). My profession means that I keep in shape, but I have a pretty average figure for an actress, rather than a bankable one. With fair skin, brown eyes, and brown hair, I can fit a variety of roles . . . including a bisexual junkie hooker with whom a bent, traumatized, substance-abusing cop had become obsessed.

We would be filming two sex scenes the following week. Segments of each of them would be used as flashbacks during various moments in the season's final three episodes, as Conway struggled to differentiate between fact and fantasy in his own mind. One of the scenes was obviously (obvious to the *viewer*, that is—not so much to Conway) just an erotic fabrication of Jimmy's troubled imagination. The other scene was grittier and more realistic, and possibly a memory of actual events from the night of the shooting—though Kathleen wasn't telling us whether this was the case, and I had the impression she didn't know. While angrily questioning Jilly on a dark (and conveniently empty) street, anger would turn to lust and Conway would shove her up against a wall and have his way with her in a rough, clawing, and very unwise exchange of bodily fluids.

So, all in all, it was easy to understand why, by the final episode, Jilly would want to see the cops of the Three-Oh lying in a shallow grave.

I doubted she would get her wish, though, since the show had been renewed for another year. And although the season finale wasn't firm yet, I had the vague impression from Kathleen that Jilly would wind up dying nastily, as so many guest characters did on

D30. But this plot thread about Jimmy Conway's grad-ually returning memory was still new, and the writers didn't yet seem sure how they'd resolve it, so it re-mained to be seen whether I'd get a death scene.

In any case, I would get to keep my clothes on for both sex scenes next week. The fantasy scene and the gritty one each took place on city streets, outdoors, standing up. There was no disrobing involved, let alone partial nudity. I had never yet taken off all my clothes for a role, and although it wasn't completely out of the question, it was a decision I'd rather not face. (Realistically, it might someday be required by a job I really wanted to do, but I'd cross that bridge if and when I came to it.)

Fortunately, I knew from my previous experience of working with him that, despite how unappealing No-lan's personality was, he was very professional about filming intimate scenes. And although we didn't like each other (I wondered if *anyone* had ever liked Nolan), we worked well together. Even just doing this first read-through, which was certainly not an immersive acting experience, our characters were already making a connection with each other, and I could feel the po-tential for interesting energy and tension between them.

Benoit made a few notes about the scene we'd just read, then suggested we continue to the next one in-volving Jilly. We were just starting on that when the door opened and a bright-eyed staffer with messy hair stuck his head in the room.

"Kathleen? I'm sorry to interrupt. There's a call for you from the location shoot. Emergency."

"Emergency?" she repeated, rising to her feet. Her assistant rose, too.

"A water main has burst right where they were filming."

"Yikes," said Kihm, as Kathleen hurried out of the room to take the call, with her assistant right behind her. "We can't afford to lose another day of shooting. What are they going to do?"

"Jesus fucking Christ," said Nolan. "It's one thing after another since I came back."

Seeing my curious expression, Kihm explained, "This is the third week in a row that something has screwed up our filming schedule."

"That's trouble," I said in commiseration.

Filming is expensive, and full-length TV dramas have very tight, demanding schedules. In addition to being costly, the problems Kihm mentioned probably meant that everyone had worked extra long hours to compensate for the wasted time and unexpected changes.

"Last week," Nolan said, "the whole studio lost power for half a day. Can you believe that shit?"

He sounded as if he had taken it personally.

"The week before that," said Kihm, "one of the

show's equipment trucks skidded on ice when it arrived at the location to set up. The driver lost control—"

"Incompetent bastard," Nolan grumbled.

Kihm exchanged a glance with me, then continued, "No one was hurt, thank God, but the truck plowed into a storefront. It was a huge mess, lots of equipment damaged, the site couldn't be used . . . We lost a whole day that time."

I wondered briefly if Lopez's buddy in the NYPD's film unit had dealt with any of this.

A stab of anxiety pierced me. What was Lopez going to say when we talked about our relationship? What was I going to say? And when were we going to have that talk, anyhow? We'd left things pretty loose . . . and, I recalled, pretty tense, too.

That led me to thinking about Quinn.

Is he in danger—or is he dangerous? And how much danger is Lopez in because of him?

"Oh, come, you don't believe in that shit, do you?" said Nolan.

"Huh?" I realized I'd missed part of the conversation.

"Okay, maybe we're not *cursed*," Kihm said with a self-deprecating smile, "but something's off, you know? Our energy, our karma. Whatever. Three accidents in three weeks? It wouldn't hurt to get a shaman to come do a cleansing of the whole production."

"That is so fucking California." Nolan picked up his

coffee mug and held it up in the air. Behind him, a young woman hopped out of her chair, took his cup, and left the room to go get him another hot beverage.

Which was definitely not coffee. He was drinking some sort of designer herbal tea whose leaves were plucked ceremoniously by mute Buddhist saints in the mountains of Sri Lanka and then processed organically in a diamond mine in Finland. Or something.

Nolan, I had learned within minutes of arriving for work today, had become a health nut since surviving his second heart attack. There being no zealot like a convert, he no longer allowed caffeine, alcohol, sugar, red meat, saturated fat, or refined starch to pollute the sacred temple of his body.

This voluntary deprivation did not, I noted, make him any better company than he had been before his brush with mortality.

"Okay," said Kihm, "if a shaman makes you uncomfortable—"

"I'm not uncomfortable, it's just a stupid idea." Nolan spoke with all his habitual charm and tact.

"—then how about a priest doing a blessing? Or," Kihm added with a courteous nod to me, "maybe we could get a rabbi. Would a rabbi do a blessing, Esther?"

"I don't know," I said. "Maybe if you ask nicely."

My parents tried, but my religious education is pretty shaky. Fortunately, we had a very nice Reform rabbi who let me explore the history of Yiddish theater for my bat mitzvah—the ceremony in Jewish tradition where a child becomes an adult—after it became apparent that a more traditional course of study just wouldn't go well for me.

"Or how about we just fire the idiots causing these problems and hire some competent people?" Nolan said.

"Who do you think *caused* a water main to break?" Kihm challenged.

"Someone should have known it was going to happen."

Benoit, quite sensibly, rose to his feet and made a vague excuse to absent himself from the room until Kathleen finished her call and we could recommence the read-through.

"Well, I just don't think it would hurt to do something to create a little positive energy around here, is all I'm saying," Kihm concluded with a shrug. Then he changed the subject, turning to me to ask what I'd been doing since I had last worked with them back in August.

The Vampyre, the Off Broadway play I'd been in all autumn, was the only thing I'd done since then that I was willing to discuss.

"Oh, right," said Kihm, looking interested. "That was in all the tabloids for a while because of that weird murder where some vampire groupie was bled dry. They got the guy, didn't they?"

"Sort of. He died while fleeing the police." More or less.

During the run of that play, I had nearly been eaten by that vampire serial killer. Thack, whom Max had drafted into helping us with that problem, had found the whole thing deeply distasteful and was eager to put it out of his mind afterward.

Kihm asked, "Wasn't the lead role played by an actor who pretends he *is* a vampire?"

"Yep." And pretending was all there was to it. "He went to pretty extreme lengths to maintain that image."

"*You've* done Off Broadway?" said Nolan with unflattering surprise.

"Yes."

"*I've* never done Off Broadway," he said, as if this were relevant.

"That must have been weird," Kihm said. "What was that guy like?"

"An ego the size of the planet Jupiter."

"Wow," said Kihm, absolutely deadpan. "That must be hard to work with. I'd sure hate to deal with someone like that."

"Indeed."

We both glanced at Nolan as he grabbed his cup of steaming herbal elixir from the returning staffer without even looking at her. "Who the hell is this guy?"

I said to Kihm, "He's making a cable movie now."

"Let me guess—still playing a vampire?"

I smiled as I nodded.

"*I* could do a vampire," said Nolan. "But I just don't think it would stretch me. So what would be the point?"

"But would you do it if it was Off Broadway?" Kihm asked him, with an amused glance at me.

"Fuck theater," Nolan said dismissively. "Who's got time for that shit?"

"So what else is going on?" Kihm asked me politely. "Did I hear Kathleen say that you're working in an indie film at the same time you're doing this show?"

I abided by Thack's instructions not to tell anyone here that my movie had been canceled, but I didn't want to manufacture lies about it. So I quickly changed the subject by asking Kihm if he had any projects lined up for his downtime after the end of the shooting season.

"No, our schedule has been such a killer this year, I'm just going to take some time off. Get reacquainted with my wife and kids." He glanced at his watch and added, "In fact, since we're not doing anything right now, I think I'll go call home and tell them I'll be working late again. I'm supposed to go to today's location and film a scene after we're done here, and they'll be running way behind schedule today."

I didn't realize until after he exited the room that he was leaving me alone here with Nolan.

I liked Kihm, but the words *rat bastard* did briefly cross my mind.

Okay, Nolan and I weren't *alone*, exactly, since there were a bunch of staffers in the room with us. But I didn't know any of them, and Nolan barely regarded them as people. So there was a real danger that he'd talk to *me*.

Seeking salvation, I picked up my coffee mug, hopped to my feet, and turned toward the door.

A production minion immediately leapt to his feet, blocked my escape path, and asked, "Do you need anything, Miss Diamond?"

"No, thanks. I'm just going to get some coffee."

Nolan said, "That stuff will kill you."

"I'll get it!" The minion reached for my mug.

I held onto it. "No, that's okay. I can get—"

"No, no, you sit," he insisted, tugging on my cup. "I'll get it."

Rather than engage in a wrestling match, I surrendered the mug. Then I realized in exasperation that, having sent him off to get coffee for me, I couldn't make some other excuse to leave the room now, since then I wouldn't be here when the guy got back with my beverage. And that would be rude. (Did I mention I'm from the Midwest?)

Hoping that Kathleen and the others would return momentarily, I sat back down and resigned myself to enduring a few minutes of conversation with Nolan—who did not, of course, ignore his captive audience.

"I'm doing five miles a day on the treadmill now,"

he said, as if I had asked. "I work on increasing speed for a couple of weeks, and then I increase distance for a couple of weeks. You should try it."

"Hm."

He talked for a while longer about his exercise regimen. Then he switched to the fascinating subject of his one hundred percent organic diet. Next, we covered the scintillating topic of how young and vital he thought his lifestyle change was making him look. At some point during this deluge of unsolicited personal information, I received my cup of coffee, which I drank while Nolan explained that it was prematurely aging me and probably accounted for the dark circles he thought he saw under my eyes.

When I realized I was thinking longingly of throwing myself out of the window and onto the slush-covered street below, I decided to change the subject. There was, of course, no realistic hope of getting Nolan off the topic of himself—not without others here to assist me, *damn* them all for abandoning me with him! But I had to get him off the subject of his health. I had reached my limit and was feeling ready to give him one of *my* ventricles if that would get him to stop talking about his own.

So I asked, as if I cared, "How long were you off work?"

He grimaced. "Four months, more or less. They filmed me lying unconscious in a hospital bed a couple of times early on, but since it was my real hospital bed, it didn't exactly count as 'work.'"

"I guess being back feels good?"

He shrugged. "I guess."

That surprised me. I figured a narcissistic workaholic like Nolan would be delighted to be back in the game, in front of the camera again, and getting the show rewritten at the last minute in order to accommodate a new subplot featuring his character.

"Do you feel like you came back to work too soon?" I asked.

"No, the opposite. I think I let the damn doctors talk me into convalescing for too long," he grumbled.

I thought he meant he should have come back sooner to prevent Jimmy Conway from losing the spotlight to other characters.

But then Nolan looked around, saw that the other bodies in the room were ignoring our conversation (and who could blame them?), leaned close to me, and said in a low voice, "I feel like I've lost my edge. You know what I mean?"

"Oh . . . Well, this was just a cold read-through," I pointed out. "When we're in costume and on set, you'll—"

"No," he shook his head. "I can't just wait around and hope that'll bring it all back."

"Bring all what back?" I didn't feel compelled to be nice to him, but he was a fellow actor and I thought I could guess what was bothering him. So I said, "Look, you've been very ill, and you haven't worked for a while. Not really." A couple of brief appearances recently as the heavily drugged Jimmy still lying in a hospital bed and muttering a short, drowsy line or two of dialogue probably didn't count. "So it's natural to feel a little cold or stiff or anxious. But if you focus, do the work, and trust—"

"I'm not worried about my *craft*," he said, apparently taking offense. "That's as top-notch as it ever was. What, you think I was just sitting on my ass the whole time I was recovering?"

"Okay, I guess you're fine then." I regretted that I had shown an interest, even for a moment.

"It's not focus or technique I'm worried about, it's *edge*. Like I said."

"Edge?" I repeated without interest, about to rise to my feet and excuse myself for an unnecessary trip to the bathroom so that I could get a break from his company.

"Yeah, edge." He gripped my forearm, as if realizing that I was about to flee. "Jimmy is very *street*. Very gritty. He's part of the primal pulse of the alley, the gutter, the fresh crime scene, the wailing sirens of a nine-one-one call. He has that energy. That texture."

"Right."

"*I* don't fake it. *I* have to be authentic." Nolan's tone suggested this was a major difference between himself and other actors—including me. I resented this; I also suspected the regular *D30* cast was accustomed to resenting it on a weekly basis. "My fans expect *truth* from me."

"Uh-huh." I tried to pull my arm away. He didn't notice.

"If I don't make Jimmy believable for them, I'll be letting them down," he said tragically.

"You've been making him believable for them ever since the series began." I hated coming so close to complimenting him, but there was no denying that Nolan's compelling portrayal of Jimmy Conway was a crucial component in *D30's* success.

"And I have a responsibility to maintain that level of quality. Of *reality*."

Reality? His character was an alcoholic, morphine-addicted cop with occasionally debilitating PTSD who'd been gunned down twice in two years, in a squad so blatantly corrupt that real NYPD cops either guffawed or hyperventilated with aggravation when criticizing the program.

Okay, fine. Whatever.

In the hope that Nolan would let go of my arm, I decided to bring these flights of grandiosity down to a more prosaic level to close the subject. "In that case, what you're talking about is research."

"Research?" He frowned thoughtfully. "Hm . . . *Research.* You know . . . you may have something there."

"Go shadow some cops for a few days," I said with a nod. "That'll get you back in the saddle."

"It's not a bad idea." Coming from Nolan, this was a huge compliment. "I guess I haven't been out on a ride-along with real cops since before we started filming the first season." He added petulantly, "No cops were willing to take me after the show started airing."

That didn't surprise me, but I said, "Oh, I'm sure your production department can talk *someone* on the NYPD into letting its Emmy-nominated star shadow them." I tested his hold on my arm again and was pleased to discover that he was so absorbed in contemplation of this suggestion that I could pull away easily now. I did so, and I started rising to my feet to make my escape. "You can get back some of that texture you lost during convalescence by following a streetwise cop around for a few days." Standing now, I looked down at Nolan. "Watch him work, follow his every move, go wherever he goes, and . . . and . . ." I stopped jabbering at Nolan as I realized what I was saying.

"I like it," he said, nodding. "They really don't have me doing much around here until we start filming the next episode. I've got time to shadow someone for a few days."

Follow his every move, go wherever he goes . . .

I sank slowly back down to my seat. *This* was the solution. My way in. Our path to finding out more about Detective Andrew Quinn!

And Lopez was going to *hate* me for this.

But it's for his own good. It may even save his life. Who knows what kind of time bomb Quinn might be?

Max had said we couldn't know more about the ramifications of Quinn's (probable) demon situation without knowing more about the demon itself. There were tens of thousands of demons (maybe millions or billions, if you included all possible dimensions of existence). Some were common and easy to identify, while others were rare or still unknown. Some were relatively straightforward to expel and vanquish, while others had the power to destroy most of the tri-state area. We had dealt with a couple of the latter type by now, and it was a terrifying prospect.

Lopez would be so mad at me he might keel over in an apoplectic fit the next time we talked . . . but we *had* to learn all we could about Quinn, and this was the obvious way to do it.

"You know, Mike . . ." I said a little awkwardly. Natural revulsion usually prevented me from trying to sound friendly when I spoke to him. "I think I know exactly the team you should shadow."

Accustomed to being dismissive of me (and of all women, guest performers, and people less famous than he was, I assumed), he brushed this aside. "No, Esther, I'm going to need to shadow someone really *experienced* and—"

"These are a couple of detectives working that big Gambello case that's been in the news."

"Gambello?" He frowned. "The pizza chain that's turning away gay customers?"

"No, the Mafia crime family implicated in decades of murder, extortion, armed robbery, racketeering—"

"Oh, *that* Gambello. Right." He looked at me with unaccustomed interest. "You know cops investigating the mob?"

"I do. And these are very gritty guys, very street," I lied.

"Yeah?"

"Oh, *yeah.*" I nodded emphatically.

Actually, Lopez was a college-educated man with nice manners (when he wasn't mad at me) who'd grown up in a stable, loving, and fairly religious family in Nyack, a pleasant suburb across the Hudson River. But he was a shrewd and experienced cop, though only thirty-one years old. As for Quinn . . . well, I suspected him of demonic influences, which ought to compensate for any lack of "grit" there.

"Plus," I added enticingly, "they've got some problems with the Chinatown underworld now. So you might see some action."

Okay, I embellished. So sue me.

"Yeah?" Nolan was *very* interested now. "Can you talk to these guys for me? Set something up?"

There was no way Quinn and Lopez would agree to this plan if I asked them. It had to come from a superior, and it would have to be presented as an order rather than a request.

Thinking quickly, I advised Nolan to go through channels, so there'd be official cover for the two cops if he got hurt during one of their wild and crazy shifts. He liked that a lot.

"You might even want to go through the Police Commissioner's office." I added ruthlessly, "One of these guys—Detective Connor Lopez—is getting a lot of heat right now. He's being accused of driving a . . . a suspect to suicide."

"Hey, that's great!" Nolan looked around the table as he said, "This is terrific stuff. I should take some notes." Not seeing what he wanted, he snapped his fingers in the air. "Someone get me a notebook!"

A production assistant jumped up to do his bidding.

As a company that filmed four successful TV shows here, which meant a lot of revenue for the city (including the tourism that crime shows inspired, though I found that strange), C&P had influence with local government. Despite the negative image of the NYPD that was promoted by *The Dirty Thirty*, as well as the ill feeling (or weary exasperation) this caused, C&P Productions also had influence with the police department. So I suspected the NYPD would cooperate with a formal request from C&P for a TV star to shadow a specific detective who, through no fault of his own, was getting some bad publicity these days.

I suggested to Nolan, "The company could present this request as your attempt to reframe the media story by showing your support for the hardworking detective accused of making some scumbag throw himself off a sixth floor balcony."

Well, it wasn't as if Uncle Six had been a nice man, after all. And the prospect of using his own celebrity this way appealed to Nolan.

"Oh, man, I can't wait to meet these guys!" A notebook appeared under his nose. He grabbed it and, without looking at the young woman who'd handed it to him, said, "It's about time."

"Here, let me write down the cops' names for you." I took the notebook from him and picked up my pen, determined to make sure C&P asked for the right detectives when arranging this with the NYPD.

After I handed the notebook back to Nolan, he read the names aloud. Then asked inquisitively, "Connor Lopez?"

"Irish-American mother, Cuban father."

Nolan snorted. "I hope his father did the cooking."

I recalled that Lopez had mentioned his mom wasn't the greatest cook.

"I'm going to go tell them to organize this right away. I want to start the day after tomorrow. If Kathleen and Benoit come back before I do, tell them I'll only be a few minutes." Nolan rose to his feet and headed for the door. Right before he exited the room, he turned around and looked at me. "Thanks, Esther."

You would think a thunderbolt had flown out of his mouth. Everyone in the room did a double take and stared at him in surprise. He didn't notice.

After he disappeared through the doorway, they all turned to look at me.

I realized that Nolan thanking someone must be unprecedented around here.

"What did you *do* for him?" one of the minions asked.

I said wryly, "I have a feeling he was thanking me because he thinks I'm helping him do something dangerous."

And, in fact, I supposed I was. Whether Quinn was evil or, as Max now suspected, something evil was hovering around him, Nolan's intrusion probably wouldn't be welcome.

I realized I might not have thought this through as well as I should have . . .

But it was too late to change course now. Persuading Nolan had been easy; talking him out of this would be close to impossible. It was all for his fans, after all. For quality, truth, and gritty reality.

And since he was appreciative enough to have thanked me (the staff still look amazed) . . . I thought it likely I could convince him to confer with me by phone about what he was learning, and to observe whatever details Max wanted him to report. I'd need to ask Max what Nolan should be looking for, then figure out how to phrase these suggestions when talking to the actor.

Pleased that I had a workable plan for what I feared was an urgent situation, I sat back in my chair and waited for people to return to the room so we could read the next scene.

I just regretted that Lopez would probably never forgive me for this.

9

"I will never forgive you for this," said Lopez. "Do you hear me? *Never.*"

I had been expecting this call since talking Nolan into my plan two days ago, but that didn't mean I was ready for it. Nonetheless, I put on my game face and gave Max a reassuring look as I shook my head, indicating that the actor was not my caller.

We were alone at the bookstore, along with Nelli, who was dozing in her usual spot near the gas fire. Lucky was at the funeral home. Mr. Capuzzo's send-off had gone smoothly and he was now safely buried; but after witnessing that frightening and bizarre reanimation, Nathan was still feeling tense and anxious. Joe Ning's body had been released to Chen's, where it now rested in a closed casket. The wake was scheduled for this evening—due to start soon, in fact. But Sam, Na-

than's eldest son, was at home today with two sick toddlers and an exhausted wife who'd caught their cold.
So John and Lucky were pitching in to help Nathan
deal with the event. Uncle Six's status in Chinatown,
both among respectable people and the not-so-
respectable, made this a particularly important occasion for the mortuary.

I glanced out the storefront window, noting that it
was a rotten evening for attending a visitation—or anything else. Heavy, wet, icy-cold globs of snow were falling, slippery slush covered the streets and sidewalks,
and a bitter wind was making awnings flap and windows creak.

"Never," Lopez repeated into the phone. "Do I make
myself clear?"

Max had been pottering around the place, dusting,
shelving, and reorganizing books, while I sat at the big
old walnut table and studied my preliminary script for
next week's *D30* episode. I'd had my first costume fitting yesterday and would have to go back tomorrow
for another one. The location shoots were going to be
uncomfortable for me at this time of year; Jilly C-Note
put her merchandise in the window, so to speak. But
maybe there would be a medical team standing by to
administer treatment for my hypothermia between
takes.

"Lopez! I'm happy to hear your voice," I lied.

Normally, I *would* be happy to hear it. But since he

was obviously calling to chew me out, my comment was absurdly disingenuous. I realized this a moment after making it and wished I had come up with something better.

Max whispered to me, "Do we have confirmation that Mr. Nolan is in place?"

"Happy?" Lopez sputtered. "I don't want you to be *happy*. I want you to suffer the way *I'm* suffering."

I covered the receiver and said to Max, "Yes. I'd say we have definite confirmation."

"This is *your* doing!" Lopez accused.

Max whispered, "Then this being in the nature of a personal phone call, I suspect, I shall recommence my tidying." He disappeared around the corner of a bookcase, duster in hand. Not really out of earshot, but not hovering.

"Since I assume Nolan told you that," I said to Lopez, "I'm not impressed with your deductive reasoning."

"How could you do this to me?" he demanded in a wounded, betrayed tone. "Are you *that* angry at me?"

"I'm not angry at you," I protested.

"Oh, really?" he said skeptically. "You didn't do this to get back at me?"

"For what?" I asked in bemusement.

"For my reaction to your crazy cursed cookie crime."

"Oh! No," I said. "You reacted pretty much the way I expected."

"So you didn't do this to punish me for that?" he asked suspiciously.

"No." I decided to take the offensive. "My God, is that really what you think of me? That I'm that petty?"

It didn't work. "Then why the hell *did* you do this?"

"I thought it might help you with your PR problem to have, you know, an Emmy-nominated TV star showing public support by using you as his role model," I lied.

"Right," said Lopez. "You thought it would be *good* for me right now to be identified as the inspiration for Nolan's portrayal of a drunken cop who steals money from drug dealers, beats up suspects, and extorts sex from hookers."

"So you do watch the show!" I said brightly.

"Show me another explanation, Esther," he said tersely. "I'm not buying that one."

"But the department must have liked the idea," I said, "or else Nolan wouldn't be shadowing you now."

"They like the idea of using me right now to play nice with C&P," he said grumpily. "The details don't seem to matter much to them."

"Then you shouldn't let the details bother you, either."

"Don't *even* . . ." He took a breath. "Esther, you know what this guy is like. How could you inflict him on me?"

"I didn't inflict—"

"Oh, yes, you did. Why?"

Okay, I did. So I tried another explanation. "I thought you'd like to do something nice for me, after the way you treated me on the phone the other day."

"But you just said you're not mad at me about that," he protested.

"Well, you were . . . not pleasant," I said. "And you should make it up to me."

"So you *are* mad." His voice had the tone of a man reconciling himself to a woman's irrationality.

"Oh . . . maybe."

Not really, but I realized that it would be better to let him think so than to start suspecting that I'd inflicted the actor on him in order to spy on Detective Quinn. Luckily for me, Nolan's self-absorption made him such an unlikely infiltrator that the truth hadn't yet occurred to Lopez. I'd like to keep it that way for as long as I could, given the way Lopez had drawn a line in the sand about Quinn when we talked about him a few days ago.

"I had no idea you could be so vindictive," he said in amazement.

I shrugged. "A woman scorned."

"Okay, look, if I . . . Jesus, if I *apologize* for our conversation the other day—"

"You don't *sound* sorry."

"—will you get rid of him?"

"I've already cried havoc and let slip the dogs of war."

"What the hell does that mean?"

"It means I doubt I can influence him now that he's having a great time getting all *street* with a notorious real-life cop like you."

"I'm only notorious if you're Alan Goldman or one of his dimwitted media patsies," Lopez said stonily.

"Of which there seem to be many today," I noted, having taken a long look at local news online this morning.

Lopez's parents, with whom I'd had one memorably disastrous encounter, were bound to see this coverage. They were a devoted family, and I suspected they'd be upset (his father) and infuriated (his mother) by Goldman's insinuations about their son. There had been tension between Lopez and his family in recent weeks (there had been tension between Lopez and *everyone* lately, mostly because of me), but I thought this mess would make them forget their vexation with him.

"How are you parents taking this?" I asked.

"I doubt they know, thank God," he said.

"How could they miss it?"

I assumed that headlines like "Did OCCB Detective's Harassment Drive Businessman To Suicide?" were bound to get their attention.

"They're on a cruise in the Galapagos Islands."

"Seriously?" I said. "Well, that's reassuringly far away."

"Yeah," he said. "I encouraged it."

I knew he loved his parents, but they could be a bit overpowering. And since his two older brothers didn't live in the greater New York area anymore, Connor—his father's little *perrito* (puppy)—was the one who had to deal with them the most.

"Going there has been a dream of theirs for years," he added. "My father loves all those wildlife programs and nature documentaries on TV. And my mom loves the ocean."

"When do they get back?"

"Next week."

"Well, maybe this Goldman thing will have blown over by then," I said, though I didn't believe it for a moment. Goldman seemed like he was just getting started.

"From your lips to God's ears," Lopez muttered. "Look, Esther, this is *not* a good time to pull this Nolan thing on me."

I doubted there would ever be a good time to be shadowed by the actor, but considering the professional pressure on Lopez right now, combined with the stressful effects of the (suspected) demonic presence, I wasn't surprised that he sounded like he was all out of patience. However, his life was more important to me than his mood, so I hardened my heart. We *had* to learn more about Quinn.

I said, "You should have thought of that before you were so mean to me the other day."

"Oh, come on."

"Buck up," I said. "Be a man if it kills you." I regretted those words as soon as they were out of my mouth; they seemed to invite bad luck. But I interrupted his outraged reaction to point out, "We start filming the new episode on Monday. Nolan has a bigger role in this one than he's had since his character got shot."

"*Again*," Lopez said. "Why is that character always staggering in front of bullets?"

"So he'll be working long hours—and he's a recovering heart patient who's obsessive about protecting his health."

"You don't say."

"Plus, the guy spends, like, two hours exercising every day."

"I know. He's told us. Over and *over*, he's told us." He added with a touch of desperation, "I can't believe this is only his first day with us. It seem so much longer."

"So from Monday onward, he won't have time for you," I said soothingly. "Probably never again."

"Don't try to be consoling," Lopez said irritably. "It's your fault we're stuck with him in the first place."

"You've just got to get through a few days of this, and then it'll be over."

"Why do I have to get through a few days of this? Why? *Why?*"

"You're sounding perilously close to a tantrum."

"You should have just let your damn cursed cookie kill me," he said bitterly. "It's wrong to make me suffer like this."

"Where is Nolan now?" I asked. "Not with you, I assume."

No matter how aggravating the guy was, Lopez wouldn't talk about him this way if he were standing right there.

"He's with Andy," said Lopez. "I won the coin toss."

This was good news. Nolan would be more focused on Quinn this way. And I was more comfortable with distance between Lopez and his partner.

"And where are you?" I asked.

"Police garage." He sounded morose. "Returning another goddamn car."

That got my attention. "What's wrong with this one?"

"I have no idea. The police radio stopped working, so I brought it back to the garage. But they looked at the thing, and it's working just fine now. So I guess I'm taking the same car back out." He made an exasperated sound. "*God*, I'm tired of this."

"How's your computer?" I asked cautiously.

"That's where I'm heading next. Back to the office to stand guard over the IT guy—at gunpoint, if need be—until he finishes fixing it. I've *had* it with all this crap. Can't the department provide me with one single piece of equipment that *works*?"

I wondered if it was relevant that the radio had started working again after being removed from Quinn's presence. I wanted to get off the phone to tell Max about this.

"Well, it sounds like you've really got your hands full—"

"Thanks in no small part to *you*," Lopez said. "You and I really need to talk, Esther. And not by phone."

"We'll do that. Real soon. I've got to go now. Bye."

I ended the call while he was in the middle of saying something else. It sounded cranky, so I figured it was just as well I didn't hear the whole sentence.

"Max?" I called.

"Is there news?" he asked as he came trotting toward me from the rear of the store.

I brushed a cobweb off his woolly sweater as I recounted the relevant portions of the conversation.

"Hmm. My instinct is that the renewed functionality of the police radio is deliberate," Max said as he sat down at the table with me. "I doubt it represents a limitation of the demon's power. Consider, for example, the car that broke down on the Bowery, where Detective Lopez waited in the cold for help for some time."

I saw Max's point. "Quinn wasn't present, yet the car remained dead."

"I hypothesize that the radio today has resumed functioning because the demonic entity intended it to do so."

"Why? That makes it seem like a . . . a *prank*." I always thought of demons as more serious than that. More menacing.

"Oh, many demons are prone to pranks," said Max. "Especially demons that attach to humans, as we suspect is the case here. But the pranks are never harmless, though the word itself has a lighthearted connotation."

"This one seems harmless," I said. "Pointless, but not harmful."

"We should consider the intent. Demons are clever, manipulative, and usually very malevolent. And they typically function with intent."

"What could be the intent of sending Lopez on a wasted trip to the police garage?"

"The most obvious one would be to increase his stress and frustration."

"Ah." I nodded. "Well, yes, it accomplished that."

"You indicated the other day that these events are taking a toll on his equilibrium, I believe?"

"You bet," I said. "The stress of cars breaking down, phones going dead, his computer not working, his communications being unreliable . . . It's really wearing on his nerves after several weeks of this kind of thing happening over and over."

"Stress, tension, irritability, frustration, anger . . . demonic entities feed off these negative emotions in the way that you or I derive strength and sustenance from food or a stimulating beverage," said Max.

"Not only those particular negative emotions, of course. They also feed off fear, sorrow, depression, hate, despair . . ." He continued, "But, particularly in the modern world where people are so reliant on mechanical and electronic devices, numerous species of demons find it conveniently easy to stimulate negative emotions by interfering with such things. Even a patient, contented individual will start reacting with predictably negative emotions to the sort of incidents that Detective Lopez has been experiencing."

And a man who was already stressed and frustrated due to his volatile relationship with a woman and various complications arising on the job would be even easier to manipulate that way, I guessed.

"So you think the demon is inflicting these—okay, let's say *pranks*—on Lopez to generate the negative emotions that it feeds off." I asked, "Will it get full and stop, the way we stop eating and drinking?"

"No, the appetite of Evil is voracious and always feeds on its own hunger. The entity will escalate its efforts as it keeps growing stronger," Max said gravely. "This is a very typical pattern when demonic influence is at work."

"But growing stronger for what?" I wondered. "What's the thing's goal?"

"That is what we must learn before it becomes powerful enough to achieve its aim," he said. "We must also ascertain Detective Quinn's precise role in this. For example, I am concerned that the intent in today's prank may be manifold."

I wasn't sure what that meant, but this often happened when Max spoke, so I just said, "Go on."

"In addition to increasing Detective Lopez's frustration—and adding confusion to his state of mind, which the demonic also finds stimulating . . . This prank also had the effect of separating Detective Lopez from his two companions."

"You think he's in danger now?" I asked in alarm. "He's being deliberately isolated?"

"No, since our hypothesis is that the entity is attached to Detective Quinn," said Max, "I am more concerned about the safety of Mr. Nolan, who may now be alone with him somewhere."

"Oh, I see. Lopez isn't under attack," I said. "You think he was gotten out of the way?"

"He is a trained police officer, he has weapons and a strong protective instinct, and he is also a very observant, decisive individual . . ." Max nodded slowly. "I believe that manipulating Detective Lopez into leaving its presence, as has just happened, would be the demon's strategy if it senses a desirable opportunity in its path."

"An opportunity for what?"

"For whatever it's trying to achieve."

"Back where we started," I said in frustration. "All right, I'm going to call Nolan right now, find out where he is, and make sure he's okay."

To my relief, Nolan answered his phone on the third ring.

"How's it going, Mike?" Subtle as a freight train, I reminded him, "This ride-along you're doing with my friends was all my idea, so I wanted to find out if it's working out well."

"Oh, yeah, great!" Nolan sounded enthusiastic—which was still an unfamiliar tone, coming from him. He also sounded like he was eating while he was talking to me. "I'm getting loads of material. Really good stuff. I should do this more often."

I hoped he didn't say that around Lopez.

"I'm glad to hear it. You've hit it off with the guys, then?"

"Well, that Lopez guy is a wet blanket." Yes, Nolan was definitely chewing. I tried to ignore it. "I mean, sure, he's a smart guy, and he really knows his stuff. And you can tell he's someone you'd be glad to have at your back if you were in a tight spot. But he's got no sense of humor, he only talks if you ask him a direct question, and he's really got a poker up his ass."

Those last few bits didn't sound like Lopez at all, and I figured it was an indication of how much he had loathed Nolan's company. I felt a little bad about that. A *little*.

"Quinn is an okay guy, though." As Nolan continued speaking, I realized I'd never before heard him talk this much about anything other than himself. This ride-along was having a remarkable effect. Maybe the demonic entity was bringing out the best in him? "He's kind of morose, but a lot more relaxed than Lopez."

"Morose?" I repeated, thinking of what Max had said about negative emotions feeding demonic appetite. Using my pretense that this was acting research, I said, "Let's explore that. Is it something you can use for Jimmy Conway?"

"Maybe, but Quinn is more of a sad sap than Jimmy is."

Well, sure. Quinn had to deal with his own problems, after all, whereas Jimmy weekly got to vent his spleen on suspects, hookers, dealers, and other cops.

Max whispered to me, "Who is morose?"

I mouthed Quinn's name, and I could see from Max's expression that he wanted me to keep pursuing it. Still treating it like an acting exercise—we spend a lot of time observing human behavior so that we can portray it well—I asked, "Why is he morose? What's the trigger?"

"A woman," said Nolan, eating again. "What else?"

"His second divorce," I guessed, recalling what Lopez had said.

"I think he really thought she was the one, you know? She walked out a year ago, and he's still not over it." He slurped a drink, then added, "And she took him to the cleaner's in the divorce, too. He'll be paying for *that* marriage for a few years, that's for sure." Nolan added darkly, "I can relate."

"Does he seem angry about it?" I asked.

"Sure, a little. Hey, maybe that's what I can use. He channels it into this kind of brash, edgy attitude that's got some potential."

I put my hand over the receiver as I explained quickly to Max what Nolan was telling me.

"Has he told you what he was doing before he joined the OCCB?" I asked Nolan.

"Worked in some god-awful part of the Bronx where drugs and gangs have overrun the place. Sounds like he investigated a lot of ugly homicides there. I'm glad you reminded me. I don't want to do it while I'm eating—"

"Oh, you're eating? I never would have guessed."

"—but I want to get some details about that. I should take notes."

"That's a good idea. It would be great stuff for us to discuss." I did not look forward to hearing about a bunch of grisly murders, but it might be necessary.

"This guy's been around. There's a lot of texture there."

Assuming Quinn would have objected to this discussion before now if he were present, I asked where he was.

"On the phone, getting a ride for us. The weather's rotten out there. Oh, and he was going to check in with his partner, too—wherever the hell Lopez is. He's been gone a while. Anyhow, Quinn's phone stopped working about an hour ago, so he's using the restaurant's."

I covered the receiver to tell Max that Quinn's phone had died. Yet another electronic device. More disrupted communication. The pranks were escalating.

Max told me to ask if the detective seemed like a religious man.

"Lapsed Catholic, from the sound of it," replied Nolan.

Which is what Lopez had said about him, too. I had to hand it to the actor. He'd gotten a lot out of the guy in only a few hours. I wondered if Quinn suspected anything, or it he was just flattered by the interest that a TV star was showing in him.

While Nolan had been talking, Max had been scribbling on a notepad in his elegant, archaic handwriting. Now he pushed his notes over to me. I saw he'd made a list of questions he wanted me to ask Nolan.

I read them, then gave Max an uncertain look. He nodded encouragingly. So I sighed and dived in.

"Say, Mike, have you guys entered any churches or houses of worship today?"

"No. Well, not yet."

"Does Quinn appear to avoid them?"

"Huh?" Nolan sounded puzzled. "No. We just haven't had any reason to—"

"Does he exhibit any ritual behaviors?"

"He chews on a pen sometimes. He says it became a habit when he quit smoking."

Probably not the sort of ritual Max meant.

"Have you observed him encountering any dogs or other animals?"

"No. Not many people are out walking their pets in this weather. Why?"

"Has he appeared violent or menacing at any point today?" I asked as casually as possible.

"Uh, no . . . but that's something I'd like to see. It could give me some background i—"

"Have you noticed any odd smells or odors in his presence?"

"What kind of odors?" Nolan sounded perplexed.

I made a gesture to Max indicating I needed more information, then I read what he quickly jotted down. "Excrement? Rotting flesh?"

"*What?*"

"Sulfur? Decay? Putrescence?"

"*No.*" Nolan added, "Jesus, Esther, I'm *eating.*"

I moved on to the next question. "Have you observed any peculiar changes in his eyes?"

"Whoa, does Quinn have a drug problem or something? Is that what you're getting at?"

"I'm just worried about him," I said, which was not entirely untrue. "He, um, doesn't look after himself."

"Yeah, that's obvious. Have you seen his posture?

It's no wonder he talks about aches and pains. I should make him an appointment with my chiropractor."

"He talks about aches and pains?" I prodded, meeting Max's gaze.

"Yeah—in fact, about an hour ago, he kind of doubled over for a few seconds when he got this stabbing pain in his stomach. I think something's wrong with his appendix. But, you know, that could be referred pain from his heart. My cardiac doctor tells me—"

I held the phone away from my ear as Nolan prattled on, and I relayed this information to Max, who looked gratified.

"Recurrent, unexplained pain like that is another common sign of demonic presence," he said, keeping his voice low. "The evidence is mounting to the inescapable conclusion that Detective Quinn is oppressed."

"Oppressed?" When Max started to explain, I said, "Wait, not now. Is there anything else you want me to ask Nolan?"

"Find out where they are now," Max instructed. "This is an opportunity for us to confront Quinn without Detective Lopez being present." He didn't need to add that Lopez would be an impediment to such a confrontation.

When I held the phone to my ear again, Nolan was still talking about cardiac stuff. I interrupted him. "You said Quinn is on the phone calling for a ride? Where are you—"

"Whoops, not anymore," said Nolan. "Quinn is waving at me to get up and come to the register. I guess we're paying and leaving."

"Where are you going?" I asked.

"A funeral in Chinatown."

"What?" I blurted.

"Hell of a night for it. Quinn suggested I might want to skip it and go home, but it's for that tong boss who flew off a balcony last week. The guy Goldman is claiming killed himself because of Lopez," he said with relish. "As if I'd miss *this*."

"You're going to Joe Ning's wake?" I asked shrilly.

Max's eyes widened and our gazes met.

Chen's Funeral Home. Quinn. Another corpse in a coffin.

"This is gonna be great," Nolan enthused. "Loads of texture, a tong boss's wake, authentic underworld characters . . . *Jackpot*."

"Mike, listen to me very carefully," I said. "You mustn't let—"

"Gotta go, Esther."

I sighed heavily and set down my phone in frustration when I realized he'd ended the call.

"*That's* what it wants," Max said, rising to his feet. "And that's why it manipulated Detective Lopez into leaving his companions. The entity suspected he would interfere if he were present."

I rose, too, and followed him to the coat hooks by the

door. He started donning his heavy outerwear (all new stuff, since his things had been ruined in the Yees' fire last week). I grabbed my coat and started putting it on, too, since I gathered we were going to Chen's now.

"Max, I still don't understand. What does the entity want?"

"It wants a cadaver!"

"A corpse?" I said with a frown. "A dead body?"

"Yes!" He turned to his familiar. "Arise, Nelli! The game is afoot!"

10

Nelli had been very reluctant to wake up and leave the dry warmth of the bookstore for the cold, cruel, wet elements of this miserable Manhattan night.

After standing outside for twenty minutes in the pouring snow (the best description of the frigid, wet, semisolid stuff falling steadily down on us), I wished I had sided with her instead of with Max.

Fine, let the demon have a dead body. What do I care?

In our eagerness to get to Chen's Funeral Home, we had not considered the difficulty of getting a cab on a night like this, let alone the challenge of finding a taxi that would agree to carry Nelli. After a few minutes of exposure to the elements had drenched the dog and her winter vest and coated her big paws with slushy filth, we accepted the impossibility of our foolish quest, and I phoned Max's pet transport service. Although Max was a regular customer and known for tipping well, they were having a busy night, so we wound up waiting much longer than expected—which was why we hadn't returned to the store to wait inside. As a result, we were shivering and very damp by the time a sleek black SUV collected us from a curb in Greenwich Village.

After giving the driver the address of the funeral home, I closed the plastic partition so the driver wouldn't overhear our conversation. Sitting in a cold, dripping huddle, I asked Max, "Why does the entity want a dead body?"

"I don't know. We'll have to ask it."

I tried to picture chatting about this with a demonic being that reanimated corpses. It didn't seem like something I wanted to do.

"How did it know Lopez would interfere?" I asked.

"By virtue of being attached to Quinn, it has been in his company for weeks. Detective Lopez is not aware of the entity, but it is aware of him and has learned things about him."

That made me shiver again. Then I thought of something else.

"Max, when Susan was running around Doyers Street with a gun in her hand, at one point she turned that thing on me. I think she really intended to pull the trigger. Lopez was there, and he saw. I could hear him shouting to me. And then projectile flames suddenly burst out of the mouth of John's lion costume and shot across the street. It scared Susan and startled her into the dropping the gun." Then Lucky had tackled her, followed by some cops. "Those flames probably saved my life, Max."

He nodded, having listened with intent interest. "And there was, of course, no evident explanation for what had happened."

"Everyone who examined the lion costume afterward was perplexed. Including Lopez."

"He had reacted instinctively, unconsciously calling on power he doesn't realize he possesses," Max mused, "at a moment of supreme stress when he saw a madwoman pointing a loaded gun at you."

"Quinn was there," I said.

"Ah." Max realized where I was going with this. "That means the entity was present and witnessed the incident, too. And you're wondering . . ."

"Does it know about Lopez? Does it know what we know? Well, I mean . . . what we strongly suspect."

Although I couldn't have explained why, it struck me as threatening for a mysterious demonic entity to realize there was something special about Lopez—in a mystical sense, I mean.

"That probably depends," said Max, "on what the entity can sense." He thought it over for a few moments. "But I am skeptical that a single isolated event would be revelatory. As I understand it, there were many people on the street at the time, and quite a few of them were emotional, alarmed, and shouting. There was also a mystical familiar present."

"Yes." I looked over my shoulder, to where Nelli lay in the back of the vehicle, making a halfhearted attempt to clean her front paws. She had been at the scene, of course—it was where she had subsequently tried to attack Quinn.

"So it would be unlikely, I think, for the entity to pinpoint the catalyst of those flames, even if it recognized a frisson of mystical power at that moment." Max added, "If it is any comfort to you, I think the demon's effort to get your young man out of the way for this evening indicates, if anything, that it prefers to avoid confrontation with him."

"It is a comfort. But I don't think he'd go to the wake, anyhow," I said. "Given the garbage that Alan Goldman is spreading in the media, showing up at Ning's visitation would just bring more pointless trouble down on Lopez's head."

On the phone, Lopez had indicated that he intended to go back to his squad and stay there for a while. So it seemed to me that he and his partner, who was unknown to the media or the Ning family, had agreed that if there was anything more to be learned about Ning's controversial death at the wake, it would be up to Quinn to observe it.

"Oh, the demon probably doesn't understand any of

that," said Max. "They're clever, but they're not human, not part of society, and often didn't originate in this dimension. The demon is no more likely to understand why Detective Lopez will avoid this wake than you would be likely to understand the intricacies of court etiquette if you were suddenly transported to medieval Japan. So it took steps to distract him."

I nodded and sat pensively for a few moments.

The SUV entered Chinatown, maintaining a steady pace and a smooth ride on the increasingly treacherous streets. We'd be at the funeral home within minutes, so I asked what our plan was.

"I propose that we find Detective Quinn and remove him from the premises with all due haste. I believe the Chens' reputation in the community is such that it can probably withstand an alarming incident, but I assume they would nonetheless much rather that Uncle Six does *not* become reanimated at his own wake."

"That's what we're expecting then?" I asked, trying to get my head around this. "Quinn and his demon arrive at the wake and . . . what? There's a little mystical mojo and—abracadaver!—another corpse reanimates?"

"Yes, I believe that is the likely scenario." He paused before adding, "More or less."

"I still don't understand why. It is doing this just to generate fear? Is this another escalation of pranks designed to feed its appetite for negative emotion?"

"I suspect there is more to it than that," Max said.

"This entity attached itself to a police officer, someone who presumably comes into contact with many fresh corpses . . . Well, *many* compared to the average citizen, that is."

"Nolan said that Quinn investigated a lot of murders in his previous post," I recalled. "And he's bound to investigate homicides as an OCCB detective." It wasn't as if people in organized crime shied away from committing murder, after all.

"I hypothesize that the entity chose Quinn for that reason. The detective could be counted on to bring the demon into contact with the dead," said Max. "The *recently* dead."

"So that it can animate them."

"Yes." He frowned in thought. "Rather than being another prank, I suspect that reanimation may be the entity's goal—or a significant step on the path to its goal."

"Well, the Chens are not going to like *that*." I doubted the Ning family would like it, either. I pulled my phone out of my pocket. "Quinn must already be there. I'll tell Lucky what's going on."

Max nodded his approval. Unfortunately, though, Lucky didn't answer his phone. I left a message, then put my phone back into my pocket. I didn't even bother trying John, who would also be there. The Chens didn't carry cell phones when hosting a wake. Nathan felt it was disrespectful to the departed and insensitive to the bereaved to chat on a phone while standing five feet away from a newly filled casket.

As was Max's custom, he tipped the driver generously when we reached our destination. I didn't know if the Magnum Collegium paid well or if he had simply invested wisely over the centuries, but Max seemed to have a healthy income. (I just knew that the bookstore couldn't be the source of his funds, since it did very modest business.)

Uncle Six was such a big man that the wake was heavily attended despite the daunting weather and slippery streets. The funeral home was so crowded I wondered if it had been a bad idea to bring our pony-sized dog. But then I remembered there was probably a demonic entity hovering somewhere on the premises, and I was glad to have her at my side—though she was by now very damp and a bit odorous. Her feet were tracking dirt through the funeral home, but then so were everyone else's. I didn't envy the Chens their cleaning bills at this time of year.

I had been here a few weeks ago for the wake of a well-to-do local citizen—Benny Yee, Susan's first murder victim (though his death was attributed to natural causes). This occasion was even grander, Joe Ning being a more prominent man, but very similar. There were tables of offerings and traditional floral arrangements, and there were Christian symbols alongside incense burners, statues of the Buddha, and banners with graceful Chinese calligraphy. I stood on tiptoe and craned my neck to see the coffin, which was on the other side of the main reception hall, beyond this throng of people. The closed casket looked expensive, dignified, and undisturbed.

"Well, nothing's happened yet," I said.

Max and I had been just about the only non-Asians at Benny's wake, but Uncle Six's business interests had been more extensive, and apparently so had his social contacts. Although most of the people here this evening seemed to be Chinese, certainly not all of them were. But I didn't see Quinn's distinctive head of red hair in the crowd.

And searching for him would take time because the place was so crowded. Max and I could scarcely push our way through the wall of people, and having Nelli with us made it that much more difficult.

"Wait," I said, "there's an easier way to do this."

"Oh, thank goodness," Max said, brushing a total stranger's hair out of his mouth.

I pulled my phone out of my pocket again and called Nolan, intending to ask exactly where he and Quinn were. The place was so noisy I was afraid he wouldn't hear his own phone ringing, but he answered the call quickly.

"Esther?" It sounded like he was whispering.

"Yes," I shouted. "I'm here at the wake and looking for you."

I couldn't hear whatever he said next. He *was* whispering.

"Speak up!" I shouted. "I can't hear you!"

Instead of doing so, he ended the call. I stared at my phone in bemusement, wondering what to do now.

A moment later, I received a text message from him: *Can't talk louder. Tailing Danny Teng on foot.*

"He's doing *what?*" Max exclaimed. "That sounds most unwise."

I agreed. If a violent street thug like Danny Teng noticed he was being followed and felt threatened, I had a feeling the *best* outcome would put Nolan in a hospital bed.

In response to my texted query about what was going on, Nolan replied:

Teng arrived. Made scene. Claims Ning's death is murder. Says he knows who did it.

Tailing him to learn more.

"If Danny knows Susan did it, well, she's in custody. But we've got to warn Ted," I said to Max, afraid that Danny would retaliate against Susan's brother for her crime.

"Isn't that Ted over there?" Max pointed off to our left.

Sure enough, it was. He looked glum, which was understandable. I didn't see his mother with him, which was a relief. I supposed he had come here to pay his last respects to the man who had intended to finance *ABC*.

"Thank God he's here and safe while Danny is out prowling the streets," I said. "But Nolan is *not* safe. What he's doing could get him killed!"

"Agreed. I shall speak to Ted while you use your device to communicate with Mr. Nolan and convince him to halt his ill-advised pursuit before he comes to grief."

"Right," I said with a nod.

Taking Nelli with him, both of them still very damp, Max started pushing through the crowd, moving slowly and apologizing often, heading in Ted's direction. Fortunately, the ex-filmmaker was not far away from this spot, and Max had nearly reached him by the time I finished my next text to Nolan:

Stop now. VERY DANGEROUS. Danny Teng is a killer!

I was kind of guessing on that last one, but it seemed likely.

Nolan wrote back:

Getting great material!

"Oh, for God's sake."

For a moment, I hoped Danny *would* shoot him. Then I banished the thought, which felt like it invited bad luck. I texted again.

Leave this to Quinn. SERIOUSLY.

The reply came back shortly, telling me that Quinn was sick and lying down inside Chen's. In answer to my follow-up question, Nolan replied that Quinn had gotten dizzy and queasy soon after arriving here.

Was the illness a deliberate ruse of Quinn's? Or was

the entity making him ill? Well, either way, he was in the building, and so was the demon that was attached to him. So we needed to find him.

I texted again, asking exactly where Quinn was. I waited a few minutes, but there was no reply. I hoped Nolan was all right and was just absorbed in his pursuit of Danny Teng.

I couldn't just stand around all night hoping Nolan would eventually reply. Besides, he might not even know the answer to my question. We had to search the building. If Quinn was still lying down somewhere, I thought it must be in the Chens' office or one of the other workaday rooms behind the door marked "Private." We should look there.

I had no intention of confronting a cadaver-animating demonic entity by myself, so I turned to look in Ted's direction, intending to go grab Max and Nelli—and was relieved to see them coming back toward me, pushing their way through the crowd.

"Whatever Danny Teng thinks about Uncle Six's death," Max informed me, "he evidently doesn't suspect Susan."

"What did Ted tell you?"

"Danny showed up here briefly this evening, drunk and emotional. He is angry about Uncle Six's death, but shows no sign of blaming the Yee family. He was, in his fashion, cordial to Ted and expressed condolences over Susan's arrest."

I wished the police would arrest Danny for providing Susan with that gun, but since they had not, I supposed he had covered his tracks too well for charges to stick. He was an impulsive idiot, but nonetheless an experienced criminal.

"So Ted's not in danger from him?" I said. "Well, that's a relief."

But based on what Max said next, it sounded as if someone who was not involved in the murder probably *was* in danger.

"In keeping with what Mr. Nolan has conveyed to you, Ted says that Danny soon got noisy and made a scene. Upon paying his respects to the family, he told Mrs. Ning that he knows who killed Uncle Six and he vowed to extract vengeance—though his language, one supposes, was far more colorful than that."

"Indeed."

In the Chinatown underworld, Danny's wagon had been firmly hitched to Uncle Six's star. I had previously seen how the gangster fawned on the tong boss, and I thought he had probably felt an emotional attachment to him. Mostly, though, I assumed Danny's grief and rage now were caused by his career prospects spiraling due to his patron's death. Ambitious members of the Red Daggers were probably eager to challenge Danny's position as leader now that he wasn't protected by Uncle Six, and other powerful underworld bosses presumably already had their own trusted right-hand thugs and didn't want Uncle Six's leftovers.

Danny's performance at the wake sounded like he was mostly acting out . . . But just because he was an idiot didn't mean he wasn't a survivor. So I thought he might also have his eye on the ball. If he could reinvent himself as the avenger of Uncle Six's murderer, he might turn his fate back in the direction he wanted it to go.

Max asked, "Have you convinced your friend to cease following Danny?"

"Nolan's not a friend, he's a colleague," I said automatically. "And, no, he won't listen."

"Based on what we know of that lad, I am very concerned for Mr. Nolan's safety."

"So am I, but he's ignoring me now," I said. "And it sounds like Quinn is probably still here." I relayed the information I had gotten from Nolan.

"Sudden illness, such as Detective Quinn apparently experienced after arriving here, is a common reaction of the oppressed to increased demonic energy," said Max. "I think it likely the demon is gathering its strength and focusing its energy on a goal."

We both looked in the direction of Uncle Six's closed casket. If the old man rose and tried to get out of the coffin, I had a feeling that things would get revoltingly messy, given that his body had fallen six floors last week before being scraped up off a city street.

"Yuck," I blurted, shying away from the images in my head.

"Let's make our way to the back rooms," Max said. "If Detective Quinn is there, we should extract him immediately."

With Nelli right behind us and occasionally stepping on our heels, we pushed our way through the crowd, apologizing as we went and ignoring the censorious looks we got from mourners who clearly thought a wake was no place for a large, wet dog.

I kept looking around, hoping to see John, Nathan, or Lucky, but the whole funeral home was so crowded this evening that I couldn't spot any of them. I had no idea if they knew Quinn was here, and I wanted to warn them that we feared Uncle Six might stop resting in peace at any moment. But in the current circumstances, I was unable to communicate with them.

After prolonged pushing, sidling, and squeezing through the press of bodies, we reached the door to the back rooms and went through it. Once on the other side of it, it was such a relief *not* to be in that densely crowded hall anymore, we paused for a moment to take a few steadying breaths and compose ourselves.

Then I said to Max, "Let's just start opening doors. If he's here, we should find him quickly."

He nodded, handed me Nelli's leash, and stepped in front of me to open the door to the office.

A man inside the room shrieked.

Max gave a startled cry and staggered backward into me. When his skull crashed into my nose, I cried out and staggered back, too—and stepped on Nelli. Nelli wailed and jumped sideways, then gave me a reproachful look.

"*Dio mio!*" Lucky's voice sounded breathless. "Don't creep around like that! You nearly gave me a heart attack!"

"My dear fellow, I'm so sorry! We didn't expect to find you in here."

I put a hand gingerly on my throbbing nose while my eyes watered.

As we entered the office, I saw that a telephone receiver was in Lucky's hand. He put it back in its cradle on the desk and said to Max, "Well, now I know why you're not answering the phone at the bookstore."

"I left you a message," I said to him, sniffing a little. He shook his head. "My phone's dead."

A wave of cold passed through my chest. "Since when?"

"Since Detective Doom-To-Devices got here," Lucky said grimly.

"Is he still here?" Max asked urgently.

"Yep. But how did *you* know? I been trying to call and tell you." He gestured to the phone on the desk.

"You should have called *me*," I said, waving my cell phone in the air. Still no reply from Nolan, I noticed.

"When I say my phone is dead, kid, I mean *dead*. I

can't even look up the numbers." He added, "But the bookstore is listed in the phonebook, so I've been calling there."

"Where is Quinn now?" I asked.

"Don't worry. I got him tied up next door."

"Tied up?" I repeated as Lucky led the way out of the room. "Literally?"

"Yeah. He's gagged, too. Sounds don't really carry from here to the visitation rooms, but better safe than so—"

"You *bound* and *gagged* him?"

"Would you relax? I didn't hurt him." Lucky added, "Well, not much."

"You've tied up a *cop*?" I said. "Are you crazy?"

"I didn't know what else to do," Lucky said defensively. "When John told me he was here, I didn't think we should just let him roam around loose. Not after what happened the last time he was here."

Max said to me, "Lucky has a point."

"Max, we can't tie up a police officer," I said firmly.

How was I going to talk Quinn out of charging Lucky with kidnapping him?

More importantly, how would I talk him out of telling Lopez about this?

We entered a storage room. There was a narrow cot there, and I realized this must be where Lucky slept when he'd been hiding from the police in recent weeks.

Now the cot was occupied by Detective Quinn, who

had been bound and gagged with—even I could see—professional efficiency. Both wrists and both ankles were tied to the metal bedframe. He was conscious and, as might be expected, looked absolutely furious.

Nelli started growling. A low, deep sound that rumbled in her throat.

I looked anxiously at her, realizing I didn't have the strength to hold her back if she attacked the helpless man tied to the cot. But Nelli wasn't even looking at Quinn. Her eyes scanned the room a few times, then she half-closed them as she continued growling softly. Whatever she found threatening, apparently she couldn't locate it; she just knew it was somewhere in our vicinity.

Quinn's angry gaze shifted from Lucky to the growling dog, and his eyes widened with alarm. He started struggling against his bonds.

"Oh, my God," I said in a hollow voice, my heart pounding. "Ohmigod, ohmigod, ohmigod."

We were in deep shit this time.

This was a *cop* we were holding prisoner.

At the sound of my voice, Quinn's gaze moved from Nelli, who was still growling softly, to me. A little disoriented, it took him a moment to recognize me. And then his expression transformed into appalled shock. He tried to speak through the gag, addressing me. His comments just came out as muffled grunts, of course, but I had the impression he was asking what the fuck I

thought I was doing and declaring that I was every bit
as crazy as Lopez feared.

"Lucky," I said desperately. "We can't do this."

"Too late now. It's done." The old mobster shrugged.
"Spilt milk."

"Oh, my *God*." I couldn't think of what else to say.

While Quinn writhed in protest against his bonds
and continued grunting angrily through the gag, Max
leaned over his body and took a few sniffs. Checking
for odors of excrement, rotting flesh, or putrescence, I
supposed.

Then he looked in each of his ears and peered into
each of the detective's eyes. Quinn found the examina-
tion peculiar enough that he stopped struggling for a
few moments and just stared at Max in bemusement.

"Lucky, how did this happen?" I demanded.

"Well, John told me he was back here, lying down,"
said Lucky. "He'd arrived with another cop—not your
boyfriend, someone else."

"The other guy isn't a cop," I said. "He's an actor."

"After what happened last time . . ." Lucky looked
down at Quinn and added, "You *jerk*."

"Hm?" Quinn grunted.

"Well, John was really worried about him being here
in the middle of a big wake."

"Of course," said Max. "As soon as we learned this
was his destination, the alarming implications of his
presence were immediately apparent."

"Hm?" Quinn said again, frowning at Max.

"So John sees him arrive and walks up to speak to him, hoping he can get rid of him. Maybe say it's insensitive for cops to be here on such a sad occasion," Lucky continued. "Something like that. But before he can make his point, the other cop tells him—"

"Nolan's not a cop, he's an actor."

"—that Quinn is feeling really sick all of a sudden and asks if there's somewhere he can lie down until their ride comes for them."

I supposed Quinn had gotten a squad car to drop them off here and told it to come back later for them.

"And instead of refusing, which he's got a constitutional right to do, John gives him my cot." Lucky made a disgusted sound. "And him such an educated boy, too."

While Max continued examining Quinn and Nelli continued growling softly, which was starting to get on my nerves, I said to Lucky, "So you . . . what? Came straight back here, conked him on the head, and tied him to the bed before he regained consciousness?"

"Yeah." Lucky seemed pleased that I was catching up to the plot. "Then I started trying to get in touch with you two. Which wasn't working, so I'm really glad someone else told you this bozo was coming back here to reiterate another corpse."

"Hm?" said Quinn.

"I think you mean reanimate."

"*Hm?*" the cop grunted.

"Are you still feeling sick?" Max asked him.

Quinn shook his head. Then he glared at Lucky and said something.

"I think he's saying his head hurts," I said.

"I didn't hit him that hard," Lucky said dismissively.

"Even if he's better, he could have another bout of nausea," I said to Max. "We should remove the gag."

"Bad idea," said Lucky. "What if he goes into some mumbo jumbo chanting to raise another body from the dead?"

"*Hm?*" said Quinn.

"We should remove him immediately from this place," said Max.

"It's too risky," I argued. "We can't get a bound and gagged cop out of here without being noticed. Not with so many people around."

"We could haul him out through Antonelli's," said Lucky. "No one's using those rooms tonight. The exit is clear."

"But there are people on the street," I said. "Even if we use the hearse—"

"Hm?" said Quinn, looking alarmed.

"—and pull it right up to the door, the risk of being seen abducting a cop is too great."

"We'll put him in a coffin," Lucky said. "Problem solved."

Quinn protested emphatically.

"That may be the best solution," Max said apologetically to the detective. "A speedy departure is advisable, and I fear that you are not in a cooperative frame of mind. We may only have moments before Uncle Six becomes reanimated."

"Hm?"

Lucky said, "And Nathan won't like *that*."

Quinn protested some more, then choked a little on his gag.

"This is too dangerous, Lucky." I gestured to Quinn. "What were you *thinking?* A gagged person can drown in his own vomit. What would you have done if he died while you were trying to phone us?"

"I'd make sure no one ever found the body."

"Actually . . ." Max glanced at Nelli, who continued her low-level growling, then he frowned darkly at Quinn. "I rather suspect . . ."

"What?" said Lucky.

Max pulled something out of one of his pockets, and I saw that it was a crucifix. He laid it on Quinn's forehead and stared at him for a long moment.

Quinn stared back, then finally shrugged and made an inquisitive sound.

"Hmmm." The next object Max pulled out of his pocket was a small bottle of clear fluid.

"Holy water?" I asked as he opened it.

"Yes."

He flicked his wrist lightly to sprinkle some water

over Quinn's face. It flew out of the mouth of the bottle faster than he'd anticipated, drenching the helpless officer and getting in his eyes. Quinn snorted a little and shook his head, blinking rapidly.

"Oops! My apologies," said Max.

Quinn rolled his eyes.

"So where's the demon?" Lucky asked. "Ain't it supposed to appear now?"

Quinn gave Lucky a peculiar look as Max said, "It may not be responsive to Christian symbolism. Fortunately, anticipating this possibility, I have brought a variety of supplies."

The redheaded detective groaned in protest.

I realized Max had made advance preparations, anticipating an emergency. He'd certainly had no time to gather supplies before we dashed out of the bookstore this evening.

Max said, "*However*, I have a feeling . . ."

Nelli's growling got louder. I turned to look at her, and I saw her eyes were getting glassy now, her expression growing fierce and feral. Her lips drew back in a snarl, exposing her long, sharp canine teeth.

"*Max.*" My grip tightened on the familiar's pink leash.

Quinn started protesting in alarm and struggling so hard that he rocked the cot. But Nelli wasn't threatening *him*. She whirled around and started growling menacingly at the open doorway . . . or perhaps at something beyond it.

"Or maybe the demon ain't reacting," Lucky said slowly, "because it ain't with *this* guy anymore?"

Across the hall was the room where they prepared the bodies for funeral services. The door was closed. Behind it, I heard a dull thud, followed by a noisy crash.

Nelli started barking furiously, her powerful body crouched for attack, her fur standing on end.

"Lucky!" I shouted to be heard above the dog. "Is there a new arrival in there?"

"Oh, *no*," he said. "It sounds like it."

Something thudded so heavily against the door across the hall that it visibly shook. Nelli kept barking, braced for combat.

Behind me, I could hear the cot shaking violently as Quinn struggled. His inquisitive grunts were audible despite the racket that Nelli and . . . and something *else* were making. The thing in the other room thudded hard against the door again.

Max raised his voice behind me. "We should untie Detective Quinn!"

"I got it!"

As I glanced over my shoulder, I saw Lucky flip open a pocket knife and, with one stroke, cut the slender cord that bound Quinn's wrists to the metal frame of the cot. Then he handed Quinn the knife. The cop struggled clumsily to sit up and reach for his bound ankles, his eyes fixed on the dog and the door she was snarling at.

The door across the hallway creaked open. I whirled around to look at it—and then gagged as a fetid odor emerged from that room and poured into this one.

The other room was dark, but the light from the hallway illuminated the delicate form of a very petite, very old Chinese woman. Her eyes glowed with green fire and her lips were curled back in a snarl. Thick, yellow drool flowed down her chin.

Behind me, I could hear Quinn making guttural sounds as he struggled to free his feet from their bonds. Max started chanting in a language I didn't recognize. I stood frozen on the spot, clutching Nelli's leash.

The thing in the room across the hall took a step toward us.

I gasped and dropped Nelli's leash as the fearless familiar leaped and hurled herself at the infernal being coming toward us. Nelli probably weighed twice what the corpse did, and she was all bone and muscle and teeth, attacking with bold fury to battle Evil as she had entered this dimension to do.

The two forms collided, wrestled for a moment—and then the petite little corpse threw Nelli aside as if she were a twig. Nelli hit the wall like a speeding train, bounced off, landed on the floor, and lay there without moving.

"Nelli!" I cried.

The thing grinned, and then its glowing eyes rested on me and it came forward, its bony arms outstretched and a dry cackle emerging from its throat.

11

*B*OOM!

I flung myself sideways in reaction to an ear-shattering explosion right next to me. After falling to the floor and rolling, I looked up to see Lucky, gun in hand, shoot the cadaver again.

The reanimated corpse paused for a moment, swayed a little, and then kept on coming. As it entered the room, Quinn jumped off the cot and tore the gag from his mouth. He was bleeding where he had cut himself with the knife while sawing at his bonds.

"What the *FUCK?*" he shouted.

Max hurled his bottle of holy water at the moving corpse. It flung the bottle aside, said something guttural in words I didn't understand . . . then paused and swayed.

Nelli rose clumsily to her feet, lurching and slipping in

her disorientation as she reentered the storage room. She snarled as she prepared to launch another attack. I was still on the floor, and I skittered backward, trying to get away from the *thing* that was in this tiny room with us.

And then, in the blink of an eye . . . the corpse collapsed. Between one moment and the next, it simply fell to the floor like a puppet whose strings had been cut. It lay there motionless, its eyes closed, all signs of demonic presence vanished.

I became aware of the sound of fists pounding on the door from the reception hall. Beyond it, I could hear people shouting. A moment later, that door burst open and people stampeded through it. Footsteps thundered down the hall toward us.

John appeared in the doorway and his gaze swept the storage room. He took one look at the collapsed corpse, the disheveled cop, the crouching dog who was sniffing the cadaver, and the rest of us—and he apparently understood the situation. He immediately closed the door on all of us and said loudly to people crowding into the hallway behind him, "It's all right! My uncle was playing with his dog and . . . and had an accident with some fireworks."

Through the door, I heard the rumble of anxious voices, some of them speaking in English, some in Chinese. John raised his voice and said, "No, he doesn't need help. He'd like us all to just return to the other room and leave him alone. He's, um . . . naked."

"Naked?" Lucky repeated darkly.

"He's doing a . . . good job of . . . thinking on his feet," I whispered, breathing so hard that it was a struggle to speak.

Nelli was still sniffing the corpse, but she had stopped growling.

"What the *fuck* is going on around here?" Quinn demanded. "What *is* this shit?"

"Shit . . ." I repeated vaguely, realizing that the fetid odor was gone. In the hallway, I could hear John's voice, soothing people and urging them to return to the wake.

"Doc, what made that thing collapse?" Lucky asked. "Was it the second bullet? Or something else? If we knew what made it *stop*, we could plan for the next time."

"*Next time?*" Quinn repeated.

Breathing hard, Max said, "I postulate that it ran out of energy. It's not strong enough yet."

"Not *strong* enough?" Lucky repeated. "Did you see what it did to Nelli?"

"Reanimation of a dead being must be a tremendous drain on its power," Max panted. "It could only sustain the effort for so long."

"I think it said something." My voice felt weak. "Did you understand it?"

"Sounded like gibberish to me," said Lucky.

"I believe it said 'life,' " said Max. "Or perhaps 'to live.' I think it spoke an archaic form of Aramaic."

Which would explain why it sounded like gibberish to me and Lucky.

"What the *hell* are you people into?" Quinn demanded.

"Are you kiddin' me?" Lucky said to him in disgust. "This ain't our thing, you jerk. It's *yours*."

"What?" Quinn looked angry, disoriented, and shocked. "What are you . . . Jesus, what *was* that?"

John had opened the door and was slipping into the room as Quinn spoke. Closing the door behind him, he looked down at the petite corpse. "I'd say it's Grace Chu."

"Who?" Sweat was gleaming on Quinn's face.

"Grace Chu?" I repeated. "Well . . . RIP, Grace."

Reanimated, infernal, and pretty damn dangerous. Imagine if the kids and grandkids had seen *this*.

Looking at the little old lady's corpse, which now had two fresh bullet holes in the torso, I started laughing.

When I saw the way the others all looked at me, I laughed even harder.

"Jesus," Quinn said in disgust.

"She's overwrought," Max said kindly.

"Is it any wonder?" said John.

"Everyone reacts different to these things," said Lucky.

"Oh, for fuck's sake," said Quinn, as I continued laughing.

I took a deep breath and pulled myself together. "Okay, I'm done."

I hiccupped, which sent me into another peal of laughter. Then I looked at the body again—and suddenly I was ashamed and embarrassed and had no idea why I'd been laughing a second ago.

"Sorry," I said.

They all brushed aside my apology, except for Quinn.

Nelli groaned a little and lay down next to me, apparently feeling the sting of her injuries. She'd hit the wall and the floor very hard. I started petting her big head, trying to calm both of us with that soothing, repetitive motion.

"Who the hell is Grace Chu?" Quinn demanded in a strained voice. "And what . . . what . . ."

John looked down at the body again. "She died last night. Natural causes. Ninety-two years old." After a moment, he added, "I hope Sam will be able to hide the bullet holes. We don't want to have to explain those to the family . . ."

"So here I'm worrying about Joe Ning's body," Lucky said crankily, "and you don't mention there's a body back *here*?"

John looked up. "I didn't know. I mean, I knew we were expecting her, but no one told me she'd arrived." He shook his head. "Sam must have brought her over this morning before he went home to take care of the kids. And with all the preparations for Uncle Six, I guess it didn't occur to Dad to mention it."

Lucky let out his breath on a gust and sat down on the cot, his gun still in his hand. "I guess not. After all, Nathan didn't know *this* guy was here." Lucky glared at Quinn.

"You didn't tell him?" Max asked.

"Dad's been pretty high-strung since Detective Quinn's last visit," said John. "We figured he didn't need more stress in the middle of Joe Ning's wake, so we agreed not to tell him Quinn was here again."

"What does this have to do with *me?*" Quinn asked. "And what *is* 'this,' anyhow?"

"You don't know?" I asked, squinting up at him.

Instead of answering, he asked me, "Does Lopez know what you're doing?"

"Even *I* don't know what I'm doing."

"No *wonder* he doesn't want to talk about you."

"Can we leave him out of this?"

My phone rang shrilly, startling us all. I jumped and gave a little shriek. Then I fumbled in my coat pocket and found the cell. My hands were shaking so hard I dropped the thing before managing to answer it.

My caller was Nolan. "What do you want?" I asked, having no desire to talk to him.

"You wanted to know where Quinn was, right?"

I watched Max examine Quinn's hands, which were bleeding where he had cut himself.

"Oh." I said, "I found him."

It appeared that the shock of Grace Chu's reanimation had made Quinn forget that we had been holding him hostage before the corpse walked. But I had a feeling he'd remember any moment now.

After a long pause, Nolan said, "Aren't you even going to ask how things panned out with Danny Teng?"

"Who?" I realized I was sitting within two feet of the body, and this bothered me. But not enough to work up the energy to move.

"The guy you warned me is a killer too dangerous for me to follow," Nolan prodded. "Remember *now*, Esther?"

"Oh. Right." I couldn't work up any interest in Danny now. I sat staring at the corpse of the tiny, elderly lady—and remembered the way this same petite body had thrown Nelli aside as easily if she were an apple core.

Man, that thing was strong.

How were we going to defeat something that strong?

John asked Lucky to help him take Grace back across the hall. Max was suggesting to Quinn that he should sit down and listen for a few minutes. Quinn continued hotly demanding explanations.

"I think this guy's all hot air," said Nolan.

Still petting Nelli's head, I watched Lucky slip his gun into his ankle holster, then help John lift the corpse. She looked so fragile now.

I shivered.

Nolan continued, "He didn't go looking for a murderer or meet any sources."

"No?" As if I cared.

"Nah, he just went to a bar, had a few drinks by himself, then picked up a hooker—well, she looked like a hooker, anyhow—and went home."

So Danny Teng was full of hot air and making empty boasts at the funeral. Big surprise.

"Still, I got a strong whiff of underbelly by following him around for a while," Nolan said, looking on the bright side. "So are you still at the funeral home? Anything interesting happening there?"

"I'm still here," I said, watching a Gambello hitter come back into this little room to confer with a 350-year-old mage about the reanimated corpse we had just confronted. "But it's very quiet here. If I were you, I'd just go home and, uh, mentally process today's research."

"Yeah, I think that's what I'll do," he said. "Proper rest is as important as proper diet and exercise. Gotta maintain the balance."

"Uh-huh." I said goodnight and ended the call.

John came back into the room, too. "Is everyone okay?"

"No," said Quinn.

"Esther?" John stretched out a hand to help me up.

"I don't want to get up." My legs didn't feel ready to

cope with walking yet. I just kept petting Nelli, who whined a little.

"Are you all right?" he asked me with concern.

"That was fast thinking," I said to him. "The way you got rid of those people."

"Naked," Lucky grumbled. "He told them I was *naked*—alone back here where we keep dead bodies. What are those people gonna think?"

"Let it go," I advised Lucky.

"I had a feeling about what I'd find back here," said John. "I heard the barking and the shots—but when I tried to come back here, the door was . . . well, *barricaded*. It felt like someone had blocked it with a lead-lined safe or something, it was so hard to budge. A bunch of us were trying to push it open when it finally gave way—all of a sudden moving as easily as normal."

Max nodded. "Yes, of course."

"What do you *mean*, 'of course'?" Shaking his head in exasperation, Quinn strode out of the room, brushing past John. "Out of my way. I want to see that body."

We all remained where we were. Lucky and John had just handled the body, so they certainly didn't need to look at it again. And I didn't *want* to look at it.

"The entity blocked that door because it didn't want an audience," Max said.

"What *did* it want?" I felt cold all the way through when I recalled the way its arms had reached out for me a moment before Lucky shot it.

"I rather suspect it told us what it wanted," Max replied. "When it spoke."

"Life?" I said, hoping I was wrong. This was too eerie. "To live?"

"Precisely."

"Not many things give me goose bumps," said Lucky. "But that just did."

"If it wants to live," I said, scooting closer to Nelli in search of some body heat, "you'd think it would realize that the day-old corpse of a departed great-granny isn't its best possible option."

"Yes, it's interesting, isn't it?" Max said pensively.

"*Interesting?*" John repeated "I don't think that's the word I'd choose."

But I saw where Max was going with this. "If it wants life, why has it twice reanimated dead bodies?"

"Twice that we know about," said Lucky. "Might have been other times, too."

"Indeed," said Max. "Though based on Detective Quinn's reaction this evening, he is unaware of other incidents."

"Yeah," Lucky agreed. "He don't get it."

"But why doesn't it just possess Quinn?" I wondered. "He's alive, after all, if that's what it wants."

"Why doesn't *what* just possess me?" Quinn asked coldly from the doorway.

I looked up, not having realized he'd returned. "Oops."

He looked at Max. "That body in there is dead."

"Yes."

"It's been dead about a day."

I said, "No wonder they made you a detective."

"Shut up," he said.

John bristled. "Don't talk to Esther like that."

"So how did you do it?" Quinn demanded. "And *why*?"

"We didn't do it," Lucky said tersely. "You did."

"You assaulted a police officer today." Quinn gave him a hard stare. "Held me hostage."

"You assaulted him?" John groaned.

"Yeah, because I didn't want him doing *this*." Lucky's gesture encompassed the scene we'd just been through.

"And look how well *that* worked out," I said.

"You sound like you feel better now," Lucky noted.

"Binding and gagging a *cop*." I shook my head.

Quinn added, "All so you could stage this weird . . . *thing* for my benefit. I want to know *why*."

"They really breed cops dumb, don't they?" said Lucky.

Quinn shot back, "Not as dumb as they breed wise-guys who think they can get away with—"

"Everyone, please!" Max held up his hands for a moment, urging silence.

John and I exchanged a glance. Lucky scowled and folded his arms across his chest. Quinn glared at all of us.

Max folded his hands and looked at the cop with a very serious expression. "Detective Quinn, I believe . . . no, I am quite convinced that you are being oppressed."

"Oppressed?" Quinn looked puzzled. "As in, being denied my human rights?"

"No, oppressed by a demonic entity."

"Oh, come on. You can do better than th—"

"Oppression precedes possession, though possession does not always follow," said Max. "Oppression is the stage when the demon interferes with your daily life, isolating you, actively stimulating your negative emotions, and wearing you down."

"And then what?" Quinn's tone was dismissive. "I'll be possessed?"

"In this case, I don't think so. I believe that you are the entity's tool rather than its prize."

"Always a bridesmaid, never a bride."

Max did not let Quinn's flippant attitude distract him. "Am I correct in assuming that you have never been involved in any so-called occult practices?"

"Correct, and I'm not interested. So let's just—"

"Have you ever participated in a séance? Used a Ouija board? Attempted to conjure a spirit?"

"No, I live in the adult world," Quinn said impatiently.

"You have never invited a dark power into your life?"

"Not if we don't count my first wife."

Max ignored that. "Then it is as I thought. The Law of Invitation does not apply here, but rather the Law of Attraction." He explained to the rest of us, "Those are the two typical paths a demon follows to invade someone's life as this one has invaded Detective Quinn's."

"Oh, for the—"

"He didn't invite this entity into his life," I said, catching on, "which goes a long way toward explaining why he's unaware of its presence."

"Correct. The entity was drawn to him, but not because he sought or summoned it." Max spoke directly to Quinn again as he continued, "I believe the infestation is relatively recent. It may have been a factor in the demise of your second marriage, but I think it more likely that it attached to you soon thereafter, attracted by your despair, disappointment, and sense of failure."

"How do you know about my marr . . ." Quinn drew in a sharp breath and looked at me. "You scheming *bitch.*"

"That's *enough*," John said sharply to him. "You've got no business talking to Esther that way."

"You planted that actor with us to spy on *me*," Quinn said in appalled amazement. "And here I thought you were trying to keep tabs on Lopez."

"This entity has an affinity with dead bodies," Max said, soldiering on. "Particularly with the recently deceased. That is probably how it first encountered you."

"No, I've never been recently deceased," Quinn assured him.

"I assume it followed you home from the scene of a homicide or similar deadly incident."

"Followed me home? Is this thing a demonic *puppy* or something?"

"I gather you have investigated many homicides?"

"My fair share."

"Within the past year, many things have gone wrong in your life," said Max. "Haven't they?"

Quinn glared at me again.

"You've struggled with depression and anxiety. Your health has declined, yet no diagnosis explains it. You experience sharp, random pains, nausea, and severe headaches. You've been suffering for some time from disturbing nightmares, which has in turn led to bouts of insomnia."

Now Quinn looked sharply at Max. I sensed he had not told anyone about the nightmares.

I wondered how Max knew—then realized he must be reciting a list of classic symptoms. He had previously noted more than once, after all, that Quinn's situation exhibited various typical features.

Max continued, "Mechanical devices keep malfunctioning and electronic equipment keeps failing. You may be receiving phone calls regularly in which you can hear only static—particularly in the middle of the night. Things in your apartment keep disappearing and then reappearing, turning up in places you know you did not leave them. Your personal belongings are being inexplicably damaged or destroyed, particularly things to which you have an emotional attachment."

By now, Quinn was looking at Max as if *he* has just risen from the dead.

"On numerous occasions when you're alone, you feel you're being watched. You may hear sounds inside your apartment that you can't account for—footsteps, breathing, doors opening and closing."

Quinn's mouth was hanging open. "How do you know all this? I haven't told anyone about . . . about . . ."

"You've had problems at work, too," Max surmised. "Given the nature of your job, I imagine you're increasingly worried you'll make a mistake that will lead to harm."

After a long, tense moment, Quinn started to speak, appeared to change his mind, and then finally said, "You're very intuitive. Maybe you're one of those people who can read facial expressions and accurately interpret the movements of the three hundred different muscles around the mouth—like a great criminal profiler." He snorted a little and added, "Or a rich psychic."

Beside me, I felt Nelli's body go tense.

"Max is trying to help you, Quinn." I stretched my hand up to John, who took it and helped me rise to my feet.

Nelli started growling.

"This hideous thing that jumped into a little old lady's body and attacked us a little while ago?" I said. "It came here with *you*."

"Oh, yeah?" he replied. "Well, it's damn sure not leaving with me."

A foul odor crept into the room. I wanted to gag. John noticed it, too—he put a hand over his nose and mouth.

The entity had regrouped and was returning. Without a body, this time.

Nelli rose to her feet, legs stiff, eyes darting, as her growling got louder.

"Actually," said Max, looking around the room, aware of what was happening, "it does intend to leave with you. And without your cooperation, Detective Quinn, I cannot prevent that."

"Speaking of leaving, it looks like your mad dog is about to go off her rocker again." Quinn eyed Nelli. "So I think I'll be—*Agh!*"

He suddenly staggered backward as if he'd been hit. Then he doubled over in obvious pain, one hand on his belly, the other on his head.

"Ow. Ow. Ow." His face was contorted in a terrible grimace, and he was breathing hard. *"God."*

I inhaled. The odor was gone.

Nelli was staring intently at Quinn, and her growling was turning into a snarl.

I picked up her leash and said in alarm, "Lucky! I need help!"

Lucky stepped forward and seized hold of the dog's collar.

Quinn was taking deep, shaky breaths. After a moment, he said in a strangled voice, "I think I'm going to vomit."

"I'll get a bucket," said John, leaving the room in search of one.

Nelli made a little lunge toward Quinn, but Lucky held her back. Her eyes were fierce and glaring now, and her teeth were exposed in a snarl.

"The entity has attached to you again," Max said to Quinn. "That is what you're feeling. It's what Nelli is sensing."

"What a stupid name," Quinn grumbled, obviously struggling to overcome physical pain for which there was no physiological cause. "I don't want to be killed by a dog named *Nelli.*"

"She doesn't intend to kill you," Max said. "She's challenging the entity that has attached to you. She wants to confront and battle it. That is her mission. Just as you have your mission, to serve and protect."

Quinn lifted his head a little and squinted at Nelli. "No, I gotta disagree with you. She looks like she intends to kill me."

John returned with a bucket. "Found it!"

Quinn took a few more deep breaths, then straightened up. "Thanks, but, uh . . . I'm not going to puke, after all. At least, I don't think so."

"I can help you, detective," said Max. "If you'll let me."

"How? You got some good painkillers on you?"

"Exorcism," said Max.

"What?" I blurted.

"What?" said Quinn.

I hadn't realized that's where this conversation was going, or that that would be the solution to this problem.

"I know where we can get a priest on short notice," said Lucky.

"Oh, *there's* a confidence-inspiring offer," I said.

"What?" said Lucky.

"Exorcism?" I said in alarm. "Oh, Max, I saw the movie, and I really don't think . . ."

"I really don't think so, either," said Quinn.

"You need help," Max said to him. "You need to be free of this evil thing. So do those who come into contact with you."

"All right, look, guys . . . *Enough,*" said Quinn. "You seem nice enough . . . Well, apart from Lucky, who's a hitter for the mob, though we can't make any charges stick."

"I am just a businessman," Lucky insisted, "pursuing my perfectly legitimate—"

"Not now," I said to him.

"You seem sincere," Quinn said to Max. "Very *weird*, but sincere. I think you probably believe what you're saying. But, I don't. And this is all getting way too strange and heavy for me. On top of which, you've got a badly named dog the size of a New England state who wants to rip out my throat so much, she's *drooling*."

"No, she drools all the time," I assured him.

"I've got to get out of here," Quinn said suddenly.

Max tried again. "Please consider—"

"No, I've got to get *out* of here. *Now*."

He turned and left the room. Max and I followed.

"Lucky, keep Nelli here with you," I said, looking over my shoulder at him.

He nodded and tightened his grip on the familiar's collar as she attempted to pursue Quinn.

Out in the corridor, coming from the direction of Antonelli's, we heard a man calling, "Hello? Is somebody there?"

Quinn flinched.

I froze. I knew that voice.

"Lopez?" Quinn said tensely, raising his voice.

"Yeah, it's me!"

Quinn seemed more alarmed than relieved. Well, I supposed that was understandable. He probably didn't want his new partner to know anything about the things we'd just been discussing, so this was bound to be awkward for him.

Even though my heart did that little skip it often did when Lopez showed up, I found it awkward, too. I had, after all, participated in holding Quinn hostage this evening.

I really hoped the detective had forgiven us for that, all things considered.

"Andy?" Lopez called. "Where are you?"

"Coming!" He looked at me. "Not a *word*, Esther. Agreed?"

I looked to Max for a cue, unsure of whether I should guarantee my silence.

Quinn leaned closer to me and whispered, "Do you know how many charges I could file against you and your friends right now?"

"Okay, not a word," I agreed in a low voice. Apparently he wasn't the forgiving type.

"I've been waiting outside in the car for twenty minutes," Lopez said, his voice getting closer. "You're not answering your phone."

"Sorry," Quinn said. "I got, uh . . . waylaid."

We were nearly at the entrance to the reception hall that Lopez's voice was coming from. I could hear his footsteps approaching us.

And then behind us, back in the room from which we had just come, Nelli started barking madly.

"No!" Lucky shouted. "No! Stop!" Then: *"Watch out!"*

I turned around to see Nelli round the corner and

come bounding toward us in great strides, her teeth bared, her jaws dripping.

"Nelli, no!" I stood in her path.

"Andy!" I heard Lopez shout behind me. Then: "*Esther?*"

Nelli knocked me over, not even pausing in her mad beeline for Quinn's throat.

"Don't shoot!" I heard Max shout as I hit the floor— *hard*.

"Arrrgh!" Quinn screamed as Nelli's full body weight hit him and knocked him against a wall.

"Get out of the way, Max!" Lopez shouted. "Move!"

"No, please!" Max cried.

I rolled over and looked at them all from my position on the floor. Nelli was snarling ferociously, standing up on her hind legs, her dripping teeth only centimeters from Quinn's throat. Lopez was standing about ten feet away, his gun drawn and aimed at Nelli—and Max was standing between them, his hands raised, blocking Lopez's line of sight.

The demon was certainly getting a full meal tonight.

12

"Nelli! Come back!" Along with Lucky's shout, I heard the sound of running footsteps approaching.

"Max, *MOVE!*" Lopez ordered as the old mage kept himself positioned between the gun and the dog.

Nelli's big paws were on Quinn's shoulders, pressing him against the wall. Her bared fangs dripped saliva and she stared fiercely into his frightened, wide-eyed gaze. He was holding as still as he possibly could, but his chest was moving rapidly with his agitated breathing. When Nelli sniffed his carotid artery, he flinched a little and closed his eyes.

The footsteps that were thundering toward me stopped abruptly as Lucky and John arrived and saw what was happening.

"Nelli!" Lucky said sharply. "Sit!"

To no one's surprise, that didn't work. The dog snarled ferociously at Quinn and snapped at his face.

Lopez tried to circle around Max, who blocked his path, staying between him and Nelli. "Goddamn it, Max!"

About six feet tall with a lightly athletic build, Lopez had a dark golden-olive complexion, strong features, thick black hair that shone darkly under the overhead lights, and rich blue eyes—which were cold with focused anger right now.

"Don't shoot!" Max's voice was hoarse. "*Please*, detective."

I had seen Max use his power in the past to make a weapon fly out of someone's hand, but he didn't attempt it here. Probably because Lopez had too firm a grip on his gun for it to work. If he felt the weapon move, he wouldn't let go, he'd reflexively tighten his grasp—and perhaps inadvertently squeeze the trigger and put a bullet in someone.

"Put down that gun!" Lucky shouted at Lopez, sounding scandalized. "You could hurt someone!"

I was too scared to appreciate the irony of Lucky urging gun safety.

"Stay where you are!" Lopez shouted back.

An attacking dog, a cop with a gun, a Gambello killer, and a demon working overtime to inflict stress and evoke anger. This would go very badly if someone didn't do something right *now* to defuse the situation.

I took a deep breath and, fueled by adrenaline, I leaped to my feet, popping up as if propelled by a spring.

"Move away, Esther!" Lopez urged.

I ignored him, lunged for Nelli, and put my hand on the familiar's pink leather collar.

John blurted, "Esther, don't!"

"Esther, *no!*" Lopez's shout was very agitated. "Get back!"

I prayed that his stress wouldn't produce another involuntary incendiary incident. We had enough things to deal with right now.

Natural instinct made me wary of touching Nelli, but I shook her collar to get her attention as I shouted her name. Her massive body was quivering with tension as she snarled and sniffed, growled and glared. But I maintained control of my breathing, which helped me keep control of my head.

Max had said Nelli didn't want to hurt Quinn; she was challenging the entity that was attached to him, demanding that it confront her and do battle. So she was trying to protect the detective, I reasoned. Trying to free him from demonic oppression. Her way of expressing this, as a (very large) canine familiar was terrifying, but she hadn't lost her head, and she wasn't out of control. She was just trying to do her job.

This was my working theory, anyhow.

"Nelli!" I took another breath and willed myself to speak more calmly. "This won't work. You must stop."

She kept growling and snapping furiously at Quinn, menace in her eyes, her hair standing on end. The detective's face was pasty white, his expression taut and tense as he avoided the dog's fierce gaze, his chest rising and falling with his rapid breathing.

"Esther, get *away!*" Lopez shouted.

"Nelli, *no,*" I said firmly. "It will not come out and face you! Not while *he* gives it such a safe home."

"No, John, stay back," I heard Lucky say.

"But—"

"Let her handle this."

"Nelli, are you listening?" I looked at Quinn. "He *wants* to keep it. It won't confront you while he protects it!"

To my relief, the familiar reacted. I didn't know whether it was my tone, my words, or her own realization that she wasn't getting the response she sought, but Nelli paused and reconsidered what she was doing.

She remained where she was, her body weight pressing Quinn up against the wall, her paws still on his shoulders . . . But she ceased the terrifying growling and snapping and now just stared fiercely at the cop, as if trying to decide what to do next. She was breathing hard, her rib cage pumping in and out, her panting breaths ruffling Quinn's red hair.

"Esther, get *away* from that dog," Lopez insisted in a hard voice.

Quinn risked taking a look at Nelli and appeared to recognize that she was calming down.

"Nelli, *enough,*" I said. "It won't do battle. Not like this."

I could feel the tension in her big body, every fiber of her being protesting against simply letting the entity leave this place, free and unvanquished.

"We're just making it stronger," I warned her. The fear, tension, and anger among us now was so active, it felt like a small tornado was whirling around us. The walls practically vibrated with our negative emotions. "We must *stop feeding* it, Nelli. Right now."

"Max, if you don't get out of the way . . ." Lopez warned coldly.

Quinn met my gaze for a moment, and then he looked at the dog again. "Get d . . ." He cleared his throat and tried once more. His voice was faint, but functional. "Get down, Nelli. All you're doing is . . . scaring *me.*"

Nelli looked at him for a long moment, then let me pull her off him. My hand still on her collar, we backed away from Quinn, who sagged with relief.

With Nelli's teeth no longer so perilously close to a human throat, Lopez risked agitating her by knocking down Max. As the old mage hit the floor with a loud grunt, Lopez trained his gun on Nelli's head. "Get away from that dog, Esther!"

Quinn suddenly moved and staggered into Lopez's

path, putting a hand on his shoulder to halt him. "No!"

I stepped in front of Nelli, just in case. Max started crawling toward us.

"Don't," Quinn said to Lopez, still breathing hard. "Leave her be."

"Are you *crazy?*" Lopez tried to shake him off, but Quinn didn't let him.

"It's all right now," Quinn insisted. "Just a little mis . . . misunder . . .'"

"You're in shock. Go outside and sit in the car." Lopez tried to shove him aside and get to Nelli, but Quinn used both hands to grip his partner now.

"Oh, that's right, Mr. Sensitivity," I said to Lopez, my own negative reaction welling up as fear subsided. "Tell someone who's in shock to go sit alone in the cold and the dark."

"You go with him," Lopez snapped at me. "While I deal with this dog."

"You stay away from her!" I said.

"Yeah," said Lucky, wisely staying at his end of the corridor. "Pulling a *gun* on our dog? Jesus, they'll give a gold shield to *anyone,* won't they?"

John brushed past Lucky and came toward me. "Esther, are you okay?"

"Yes."

"Are you sure?" Lopez asked me, shedding his anger enough to be concerned for a moment.

"I'm fine."

"*I'm* fine, too," Quinn piped up. "In case anyone was wondering."

"Andy, you should get out of this building," Lopez said, eyeing Nelli.

John seemed to be thinking of the cadavers inside the building when he said, "Detective Lopez is right. You should go outside. Right away."

"For chrissake, could I just take a minute?" the red-headed cop said irritably. "I'm trying to catch my breath!"

Max rose to his feet and finished staggering to Nelli's side. He grasped her collar as his gaze met mine. I released her and gave Max a nod. He kept on moving, pulling her with him, clearly intending to get her out of Lopez's sight and the demon's immediate presence.

"Stop!" Lopez ordered.

He tried to follow them, but Quinn grabbed him again and insisted, "Let her go."

"What's *wrong* with you?" Lopez demanded, glaring at Quinn.

"Come on, Nelli," Lucky crooned, putting a hand on her head when she was close enough. "Let's get away from the mean man with the gun. Good girl."

Nelli turned, gave Quinn a last look and snarled once more at the demonic presence that hovered around him, warning the entity that this wasn't over.

"I'm calling animal control," Lopez said firmly. "That dog is too dangerous to—"

"She was protecting the premises," I said with sudden inspiration, while Lucky and Max led Nelli back to the working area of the mortuary, safely out of range of both Quinn and Lopez. "She mistook your partner for a trespasser."

"Why are you even wasting your breath on that story, Esther?" Lopez said in exasperation as he holstered his gun. His heavy winter coat was hanging open, probably because he'd been sitting in an idling car with the heater on.

John was at my side, so I gave him a gentle jab with my elbow, alerting him that I needed support.

"Huh? Why are you—Oh! Um. Okay." He said awkwardly, "That's right, Nelli is our . . . our watchdog!" John nodded, apparently thinking he sounded convincing.

"Yeah, right." Lopez reached into his pocket for his phone.

"She is," I insisted. "Nelli was guarding this place against an intruder."

"Yes," said John, trying so hard to help. "We need her here. Where she roams free to protect our valuable, um . . . corpses. And stuff."

And him such an educated boy, too.

Lopez said to John, "You're not an actor, are you?"

"No, I'm scientist."

Lopez searched for something on his phone's screen as he said absently, "Yeah, you don't have her flair for improvisation. Though this isn't one of her better efforts."

I gave Quinn a look, silently urging him to do something more constructive than stand around catching his breath.

Quinn just shrugged, his expression indicating that this wasn't his problem anymore. Apparently stopping Lopez from *shooting* Nelli was as much damage control as he felt obliged to contribute.

Well, we'd see about that.

I said, looking right at him, "I guess we should explain everything that's happened this evening and exactly why Nelli thinks Detective Quinn is a threat to our safety."

Lopez paused and looked up from his phone, his expression skeptical. "Is there going to be a single word of truth to this?"

Standing a little behind him, Quinn was emphatically shaking his head at me.

"Your partner wasn't answering his phone," I said to Lopez, "because it's gone dead. Isn't that an amazing coincidence?"

Quinn ran his hand sideways across his throat in a frantic gesture signaling that I should *cut! cut!*

Or maybe he was threatening to kill me if I kept talking. It was hard to tell.

"Jesus, *your* phone's gone dead?" Lopez said over his shoulder. "What the hell is going on around here?"

"We can explain what's going on, can't we, Andy?" I said, raising my brows.

Quinn glared at me.

"I know you wouldn't want our dog to be blamed for your problems," I prodded, returning his glare.

No *way* was Nelli getting impounded because Quinn was hauling a demon around with him.

But Lopez was off and running. "Jesus, doesn't anyone make anything that *works* anymore? What is this, the decline and fall of Western civilization? How the hell are we supposed to function if nothing *around* us functions? Between the two of us, that's *three* goddamn phones that have broken down in just a few weeks!"

I asked Quinn, "Should we introduce him to Grace Chu?"

"Yikes," said John.

"*No*," said Quinn.

Lopez said, "I mean, who can *work* like this? I'm not a Bow Street Runner or a sheriff in the Old West, for God's sake! I'm an NYPD cop in the digital age, and I need a working phone! Also a police radio! And a car that doesn't keep breaking down! And a computer that works! Why is that too much to ask?"

Yeah, his stress level was off the charts all right. That demon had figured out exactly how to play him.

I said firmly to Quinn, "Convince him to leave Nelli alone."

"Is this all because of outsourcing?" Lopez wondered, lost in his own fresh hell. "Is this what happens when a country surrenders its manufacturing industry to the greed of global conglomerates?"

"Please tell me," John said, looking at Lopez, "that this isn't about to turn into a diatribe about 'Made in China.'"

"You wouldn't believe how much of this I've had to listen to lately," Quinn said wearily.

"All right, everyone *stop*," I insisted. "We need to focus."

To my relief, they all shut up and looked at me.

"Why is it always up to *actors* to get things done?" I said in exasperation. "*I* have to clean up this situation, and Nolan's tailing your suspect, while you two stand around bitching and moaning. Well, I suppose it's because *we're* trained to focus, but I really would have thought that—"

"*Where* did you say Nolan is?" Lopez interrupted.

"Oh, actually, I guess he's done tailing him now." I remembered the phone call. "Nolan's gone home for the night, safe and sound."

"Who was he tailing?" Quinn asked in confusion.

"Nolan was *tailing a suspect?*" Lopez turned on Quinn. "You were supposed to babysit him! Don't I have enough problems without a TV star getting killed on my shift?"

"That guy with you was a TV star?" John said to Quinn in surprise. "I thought he was a cop."

"*What* suspect?" Quinn looked at me. "Who are we talking about?"

"Danny Teng," I said.

"Nolan is tailing Danny Teng?" Lopez said in horror. "Well, there goes my badge."

"No, I told you, he's done for the night. Nolan called me a little while ago," I said. "By now, he's probably at home, fondling his treadmill one last time before he goes to bed."

"Who's Danny Teng and why is Nolan tailing him?" Quinn wondered.

"He's *done* tailing—"

"Danny is *dai lo* of the Red Daggers," said Lopez. "Well, until the Ning funeral is over, anyhow. He was Uncle Six's boy, and no one likes him."

"Go figure," said John.

"So there's bound to be some jostling for his spot now that the old man is gone. And when Chinatown gangbangers jostle . . ."

"Run for cover," Quinn concluded. "So why the hell did Nolan tail him?"

"Why the hell didn't *you* control Nolan?" Lopez snapped at Quinn.

I resisted the urge to bang their heads together. "Quinn got sick when he got here and had to lie down," I said. "Nolan was at the wake alone when Danny showed up and made a scene, claiming that he knows who killed Uncle Six and will have vengeance. With no police around, Nolan decided to tail him when he left, to see if there was anything behind his boasting."

"Oh, my God," Quinn groaned. "There goes my badge, too."

"Nothing happened," I said. "Nolan is fine."

"Wait . . . Danny Teng says Joe Ning was murdered, and he knows who did it?" Lopez asked, making sure he'd understood my rushed account of events. "I need to talk to him."

"No, *I* should talk to him," said Quinn. "You're supposed to stay away from anything to do with Ning, remember?"

"That would include skipping the wake, right?" John asked. "The whole Ning family is here tonight. Well, except for Paul. I guess they don't let you out of maximum security for a funeral?"

"Don't worry, I'm not planning on attending. That's why I told Quinn I'd pick him up outside Antonelli's. So no one would see me." Lopez added darkly, "But I was expecting to pick up Quinn *and* Mr. Congeniality."

"Esther says Nolan is fine." Quinn promptly changed the subject. "You were right, by the way. Goldman's at the wake."

"Of course he is, that reptile," muttered Lopez. "Probably slithering all over the Ning family even as we speak."

"I wish he wasn't Jewish," I grumbled.

"Let it go, Esther," said Lopez.

"You mean Alan Goldman?" asked John. "That guy who's all over the media today, talking about Uncle Six like he was a paragon of virtue and claiming that you . . . uh . . ."

Lopez's expression was resigned. "Yep."

John cleared his throat and said to me, "If things are under control here, I should probably go help Dad. He's been on the floor running things alone ever since I heard the barking and the sh . . . Uh, I should go help him."

I nodded. "Go ahead, John."

"When I got here, I thought maybe seeing Goldman was what suddenly made me want to vomit," Quinn said to Lopez as John headed back the same direction that Lucky and Max had taken Nelli.

"And when *I* got here, I thought you were going to have your throat ripped out. Speaking of which . . ." Lopez returned his attention to the call he intended to make.

I made a reflexive motion, but Quinn beat me to it. He covered Lopez's phone with his hand and shook his head.

"The dog is not a problem," he said firmly.

"Are you kidding me?" Lopez said.

"Look, she doesn't like me, and tonight I was on her turf and I scared her." He decided to leave it at that. "Don't call it in. I want the dog left alone."

"Why?" Lopez frowned at him. "What about the next person she attacks, Andy?"

I said, "There won't be a next—"

"Shut up," said Lopez. "I'll get to you in a minute."

"We're not calling it in," Quinn said firmly.

"Andy—"

"And I'm calling it a night," he said, turning in the same direction John had gone a few moments ago. "I'll see you tomorrow."

"Where are you going?" Lopez said in alarm. "The dog is in that direction."

"So is my coat, and I'm not leaving without it."

"*I'll* get your coat," said Lopez. "And then I'll take you home."

"No, thanks," said Quinn. "I think I'll stop and get a new phone on the way home."

"I've got a car," said Lopez. "I can drop you—"

"No, you and Esther stay here and make up. Or fight. Whatever. Kind of hard to tell the difference, with you two." He snickered a little. "I'll talk to you tomorrow. And I guess I should talk to Danny Teng tomorrow, too. I've got a few questions for him, that's for sure. And it sounds like Nolan knows where to find the guy."

"Andy—"

"Wouldn't it be great if Joe Ning really was murdered and we can prove it? *That* would get rid of Goldman, wouldn't it? Or am I just a cockeyed optimist?" He was at the door to the back rooms by now. "Well, goodnight."

And then he was gone.

Lopez stood with his back to me, staring at the door through which his partner had just left the elegant old Italian funeral home for the workrooms where Nelli had been taken minutes ago. I could tell he was very puzzled by Quinn's behavior.

"I don't think Danny actually knows anything," I said. "Nolan told me that—"

"I don't want to talk about Danny Teng with you." He turned to face me. "I don't even want to talk about Nolan."

"No, I guess Nolan does enough talking about Nolan to fill up the . . . Never mind."

There was a long, uncomfortable silence between us. His face—interesting, intelligent, and good-looking without being pretty—looked strained and tired. I could see his tension and fatigue, now that we were looking at each other silently, without sparring and bickering.

The demon is really working on him, I thought.

Max was right, I realized. Whatever the entity's goal was, it didn't want Lopez interfering. So wearing him down had become almost as important as harassing Quinn. The demon had recognized the steel inside of him and knew he could pose a problem if not sufficiently distracted and misdirected.

"Two things," he said wearily, the veil of his black lashes fluttering down over his blue eyes for a moment. "I asked you to do just two things."

"Huh?"

"Leave Quinn alone, and do something about that dog."

"Oh."

"Esther . . ." He spread his hands, and I could see that he was bemused, stressed, and fed up. "What are you *doing?*"

I thought about denying that I had acted in direct opposition to his instructions to leave Quinn alone, but there really didn't seem much point, since he'd found me here with the guy.

"You didn't sic Nolan on us to punish me, did you?" Lopez shook his head. "I should have known better."

"About thinking I'd punish you?"

"About thinking I can figure you out. About thinking I have the faintest idea how your mind works," he said. "I should have remembered that my first guess is never right where you're concerned."

When I didn't respond, he said, "It wasn't about me at all, was it? You manipulated Nolan into shadowing us so you could monitor Andy."

"Yes." Keeping my voice calm and reasonable, I said, "There's something not right about Andy. He's not a bad man, and I think he can be helped. But right now, he's dangerous."

"So am I, if someone pushes me far enough." There was an edge to his voice now.

"This isn't about you," I said. "Well, okay, in a way

it is. I'm that much more worried because *you're* the person he's with most of the time, rather than some stranger I don't—"

"As soon as you found out he and I had gone off in separate directions today, you used Nolan to track down Andy." It bothered me, how cold his voice was now. "And what a coincidence, as soon as he gets here, Andy suddenly gets so sick, he has to go lie down."

"It wasn't exactly a coinci . . ." I met his hard gaze and realized what he was implying. "Oh, my God, you think *we* did something to him?"

"And then you, Max, and Lucky all show up here together."

"No, Lucky was already here." But that probably wasn't the point.

"When I got here, that neurotic dog was about to rip out Andy's throat." He asked darkly, "What would have happened to him if I hadn't arrived when I did? Would he be lying dead on the floor now?"

"No, of course not! He was on his way out the door when you got here. We were asking him not to leave, but no one was trying to prevent him. Ask *him* if you don't believe me!"

I remembered belatedly that we had taken Quinn hostage and discussed sneaking him out of here in a coffin. So it wouldn't be a good idea to encourage Lopez to probe into our behavior tonight. I tried a different path. "Anyhow, didn't Quinn just tell you he wants Nelli left alone? He's obviously not seek—"

"He's obviously not in his right mind!"

"No, he's not," I agreed. "Though not in the way that you mean."

"Did you have Nolan slip him something during dinner?" Lopez demanded. "Something that took effect when Andy got here?"

"No!"

"Who's idea was it? Max's?" He took me by the shoulders. *"Yours?"*

"We didn't slip him anything!"

"You want me to believe that he walked through the door of a place where you were all lying in wait for him—"

"We weren't lying in wait!"

"—and suddenly fell ill?"

"We followed him!"

"So you followed him when Nolan told you where he was going. And then what. You improvised?" he prodded, giving me a shake, his grip tight on my arms. "You're good at that. What did you do to him, Esther?"

"Nothing!" This wasn't strictly true, but it seemed best not to go into details. Especially given the mood Lopez was in. "He's *fine.* You can see he's fine!" I gestured to the door through which Quinn had recently departed. "So stop this! You've got to *stop.*"

I was uncomfortable by now. Lopez was right; when pushed, he seemed dangerous.

He looked down at each of his hands, gripping my shoulders, and in that moment, we both realized how tightly he was holding me. He let go abruptly as he drew in a sharp breath and fell back a step.

Our eyes met. His expression went from cold anger and frustration to shock, followed by regret. Then sad resignation.

"I think I do need to stop." His voice sounded hollow. Looking very tired, he rubbed a hand over his face, stood very still for a long moment, then shoved both hands into his pockets. "Yeah. I've got to stop, Esther."

"Stop . . . ?" I had a feeling the subject had just changed abruptly.

"I should have been stronger." He shook his head. "Should have stayed away in the first place. I tried, but . . . And I *still* feel like I can't . . ." He fell silent, staring at the floor, then said, "No, I have to be stronger than this."

My heart was thudding and my throat felt tight. I took a few deep breaths so my voice would hold steady as I asked, "Is this the talk we've been meaning to have? About us?"

He kept looking at the floor. "I think it is."

"And you're saying . . ." My voice shook a little this time, so I fell silent.

"I have to stop. Stop chasing my tail. Stop. . . . being

this quarreling, miserable idiot I've turned into." Now he met my eyes. "And stop being a cop who hides things and prevaricates and puts fiction into his reports, all because of a woman."

A few weeks ago, he had buried evidence—albeit only for a day or two—proving that my longtime employer, restaurant owner Stella Butera, was laundering money for the Gambellos. He did it because he knew that shutting down her business would be tough on *me*. Lopez corrected his misstep, but he tormented himself over it, and it led to more tension between us. I found out about it the same day Joe Ning died. Since then, I hadn't let myself think about what Lopez had done, but deep under my skin, I had been worried.

Now I said, "I *never* asked you to—"

"I know. But it's convenient for you that I'm so crazy about you I keep kicking things under the carpet for your sake. Again and again."

"That's not fair."

"Maybe not." He shrugged. "Does it make a difference that it's not fair? Does that change anything?"

I supposed not. I felt a weight pressing down on me, and I wanted to cling to him. But I didn't.

"So you're saying you want to walk away from this?" I pressed my lips together for a moment. "From me?"

"No, I'm saying I think I have to."

I heard the finality in his voice, and I wanted to cry.

So I called on anger, because I didn't want him to see my tears. "Then you're right," I said, my voice a little rough with my effort to keep it from breaking. "You should have stayed away."

I'd been on an emotional roller coaster for months—and for *what?* To wind up right back here, a moment I had no desire to revisit—a moment when most of my internal organs seemed to drop through the floor because he had decided to dump me. *Again.*

Nursing a little self-righteous indignation, I said, "After you broke up with me the first time, you should have left me alone. You should never have called me again."

"*You* called *me*," he reminded me.

"No, I didn't, I . . . Oh." Actually, he was right about that. "Whatever."

I'd had a little trouble with the police one night last summer, and Lopez came to my rescue when I asked. I tried to work out now why that was *his* fault, but nothing was coming to me.

"Look, I didn't mean to do this here and now, or like this," he said apologetically. "Maybe we should talk some more another time, when we're both more—"

"Why?" I said coldly. "Will it make a difference if we talk more? Will it change anything?"

"I'm pretty stressed right now," he said. "This isn't what I thought I was going to say. Or *how* I thought—"

"Which part?" I asked. "The bit where you accused

me of lying in wait for your partner and drugging him?"

"But, of course, I didn't even expect to see you here." He was veering back toward anger. "What the hell were you doing with Andy? What's going on?"

Oh, just tell him, I thought. *What does it even matter now?*

"We think he's being haunted by an archaic Aramaic demon that, for reasons best known to itself, wants to reanimate cadavers."

Quinn wouldn't appreciate my candor, but I didn't care anymore.

Lopez looked at me like I'd confirmed his worst fears about my sanity. I didn't care about that anymore, either.

The man I'd been obsessed with since last spring was dumping me, and I just wanted to curl up in a ball and hide until the pain passed. His opinion of my statement didn't seem important right now, not compared to the ache in my chest and the roaring in my ears.

"Okay, I don't think there's much point in us talking about that," Lopez said after a long moment. "So we'll skip it. I'm just going to tell you—*very seriously*, Esther—that you need to—"

"Oh, need to do *what?*" I snapped. "Seek psychiatric help? Get drug testing? Give up my friends? Commit myself to a mental ward? *What?*"

"You need to stay away from Detective Quinn," he said, keeping his voice level.

"You're making it awfully tempting," I muttered.

Fine, I'll let the demon do whatever it wants to you. And to him. What do I care?

"I hope I'm making it awfully *clear*," he said. "You can't mess around with people like this, Esther. Something terrible could have happened here tonight. Something that can't be fixed."

I looked at him, my heart breaking, and said, "Something terrible *has* happened here tonight. Something that can't be fixed."

13

It was a relief when the door to Antonelli's opened, carrying a gust of cold wind and breaking the mood.

A very tall, very skinny white man entered the funeral home. "What a night!" he said from the doorway. "The Almighty is really testing our mettle, isn't he?"

He came down the corridor toward us carrying a large duffel bag. He wasn't wearing a hat, and his curly, dark hair was damp and very windblown. His smile was broad and cheerful, and his cheeks glowed rosily.

As the newcomer approached us, I wiped at my eyes where tears had just gathered. "Please go now," I said to Lopez in a choked voice.

His face creased with concern, doubt, and regret. "Look, why don't I call you and we can—"

"No," I said tightly. "If you're serious about—about this . . ."

"Esther . . ."

"Don't make it worse," I said faintly, trying to control my voice. "Please."

"I never wanted . . ." He let out his breath and nodded. "Okay. You're right. I'll just go."

He turned away from me, then paused briefly to examine the other man, hesitant about leaving me alone here with a stranger.

"Good evening," the man said cheerfully. "Are you on your way out? Better bundle up!"

There was something so good-natured about the man that it put me at ease, despite the pain roiling through me as I watched Lopez walk away from me.

He agreed quietly, "Yes, it's a grim night . . . Father."

"Take care out there," the man said, turning to one side to get his duffel out of the way as Lopez moved past him. "Watch out for the ice."

When the man turned back in my direction, I saw then what Lopez had seen—the white clerical collar of a priest peeking out of the top of his coat.

"Hello." I asked doubtfully, "Are you looking for the Ning wake?"

I glanced beyond him for a moment as the door closed behind Lopez, who didn't look back at me when he left.

"No, indeed." Smiling at me with boyish enthusiasm, the priest said, "I understand you're in need of an exorcist?"

*   *   *

"I'm not really sure when it started," Quinn said, sitting in the main reception hall of Antonelli's.

Above us, on the wall that faced the street, were three attractive stained glass windows of modest size, glowing warmly in the mellow light cast by the streetlights outside. Quinn sat below them on an armchair upholstered in dark red fabric, while Lucky, the priest, and I sat in a semicircle facing him. Max was pacing nearby.

Quinn, continued, "I was really . . . *down* after she left."

"Your wife?" Father Tiano asked sympathetically.

"Yeah." Quinn nodded. "Around this time a year ago, I was drinking myself to sleep, showing up late at work, pissing off the guys on the squad . . . and screwing up on the job in a precinct where screwups were dangerous."

Father Tiano was the priest that Lucky knew, the one he could get on "short notice." *Really* short, as it turned out.

Rather than getting his coat and leaving Chen's, as he'd told Lopez he intended to do, Quinn had looked for Max and Lucky in the mortuary office and told them I was wrong, he did *not* want to protect this thing or give a safe home to the entity that was destroying his life. He was a little freaked out and still not sure he believed in any of this . . . but everything Max had surmised about him was true. The old mage's statements had described, too accurately to ignore, the nightmare his life had become. And he'd realized, while he was pinned to the wall of the corridor, feeling Nelli's hot breath on his throat as she challenged the demon, that he couldn't go on like this.

So if we could help him shake off this thing, then he wanted to get it done. Right away, in fact—before Lopez or anyone else started to think he was crazy, or worse.

And, gosh, no, we mustn't let Lopez think bad things. Imagine where that might lead?

I was going to have a good long cry about Lopez, I promised myself, but not right now. Right now, I was in a mortuary with a corpse-reanimating demon and an exorcist, so it really seemed like I should focus on the task at hand.

And the good long cry I was going to indulge in, I vowed, would be the last time I shed tears over Lopez. I would not, I swore to myself, spend any more weeks or months moping over him. I had to move on.

"So I was in kind of a fog when it all started," Quinn was saying. "It took a while for me even to notice that things kept breaking down and malfunctioning. When stuff disappeared or reappeared in my apartment, I thought I must have moved it while I was drunk and just didn't remember. In the morning, when I remembered getting phone calls in the middle of the night with static or weird voices saying spooky shit, I figured I'd been dreaming or hallucinating."

Father Tiano, who occasionally interjected a question or a sympathetic comment, was taking notes.

He was the new priest at St. Monica's, a century-old parish church that was only a few blocks away, in what was left of Little Italy. He had replaced the (now safely deceased) mystically murderous priest there who had killed several people last year and tried to kill a few others—including me and Lucky.

He was also a great-nephew of Don Victor Gambello, which made me think it could be unhealthy for us if anything bad happened to him tonight.

And based on Max's worried expression and uncharacteristic pacing, I had a feeling something bad happening was a real possibility.

Quinn's Catholicism was apparently not as lapsed as everyone thought. Having decided to exorcise the demon, he was adamant about wanting a priest. Since Lucky knew an exorcist who could be here in fifteen minutes, Quinn didn't have to insist very hard.

So Lucky and Max tied up Grace Chu's remains securely. Just in case. Nelli remained near the body, so she could alert us if the trussed corpse got lively again—and so she wouldn't stress Quinn, who was understandably afraid of her. Lucky also warned John that no one from Joe Ning's wake, which was finally winding down, was to enter Antonelli's, and he advised John to keep a sharp eye on Uncle Six's closed casket.

"The demon attached to you while you were vulnerable," Father Tiano said to Quinn now, his boyish face full of empathy. "It was drawn to your despair and preyed on your sadness."

"I was also really angry." Looking ashamed, Quinn admitted, "One night when I was really drunk, I called my ex and threatened her."

"They prey on anger, too," I murmured. "Negative emotions."

"Correct." Father Tiano beamed at me.

"You threatened some suspects, too, I'll bet," Lucky muttered.

"Why are *you* here?" Quinn asked him.

"Please continue," said the priest.

As Quinn told his story, it was clear that although he had entered a dark phase after his second wife had left him, he was not an inherently self-destructive man. After a few months of wallowing, he realized that, having lost his marriage, he couldn't go on this way without losing everything else in his life, too. He was also becoming so unnerved by the blackouts, nightmares, and hallucinations that he wanted them to stop. So he quit drinking and started applying himself to his life again.

"But the weird shit that was happening, the stuff I didn't dare tell anyone about . . ." Quinn shook his head. "It continued. No, it escalated."

He tried moving to a new apartment, but that didn't change anything.

"The demon was attached to you, not your dwelling," Father Tiano surmised.

He applied for a transfer, eager to leave behind the black cloud that seemed to hang over him at the precinct where his life had fallen apart.

"But now this thing is screwing with my new job, too," he said, sounding exhausted.

And also with his new partner, who had no idea how much danger they were both in as the demon continued gaining strength and learning how to manipulate them.

Lopez . . .

My vision got misty. I wiped impatiently at my eyes and jumped to my feet. Quinn flinched and gave me a peculiar look, then went back to answering Father Tiano's questions.

I went out into the corridor and did some breathing exercises to compose myself. When I looked into the room again, I was troubled by the way Max was anxiously pacing around rather than, as I would have expected, sitting and listening intently to Quinn.

"Max, can you give me a hand out here for a minute?" I called.

"Hmm? Oh, of course, my dear." Still looking distracted and anxious, he joined me in the hall.

"What's wrong?" I whispered. "Something's obviously bothering you."

He chewed on his lower lip for a moment, then decided to tell me. "It's this exorcist."

"You think he's too inexperienced?"

"Not necessarily," said Max. "He's fairly new to this, but he studied in Rome, and the Church's exorcism training is thorough."

"Then what's your concern?"

"I am uncertain that this demon will respond to Catholic rites. Therefore, by attempting to expose and expel it, Father Tiano may be putting himself in terrible danger." Max added fretfully, "Or, rather, *we* may be putting him in terrible danger."

"If the entity won't listen to . . . um, go along with a Catholic rite, then what kind of exorcism do we need?" I asked. "Wait, you said you thought it was speaking Aramaic. Does that mean it's an ancient Jewish demon? Do we need a rabbi?"

"I suspect it may mean that the last time this demon had occasion to speak to anyone was some three thousand years ago."

"Hmm, well, I don't think a rabbi will be of much use, after all," I said. "Judaism has changed a *lot* since then."

We don't still do animal sacrifices, for example.

"Oh, Aramaic was spoken among a number of peoples in that region, Esther, over a period of centuries. It was also spoken by the earliest Christians . . . but the phrase the entity used while in Grace Chu's body sounded more ancient than that," said Max. "A demon this skilled at manipulating two intelligent, experienced men capable of withstanding high levels of stress would typically be agile enough to learn the language of the beings it possesses and speaks through."

"Ah. You suspect the last time this entity communicated verbally with anyone was—"

"—was well before the Catholic Church even existed, let alone started developing effective rites to battle the demons it encountered."

"So Father Tiano's rite tonight will be like throwing water on a fire: effective if it's a wood fire, but incredibly dangerous if it's an oil fire."

"An excellent analogy," said Max.

"Dr. Zadok?" called Father Tiano. "I believe we're ready to begin."

I squared my shoulders. "I guess we're about to find out which kind of fire this is."

Father Tiano was unpacking his duffel bag when I sat back down, facing Quinn. He had brought half a dozen medium-sized crucifixes that he handed out.

I hesitated when he offered one of them to me. "I'm in a different union, Father."

"Take it," Lucky urged. "It can't hurt, right?"

I shrugged and accepted it. Going along with that

same theory, I also let the priest hang a smaller crucifix around my neck. He had brought a very large
cross, too, which he set up on a stand in the middle of
our group, directly in front of Quinn. Father Tiano
asked Quinn if the crucifixes were making him uncomfortable; Quinn shook his head. The priest proceeded to unpack several small bottles of holy water
in different little glass vials, a large book bound in old
red leather, and a very pretty censer—a large, decora-
tive metal incense burner that hung from a heavy
chain.

"I may have overdone it with the supplies," he admitted sheepishly. "This is my first exorcism since I returned from Rome last year. I'm so excited!"

"Knock yourself out," I said, thinking I'd like to turn
the censer into a hanging lamp for my apartment.

What followed thereafter was so boring that, far
from being on the edge of my seat in fear of demonic
attack, I wound up having trouble staying awake.

First, Father Tiano explained that tonight's rite
would be merely an exploratory process. He could not
proceed with a full-blown exorcism, he said, not even
for a friend of his Uncle Victor, without first getting his
bishop's permission.

"I'm not a friend of your scumbag uncle," Quinn
said darkly.

"That's Mr. Gambello to you," Lucky snapped.

Seeing that Quinn was about to snap back, I reminded him who had found an exorcist for him on such short notice.

Soldiering on, Father Tiano explained that in order to seek his bishop's permission, he would need to be convinced that Detective Quinn was actually possessed by a demon.

"Not possessed," said Max. "Oppressed. I don't believe this demon intends to possess Detective Quinn. It is using him to find a suitable host, which would be a cadav—"

"Oppressed, then," Father Tiano said with a nod to Max. "It is not that I doubt Andrew's account of his experiences, but we must determine whether these experiences are demonic in origin."

Recalling Grace Chu's glowing eyes as her corpse reached out for me, I said, "I'm pretty convinced."

Then Father Tiano started praying. He invited us to join him. Quinn tried to, but it turned out that he was pretty lapsed, after all, and didn't know his prayers. Lucky knew his, and he hung in there for a while, but he dropped out as the praying went on and on. And *on.*

I didn't know any of the prayers, despite having played nuns on two different occasions, so I just sat quietly and held my crucifix. Max observed Quinn and the priest with concentrated attention.

An hour later, Father Tiano was *still* praying, and I was starting to wonder if I could leave the exorcism early without being rude.

Then we heard footsteps in the corridor, approaching this spot.

Quinn, who looked like he'd been dozing off, sat bolt upright and whispered, "That's it. *That's* what I hear when I'm alone in my apartment. And there's never anyone there. That thing is *here* now."

The words gave me a chill. I clutched my crucifix tightly as I looked over my shoulder, riveted by the soft, menacing sound of those approaching footsteps.

And then John appeared in the doorway, looking handsome in his somber formal suit. "Uncle Six's wake is over, we've closed for the night, and . . . Sorry, am I interrupting?"

Father Tiano, who was holding his large, red leather-bound book open in his arms, reading from it while he prayed, looked up from the passage he was reciting.

I was about to ask if we could stop for the night when that heavy tome suddenly shot straight up in the air, about six feet above Father Tiano's head, and snapped itself shut with a resounding *thud!* Then it swooped back down and whacked the priest in the head so hard that he went tumbling across the room.

I leaped out of my chair. Having no idea what else to do, I held up my crucifix, hoping against all the teachings of my own religion that it would actually protect me.

Lucky reached for his ankle holster—and cursed in frustration when he found nothing there. Father Tiano had insisted that a firearm could not be brought to the rite, so Lucky's gun was sitting in a drawer in Nathan's office.

The heavy red book flew at Lucky and thudded heavily into his solar plexus. He doubled over, gasping for air as he clutched his torso.

"Uncle Lucky!" John dashed into the room, heading toward the old mobster.

"John, look out!" Max cried.

The big cross the priest had set up in the center of our little circle jumped out of its holder and flew like a missile, heading straight for John. An experienced martial artist, he dived to one side to avoid it, landed on his feet, and dived again when it took another shot at him.

From the depths of the building, I could hear Nelli barking furiously, no doubt sensing the dark energy that had been unleashed in here. But out of consideration for Quinn, we had left her behind a securely closed door, and that prevented her from coming to our aid now.

"Holy shit!" Quinn also instinctively reached for his gun; but, like Lucky, he had been instructed to leave it in the office. "Goddamn it!"

I held up my crucifix as a talisman as I shouted, "Stop! *Stop* this!" at the unseen force that was attacking us.

John dashed behind a standing lamp to avoid the big cross's next attempt to skewer him, then he tore off the lampshade, picked up the lamp, and starting using it like a (very unwieldy) staff to fight back.

The leather-bound book clobbered Lucky over the head then knocked him sideways. As he staggered past me, the cross in my hand turned into a hissing snake. I screamed and dropped the thing, leaping away—and when I looked at it lying on the floor, it was just a wooden cross again.

I turned around and tripped over Father Tiano, who was on his knees and praying with all his might.

Max was shouting in another language as he swept up the small vials of holy water into his hands and starting flinging them at the wall, one at a time. The glass bottles smashed when they hit the wall, spraying broken glass, and the water splashed and then dribbled downward.

Directly above this mess, one of the lovely stained glass windows suddenly shattered. A fierce, cold wind blew into the room with a force much greater than made any natural sense, even on a blustery night like this one.

My hair was whipping all around my head, interfering with my vision. The red-bound volume was still beating the stuffing out of Lucky, so I picked up the censer and swung it by its chain like a medieval mace. What with the wind, my hair in my eyes, my terror, and my inexperience with medieval maces, I missed the first few times I took aim—and I accidentally grazed Lucky's knee once, which he didn't like. But then I connected with the red-bound book and managed to hit it hard enough to stop its next attack on him in midflight.

When the book fell to the ground, though, it turned into a horde of rats that started skittering over our feet.

I shrieked and jumped around, trying to keep my feet away from them. So did the tough old gangster. (*Everyone* hates rats. Which was no doubt why that was the prank the demon chose.)

Father Tiano leaped off the floor when he saw the rats, jumped up on a chair, and kept on praying as he stood there.

"Give me that thing!" Quinn yanked the censer out of my grip and started using it to kill rats, swinging it with violent abandon and bringing it down hard with a heavy *crash!*, again and again.

But each rat he hit turned into a bat, and the little winged creatures flew at me, Lucky, and the priest, tormenting us while leaving Quinn alone as he kept trying to kill more of the things that were scurrying around the floor.

"Stop, Quinn! *Stop!*" Being dive-bombed by bats was definitely the worse of the two available choices.

I saw John stagger back and cry out when the big cross hit him hard on the hand, then he regrouped and kept on fighting it. While I dodged rats and bats, Max flung the last vial of holy water against the wall, still shouting in another language, his white hair blowing around his head in the fierce wind that whipped through the reception hall.

"What are you doing?" I shouted. "What should *we* do?"

The dripping water that was all over that wall suddenly started curling around in circles and swoops, rather than just rolling down the wall. It steamed, bubbled, and hissed, moving rapidly over the surface, forming itself into specific shapes with obvious intent.

When it was done, a few distinct shapes were painted on the wall in flowing lines made by steaming, hissing water.

Then without warning or fanfare, the bats and rats disappeared, as if they had never existed. The red-bound book appeared hovering in the air over Quinn's head for a moment, then it fell to the floor. The large crucifix that was attacking John also fell to the floor and just lay there. At the same moment, the wind stopped blowing and howling through the room, though the window remained shattered.

Our crucifixes lay scattered on the floor, but now they were charred pieces of wood, damaged by unseen fire. I touched the crucifix that Father Tiano had put around my neck . . . and it seemed to have melted like wax. It was just an indistinct little lump of metal now.

Breathing hard, Quinn tossed aside the censer and looked around the room, his expression shocked.

Max stood staring at the letters on the wall while the priest, standing on a chair, continued praying frantically. John tossed aside the lamp, tucked his injured hand against his chest, and went to help Lucky. I joined Max and stared up at the steaming letters on the wall under the broken window.

They just looked like abstract doodles to me. I said, "Let me guess. Aramaic?"

"A very old form." Max's voice was a little hoarse.

"Does it mean anything to you?"

The letters were already evaporating and fading away, disappearing as if they had never been there.

Max turned his troubled blue gaze on me. "I asked the entity what it wants. Why it's doing this."

"And?"

"If I have interpreted those symbols correctly, it has given us its answer," he said. " 'To live again.' "

14

Father Tiano left rather precipitately, not even pausing to take his gear with him. I had the impression he had just decided that exorcism wasn't his vocational path, after all.

Although Lucky must have been tired, he decided to go straight to Victor Gambello's house and tell him what had just happened, since it had involved the Shy Don's great-nephew. It was late by now, but I knew from previous incidents that Don Victor was a night owl and the two men often conferred at unconventional hours.

Quinn, the only person in the room whom the entity had not directly attacked (probably because it still needed him), decided he should leave the funeral home before anything *else* happened tonight. We all enthusiastically supported this plan.

Max wanted Quinn to return to the bookstore with him, so he could keep him (and the demon) under observation. But Quinn had had enough revelations for one night about the true nature of his problem. He said he just wanted to go home and pretend, if only for a few hours, that he was merely crazy, rather than suffering from demonic oppression.

"But I'll be in touch soon, Max," said the detective. "Believe me, I want this thing *gone*."

John quietly closed up Antonelli's and said he'd explain the ruined stained glass window to his father in the morning. "I think that Dad's had enough stress for tonight," he said, "and I'm sure that *I* have. It can wait until tomorrow."

He insisted on driving us home. It was a suggestion we welcomed, since it solved the problem of transporting Nelli and I was way too tired to take the subway.

"This was a challenging day," Max said on the ride home, as John drove the hearse through dark, slippery streets. "But we have learned a great deal."

"Such as, the entity attached to Quinn is very powerful and unbelievably scary?" I said.

"We have learned what it wants," said Max.

"To live again?"

"Yes. And we know the peculiar medium through which it is attempting to do so."

"Dead bodies." I frowned. "I still don't understand.

Why does it want a cadaver? Why doesn't it just possess Quinn?"

"I postulate that although it can oppress and manipulate the living, it can only invade and possess the dead."

John said, "That seems pretty inconvenient for a being that wants to live again, in the biological sense."

"Indeed."

"Why only the dead?" I wondered.

"Because it's a house without an owner?" John guessed.

"Well put, John." Max said, "This entity is apparently unable to move into an 'inhabited dwelling,' so to speak."

"I agree it's an inconvenient limitation, but even so," I said, "three thousand years, give or take, seems like a long time between houses."

"Not to a formless mystical entity for whom time is a meaningless construct—at least when it is not functioning in human form," said Max. "We also don't know whether it has been steadily attaching to the living for eons in search of its next host, or whether it has been drifting through dimensions and absent from this one for centuries at a time."

"What was it doing before it attached to Quinn, do you think?"

"It may have been attached to someone else, someone who was not servings its goals—a person who did not come into contact with fresh corpses," said Max. "Or it may have been long dormant and inert. In any event, when it encountered Andrew Quinn at some scene of death or despair, it felt an attraction, found his vulnerabilities, and attached to him."

"You make it sound like a relationship," John said with interest.

"It is, in a sense," said Max. "But a very negative, destructive one in which Quinn's participation is not voluntary and was, until today, unwitting."

"Hmm." I pulled my coat more tightly around myself as I thought about everything I had seen this evening. I tried to imagine Quinn's feelings as he realized all that disturbing stuff came from something which was attached to *him*. "You know, Nathan's description of Mr. Capuzzo was eerie, but it didn't sound menacing. Yet Grace Chu was definitely menacing, don't you think?"

"She also got a lot farther from her resting place than Capuzzo did," John added.

"Yes, the entity is rapidly getting stronger," Max noted.

"And it certainly got plenty of sustenance tonight," I said sourly. So many negative emotions had been generated in the past few hours, the demon could probably animate all the residents of a large cemetery at this point.

"We must prepare promptly for our next encounter

with it," Max said. "Now that it knows we have identified its nature and mean to exorcise it, it will be very intent on finding a host. And it seems clever enough to manipulate Quinn into situations that are propitious for its own intentions—and probably very dangerous for him."

"You mean it might try to get Quinn killed?" I asked in alarm. No, I hadn't really warmed up to the guy—but *still*.

The old mage nodded. "It is an opportunistic entity, and it seems to be learning quickly."

"So *how* do we prepare for our next encounter with this thing?" I asked with growing dread.

"I vote against summoning another priest," John said as he steered the hearse around a tight corner. "I'm not being anti-clerical. Just practical."

"The message we saw on the wall tonight was very useful," Max said. "Writing changes over the centuries, and its evolution is easier to trace than that of oral language. By analyzing the entity's script, I may be able to narrow down the era when it last 'lived' to within a century or two. That, in turn, will give me a region and a timeframe in which to search for references to it—and, I hope, an indication of how to combat it."

"Good. We need that information." Like Quinn, I wanted this thing *gone*.

John dropped Max and Nelli off at the bookstore. Max intended to go straight to bed, get a good night's rest, then start researching Quinn's problem in the morning.

Then we drove up to my apartment in the West Thirties. But unlike Max, I expected to toss and turn most of the night, fret in fear of the demonic entity, and weep over the loss of my stormy almost-relationship. Not looking forward to any of that, I felt like lingering in the car to chat.

So John pulled the hearse over and parked. The spot wasn't exactly legal; we were blocking the entrance to a construction site at the end of my street. But I hadn't seen anyone working there since before the holidays, never mind late at night, so I figured we were okay.

"What do you think of all this?" I asked him.

He had seemed to be a skeptic when we met, and he was never quite on board with the theory of the cursed fortune cookies. But he certainly wasn't trying to explain away the weird incidents in his family's funeral home tonight.

"Well, speaking as a scientist," he said, "it's all pretty freaking weird and really creeping me out."

I smiled. "Good summary." After a moment, I asked, "Does it change how you view the world? What you think the nature of reality is?"

"Well, sure," said John. "But that's something that changes all the time, anyhow."

"It is?"

He nodded. "That's why I like science—if you survive your undergraduate education, then after that, it's mostly about asking questions you don't already know the answers to."

I thought that was something Lopez liked about police work, too. That, and helping people.

Stop thinking about him.

"What we've seen lately doesn't seem very scientific," I pointed out.

"Maybe that's just because we don't even know the questions yet," he said. "I mean, sure, Max talks in mystical terms, but what if that's just another point of view? For centuries, astronomy and astrology were basically the same thing, for example, with people observing the heavens and recording what they saw. Whether what they observed up there was magical or 'mundane,' they were all looking at the same things. And whether what they saw foretold fate, explained human nature, or threatened the foundations of the Catholic Church with scientific principles . . . that all depended on how they *interpreted* what they saw."

"How do *you* interpret that big crucifix repeatedly trying to run you through tonight?"

"I interpret it as cause to celebrate that I'm still alive."

"Yeah." I wasn't amused now. "Agreed."

"Look, Max interprets these events in terms of a demon, an evil entity. But when I recover from my terror, which may happen in a week or two," he said wryly, "then I'll start asking myself, what if it's something else? And I'll try to figure out what else it could be. The world is an amazing place full of mysterious things we still can't explain scientifically—like what happened tonight. It's also full of things we couldn't explain a thousand years ago, or even ten years ago, that we *can* explain now—because we kept looking for the right questions."

"I like that perspective," I said. "It's got balance."

"Well that's life, isn't it? Going from day to day, trying to find a working balance between faith and intellect, instinct and reason, hope and experience." After a moment, he looked at me and said in a different voice, "The spiritual and . . . the physical."

I sensed a shift in the atmosphere between us. Less relaxed now. After a moment, he said softly, "Maybe you'll tell me it's none of my business, but I feel like I really need to ask, Esther."

I thought I already knew the question. "What?"

"Is it over between you and him?"

"I've got to stop, Esther," he'd said.

I nodded. "Yes."

"Are you sure?" John shifted a little. "I just mean . . . he doesn't look at you like it's over."

"I have to be stronger than this."

"It's over," I said.

"Okay." John nodded, accepting my word. "Then I . . . Okay."

Avoiding his eyes, my gaze landed on his hands, which were still resting on the steering wheel. The right one had two angry cuts across the knuckles, and there was some fresh bruising and swelling.

"Whoa! That thing really hurt you, John." I took his hand and pulled it closer to me, trying to see the damage in the dim light from the streetlamps.

He flexed his fingers, then drew in a sharp breath through his nostrils. "Yeah, I guess it stings a little."

"You should put something on this."

"Oh, it'll be okay," he said dismissively.

"What *is* it with guys? You'd better come upstairs with me," I said, getting out of the car. "Germs breed like rabbits in this city, even in winter. I've got lots of first aid supplies, and I don't want your father blaming me for your hand turning gangrenous and falling off."

"He wouldn't blame you," John said as he got out of the car. "He'd blame Uncle Lucky, who's supposed to look after me when Dad's not there."

I smiled at that. John's mother had died while her two sons were still young, and what little I knew about it was that Lucky had been there for the family then— and ever since.

A bone-chilling wind whipped down the street as I picked my way gingerly over the icy sidewalk.

"Here." John offered me his good hand, which I took, and we kept each other from falling down as we made our way down the slippery street, going toward my building.

I knew what I was doing. Of *course* I knew. It was after midnight, and I had just invited a man up to my apartment. A man who had made his interest in me clear, and to whom I was attracted. And I was doing this under the influence of a wounded heart and a bruised ego, having just been dumped by my lover (though we'd only spent that one night together, almost a month ago).

I didn't have any specific intentions, and my judgment wasn't as its finest just then—but I knew what I was doing.

We got to my building and climbed the steps, then I let go of John's hand to unlock the door. Once we were inside, he took my hand again, hesitantly, and met my gaze. There was no pretense now of helping me balance. He just wanted to touch me, and he let me know it—and silently asked if this was all right.

"So you're saying you want to walk away from this?" I had asked. *"From me?"*

"No, I'm saying I think I have to."

I stared at John uncertainly, my feet frozen to the spot. "Esther?"

"It's convenient for you that I'm so crazy about you I keep kicking things under the carpet for your sake."

Memories were crowding in on me. Surrounding me, taunting and hurting me.

"Are you okay?" John asked.

Get out of my head, I thought. *I want you out of my head!*

I wanted him out of my *heart*, which suddenly hurt so much it felt like it was screaming.

Seeing me standing there before him in numb paralysis, John said, "Maybe I should go, huh? I'll call you and—"

"John. No." I grabbed his coat collar as he turned away and pulled him toward me.

A tall, strong man, and an agile, experienced martial artist, he fell against me without resistance and let me have my way with him.

His cheeks were cold from the bitter night air, his mouth warm, his tongue soft. I slid my arms around him and clung, kissing him hungrily, beating back the bitter hurt inside me. I chased his warmth like it would save me, stroking his soft black hair and closing my eyes so I wouldn't think of another man's equally dark hair. We kissed and clung and kissed harder, and he fumbled through the folds of my coat to touch my body, no longer hesitant or asking permission.

I was dizzy, warm, and breathing hard when he finally pulled away.

Laughing a little as he nuzzled me, he said, "You don't actually live here in the hallway, do you?"

"Oh! No. Hm." He kissed me again. "Upstairs." And again. "One flight."

"Good," he said. "That's about all my legs can handle right now."

I took his hand and led the way, practically flying up those narrow, uneven stairs to the next floor. When he reached the landing, he pulled me into his arms again, and we slumped against the wall together, kissing dizzily and fumbling at each other's heavy clothing.

"Mm. *Mm.*" My mouth still on his, I was gesturing to and stumbling toward my front door, trying to get to it while I still had enough dexterity left to open it. As I turned away from him to wrestle the key into the lock, his hands were—"*Oh!*"—not at *all* shy with me now.

As soon as we were inside the apartment with the door locked behind us, we both dumped our coats on the floor, and then his arms were around me again. He backed me toward the couch as his mouth clung to mine. John and I fell onto the thing in a heap, jostling it hard enough to make it slide a little and thud against the wall, and we both laughed breathlessly.

We writhed around together, kissing, stroking, shifting to get closer—and my whole body went *zing!* with primal excitement when our hips slid neatly together and I could feel, through the weight of our winter clothes, how excited he was, too. I sighed mindlessly and pressed myself against him, moving without inhibition.

He whispered my name and sat up, breathing hard, to pull off his suit coat, his tie, and his shirt as fast as he could. I sat up to pull his undershirt over his head, and when his torso was finally naked, I ran my hands over him, enjoying his body, his kisses, his whispers.

He pulled my turtleneck sweater over my head, then his warm lips explored my neck and my cleavage while his hands sought the fastening of my bra. I held his head, sighing as I arched against him, and felt him unhook my bra and start to peel it away from my breasts.

And that was when I panicked.

One moment, I was passionately craving John, clutching him as if trying to absorb him into my body—and the next, I gasped in cold shock, rolled frantically away from him, and scooted to the edge of the couch, where I sat with my back to him, clutching my bra to my chest with one hand and holding the other hand over my mouth in stunned mortification.

Behind me, I could hear John breathing hard. So was I. I felt him shift a little on the couch, but he didn't come closer.

"Esther?" he murmured, sounding confused—as well he might.

I felt like someone had gathered a big bucket of icy slush from the street below and dumped it all over my half-naked body.

John shifted a little more and risked touching my shoulder. Just his fingers. Gently, no pressure. "What's wrong?"

Oh. My. God.

Well, wasn't this just a *perfect* ending to another perfect day? If my life got any more wonderful, I might ask Quinn's demon to move in with me so we could share the joy.

"Esther?"

How could I possibly face John now?

But I had to. There were some things in life you simply *had* to do, and this was one of them.

So I removed my hand from my mouth and choked out, "Sorry."

"Are you okay?" he asked with concern.

"I'm really sorry," I said, my back still to him.

"Did I . . . did I do something?"

"No." I took a few breaths, braced myself, and looked at him over my shoulder. "I'm so sorry, John. I can't tell you how sorry."

He looked concerned, confused, and uncertain. "What's wrong?" he asked again.

No, we weren't going to talk about that.

"I should never have . . . I wasn't ready . . . I'm *so* sorry, John." I looked at the floor, deeply embarrassed.

"Oh."

There was a long moment of silence, and then he sighed. When he moved again, it was to sit upright at the other end of the couch.

I glanced at his face, and I could see from his pensive expression that he had correctly interpreted my short stream of babble.

Not knowing what else to do, I apologized again as I fumbled around behind me on the couch, in search of my turtleneck. When I found it, I turned away to pull it over my head, then I reached underneath to refasten my bra.

Still mortified by my behavior, but feeling a little more secure with my clothes back on, I said, "It's my fault. This should have gone well."

"I thought it *was* going well," he said with rueful sadness.

"It was," I assured him. "Very well. You must know that."

Like my apology, the statement was sincere. John was another guy who seemed like such an altar boy when his clothes were on and then revealed a whole different side of his nature when they came off. I seemed to have a terrible weakness for men like that.

"Okay." He nodded and let out a long, slow breath. "I get it."

"I wish *I* did," I said morosely.

"Things being over between you and him . . ." John looked at the floor and shrugged. "It's not the same thing as you being over him. Is it?"

"No."

Goddamn you, Lopez.

But to share the blame fairly, I probably should not have tried to sleep with someone only a few hours after Lopez broke my heart. *Again.*

"Not my finest hour," I said, sensing John really didn't want to hear the word "sorry" again.

"I should go." He rose to his feet, slipped quickly into his clothes, and picked his coat up off the floor.

When he put his hand on the doorknob, I said anxiously, "Maybe I shouldn't ask right now, but are we still friends?"

He met my gaze. "Of course we are." And I could see that he meant it.

"I don't want things to be awkward the next time we meet."

"Oh, of course it'll be awkward, Esther," he said with a snort. "Come on."

"Oh. Yeah," I said wryly, "I guess so."

"But it'll pass and we'll be okay again."

"All right." I smiled. "Thanks, John."

He left, and I finally got off the couch so I could lock the door behind him. Then I leaned my back against it and covered my face with my hands, utterly mortified.

On the bright side, though, at least I was too swamped by remorse and embarrassment to spend the rest of the night crying, as I had planned.

Damn you, Lopez.

Yet despite how rotten he had made my whole night—and, in some ways, my whole year—when I found out the next day that he was marked for death, I was willing to do anything to save him.

15

After a restless night and a late morning, I bundled up and left my apartment the next day for another *D30* costume fitting. It was still windy, snowing intermittently, bitterly cold, and the streets were an icy mess.

I was too tired and cranky to do anything with my appearance, so my hair was pulled back in a ponytail, my head was ringed by a red knit ear warmer, and my face was bare of makeup. This look didn't really blend that well with the tiny black dress and thigh-high boots the wardrobe designer was squeezing me into for one of my upcoming scenes on the show as Jilly C-Note.

I thought this sleek, off-the-shoulder outfit looked a little upmarket for a streetwalker with a heroin problem. Sure, it was slutty (I could just imagine my mother's expression when she saw the show), but it seemed more like an outfit for an uptown party girl than for a gritty hooker suspected of involvement in shooting a cop—which, it was clear from today's new pages, was where the Jimmy Conway subplot was headed. He was having sexual fantasies about a hooker who—Cal Donner would tell him in the final episode—had probably tried to have him killed.

The costume designer wasn't entirely happy with the fit of my little black dress, so I sat around the costume shop in a bathrobe while she plucked out some seams and made some adjustments. She was pleasantly gossipy, and delighted to tell me that many people in production were grateful that I got Michael Nolan out of their hair for a few days by arranging for him to shadow some OCCB cops I knew.

Okay, Quinn and Lopez were probably still unhappy about it, wherever they were today, but at least I was scoring some points with *D30* for that desperate measure.

No, don't think about Lopez. Don't even start.

After the alterations were finished, I tried on my costume again. While I was changing into it, the costume department received a phone call from the C&P storage warehouse, and it sounded as if there was a serious problem. I stood around for a few minutes, and once it was clear that no one seemed ready for me, I excused myself to go to the bathroom—something which took some careful maneuvering in a skirt that tight. When I returned a few minutes later, the costume shop was empty.

I was surprised, and I realized the problem must be bigger than I had supposed. The designer and the two assistants who had been here earlier must be conferring with the producers or something. I assumed the best thing for me to do would be to wait here until it was convenient for someone to take a final look at the fit of my costume. So I sat down with next week's finished script, which I had been given upon arrival today, and started reading.

I was pleased that another scene with my character had been added to the episode. It supported the developing subplot that implicated (always inconclusively) Jilly C-note in the unsolved shooting of Jimmy Conway. The scene also portrayed Jilly's bisexuality, a feature mentioned in her character description but not included in my previous appearance on *D30*. In this scene, Jilly would use sex to convince another prostitute to give her a phony alibi—but whether she wanted it for Jimmy's shooting or for an unrelated matter remained murky.

So apparently I would be kissing and fondling another woman next week. I didn't have a problem with that—it's a lot like kissing and fondling a male actor. Either way, you're getting physically intimate with a person you aren't *actually* intimate with (and probably aren't personally attracted to), and you're doing it in front of cameras and microphones, with more than a dozen crew members crowded closely around.

In other words, it's just acting.

But I did have a brief moment of discomfort when I pictured my parents watching me kiss and fondle another actress.

That's where focus comes in handy. The thought of my parents bothered me now, and it would bother me when the episode aired; but while I was rehearsing and filming, I'd put it out of my head and focus on the work.

Thinking about sex and personal attraction brought last night to mind, of course—but I was *not* going to think about *that*. It would be at least a few weeks—and maybe a few months—before I'd be able to think about last night without immediately cringing and trying to put it out of my mind.

So I turned my attention back to the script.

But my thoughts drifted. What was I *doing?* A good man like John . . . an attractive, engaging man who'd been patient and gallant ever since I'd met him. And last night, I . . .

Script! Focus on the script.

I shifted in my seat, gave myself a shake, and resolutely put John Chen—and my mortifying folly—out of my mind.

As written, the new scene was pretty raunchy. There was nothing tender or emotional about Jilly's sexuality.

It was always commerce for her, whether she did it for money, to coax another hooker into giving her an alibi, or to string Jimmy Conway along. I was pleased that in the revisions Kathleen had done since our first read-through, Jilly now had a little more power. She wasn't just being used and discarded by Conway, as was previously the case. She was also using him, playing him, and making sure he stayed off balance. This dynamic also made Jimmy more vulnerable, which made him more interesting.

With still no one turning up to finish my fitting, I started learning my lines. I had a comfortable chair in a quiet room and nothing else to do today, so I might as well use the time productively.

It was nearly dark outside by the time I was letter-perfect on my lines, getting bored here by myself, and wondering if I should just leave. Obviously, something much more serious than I'd suspected must have happened.

Still wearing my slutty black dress, I left the costume workshop and went looking for someone who might know what was going on. Before long, I found a production assistant who informed me that, in yet another tedious mishap, there'd been a messy accident at the warehouse where C&P's costumes and props were stored. Due to snow and ice building up in the gutters, the roof had wound up leaking, and no one had known about it until a big part of it collapsed earlier today. The upshot was that about a quarter of C&P's costume and prop stock was damaged or destroyed. Everyone available from both departments had gone straight out to the warehouse to sort through the damage and rescue whatever could be saved.

The production assistant was practically prostrate with distress upon learning that no one had told me and I'd been sitting in the costume shop all afternoon, waiting to finish my fitting. But I insisted the abject apologies weren't necessary and this wasn't a big deal. This was the most peace and quiet I'd had for some time, and that was a luxury I didn't take lightly. I'd had time to read the script and learn my lines, and I'd been warm and dry for several hours in a row. All in all, it was hard to find cause for complaint.

When I went back to the changing room, I reached into my coat pocket and pulled out my phone. As a professional courtesy, I had turned it off upon arriving for the fitting, and I hadn't checked it since then. This was, of course, another reason that I'd had a peaceful afternoon.

I now saw that I had missed a phone call. The number was unfamiliar, but when I checked the message, I wasn't that surprised to find that it was from Lucky. His phone had died under the influence of Quinn's malevolent prankster, but he changed phones and phone numbers regularly, anyhow. It was one of the habits that ensured he remained too "lucky" to be prosecuted.

The message just said he had urgent news, and I should call him as soon as I got this. I felt a little guilty when I realized he had called more than an hour ago. I should have checked messages sooner.

Hoping that no one was hurt or maimed or malevolently possessed, I returned the call. I expected some cranky criticism about taking too long to get back to him. But he didn't say anything like that. He just launched right into his reason for phoning me. So I realized this must be pretty serious. Even though, at first, it didn't sound like it.

"Kid, it bugged me last night, what I overhead you tell the cops about Danny. Because you and I know who was responsible for the deed in question."

"Uh-huh." I assumed the deed was Joe Ning's murder, about which Danny Teng had made a scene. Lucky believed in exercising discretion on the phone.

"And we know Danny *don't* know who done that."

"Agreed," I said. All indications were that he had no idea Susan Yee was behind Uncle Six's death.

"So I wondered, what does a coke-snorting rapist with the IQ of overcooked ravioli *think* he knows about that death?"

I hadn't known Danny was a rapist or a cocaine user, but neither thing surprised me.

"This kind of thing can be very messy, and also bad for business. Hot-headed young thugs looking for vengeance in all the wrong places," Lucky continued.

"And since my boss's business interests are extensive, I decided he should be made aware of this development. There is already too much attention on our family, and we don't need more."

"Ah." It did not surprise me that Victor Gambello had interests, so to speak, that had intersected with those of Uncle Six. They were both big men, after all.

And if Victor Gambello felt that Danny Teng was becoming a liability . . . well, then Danny's future might be even shorter than previously expected. I was, due to the strange twists and turns of fate, on cordial terms with the Gambello family; but that didn't mean I ever fooled myself about how they conducted their business.

"So I received instructions late last night to look into this matter, which I been doin' today."

"And?"

"And this is not the sort of thing in which we usually interfere, Esther, but you are a friend of the family. So we will take what steps we can."

I frowned, more puzzled than scared. "What are you saying? Danny Teng is after *me*?"

"No, he's after your boyfriend," Lucky said seriously.

"What?" I blurted.

"That stupid jerk believes all this crap that TV lawyer is spouting about Wonder Boy being responsible for Uncle Six's death."

"But—"

"And in his half-baked little brain, he's taken it a step further and convinced himself that Lopez shoved the old man off that balcony and the cops are covering it up."

"Seriously?"

"You see, Danny talks a lot when he's, uh, in a woman's company."

"You found the girl he took home last night?" I guessed.

"Yeah. And she don't like him any better than anyone else does, so it wasn't that expensive to find out what he said to her. Especially since she don't want to be an accessory to killing a cop."

"*That's* his plan?" I blurted. "Danny intends to kill Lopez?"

"We'll take care of this, Esther," Lucky said formally. "You've been a good friend to the family, and we don't forget our friends."

I knew what that meant. And given what he had just told me Danny planned to do, I had no intention of telling the Gambellos I didn't want their help. Lopez wouldn't want it, but he didn't have to know.

I also suspected there was an element of self-interest at work here. The Gambellos would not like to see a cop who was investigating them get blown away by a thug who'd worked for someone they did business with. It was too likely to attract more unwanted attention to the family.

"Where's Danny now?" I came to my senses a second later and started to ask him not to tell me. The less I knew, the better, I suspected.

But Lucky said with regret, "We don't know. He's gone to ground."

"What do you mean, you don't know?" I demanded. "How hard can one swaggering, self-advertising gangster be to find?"

"Last time anyone saw him," Lucky said, "was a few hours ago, when he went looking for Detective Lopez with a loaded gun."

"He's planning to do it now? *Today?*"

"You'd better call your boyfriend and warn him," said Lucky. "I'll be in touch as soon as I've got news."

I was in my coat, out the door, and hailing a cab before I even realized where I was headed. I rarely spent money on cabs, but this was obviously an emergency.

However, when a taxi stopped and the driver asked where I was going . . . I realized I didn't know.

I hopped into the car anyhow, since it was cold and snowing, and it might not be easy to get another one later. "Just turn on the meter and drive. I'll give you an address later."

"Okay!" the driver said cheerfully. "Take your time!"

I phoned Lopez and got his voicemail. After the beep, I started babbling. "It's me. This is really important. Danny Teng is looking for you with a gun. *Right now.* He plans to kill you! Never mind how I know. *Be careful!* And call me as soon as you get this. I *mean* it!"

"Whoa!" said the driver. "Sounds serious."

I closed the partition and tried to think. I didn't have Quinn's phone number. And Lopez was the only person I knew who did.

Damn.

And then I remembered: Nolan!

"Oh, thank God for Nolan." Those were words I had certainly never expected to say. I called the actor.

To my relief, he answered on the second ring.

"Are you with Lopez and Quinn?" I asked eagerly.

"No, I'm at dinner. I'm done with—"

"Where are they?"

"Off protecting and serving, I guess," he said without interest. "My entrée is going to be put in front of me any second, so I'm gonna g—"

"Why aren't you with them?" I asked shrilly. "You're supposed to be with them!"

"Look, today was a bust, so I'm done with this," he said. "I don't even know where Quinn was today, and Lopez . . . Jesus, you'd think *rats* had crawled up that guy's ass, the way he's acting."

"We broke up again last night," I said by way of explanation.

"Oh. Figures," Nolan said. "I thought it must be something to do with a woman—but when I asked nicely, the guy bit my head off and then just brooded.

You know, I just can't stand people who are that rude and self-absorbed."

I was in no mood to appreciate the irony of this.

"Where is he now?" I asked. "Do you know?"

"At the police garage, I suppose, unless he's still sitting on FDR Drive."

"Why would he be sitting on . . . ?" I realized what must have happened. "Another car broke down on him?"

"He really lost his composure," Nolan said critically. "You'd think a cop could handle stress a little better."

I said, "So you hailed a cab and left?"

"Did I need to listen to this guy rant and rave about the failings of the twenty-first century while punching the hood of the car and kicking the tires?"

"I guess he really did lose his composure." And now Nolan was sitting down to dinner somewhere while Lopez was probably still waiting for a tow truck, in the snow, during rush hour, on that bitterly windy highway that ran along the East River. "Where exactly on the FDR did you leave him?"

"Under the Williamsburg Bridge. Of all the places to break down . . ." He sounded as if he thought Lopez had deliberately chosen the spot.

I opened the partition and said to my driver, "FDR Drive under the Williamsburg Bridge. And step on it!"

"Is this a scavenger hunt?" the driver asked.

I closed the partition again. "One more thing, Mike."

"Esther, they just put my dinner in front of me, so—"

"Have you got Quinn's phone number?"

To my relief, he did. Quinn had given it to him yesterday (perhaps with great reluctance) in case they got separated while Nolan was shadowing him.

I left Nolan to his dinner, and I dialed Quinn's number. To my relief, he had replaced his dead cell phone, and he answered the call promptly.

"Where are you?" I asked him right after identifying myself.

"Trying to find my partner," Quinn said irritably. "He's fallen off the radar."

I explained about the dead car. "I have a feeling his phone might be dead again, too. Otherwise he'd have answered my call or phoned me back by now."

"I left him a message about thirty minutes ago," said Quinn. "I haven't heard from him, either."

"Danny Teng is looking for him with a gun," I said. "He plans to kill him."

"Shit. I've been looking for Danny all day!" Then he asked, "Where did you get this information?"

"All you need to know is that my source is reliable," I said. "And Lopez has no idea. We need to find him and warn him."

I gave him the information I'd gotten from Nolan about Lopez's last known location.

"All right, I'm in a police car that actually works, for a change," said Quinn. "I'm on my way to find him right now."

"I'm on my way, too. I'll meet you there."

"Why are *you* going there?" he asked.

"Because his life is in danger."

"No, you go home and stay out of trouble. One of us will phone you—"

"Right, because a guy who's being oppressed by an Aramaic demon that loves fresh corpses and violent pranks is *exactly* who I want Lopez to be alone with in the dark on a deserted highway while Danny Teng is look—"

"The FDR isn't deserted," Quinn said. "It's probably a parking lot right now. Do you have any idea what accident statistics are like on a night like this?"

"I'm meeting you there," I said firmly.

"You're a pain in the butt, Esther Diamond," Quinn said. "You two deserve each other."

I called Lucky to give him an update. There was still no news on his end about Danny's whereabouts.

I sat back in my seat and tried to manage my agitated nerves. My sense of urgency was probably unnecessary. After all, as far as I could tell, only three people in the whole world knew where Lopez was right now: me, his partner, and a tow truck driver who probably had a lot of calls this evening. The snow was really coming down heavy now.

Quinn was right about the FDR being a parking lot. Once we got on the highway, I was frustrated by how slowly we were moving forward. By the time we reached East River Park, which the bridge runs above, I was so impatient that I rolled down my window and stuck my head out, squinting against the blowing snow as I searched for a stranded car. We were practically under the bridge ourselves when I finally spotted a four-door sedan pulled way off to the side of the highway. It crouched in the shadows of one of the massive concrete structures that supported the bridge, which loomed high overhead.

And there was Lopez, pacing back and forth beside the car, stomping his feet, his shoulders hunched against the cold, his arms folded across his chest.

Behind him was the dark expanse of East River Park, then the river itself, and beyond that were the lights of Brooklyn.

"Oh, thank God." I was so relieved to have found him. I said to the driver, "Over there! Do you see? Drop me off right by that car."

I had a cold, sobering moment of shock when I paid the driver. The fare was more than I spent on groceries in a week. I tried to comfort myself with the knowledge that I had three weeks of filming on a TV series coming up. Plus, I had spent this money in an unusual emergency.

Even so, it stung.

Just as my taxi drove away, another car pulled up to this spot, a police light flashing on its roof. Quinn got out of the vehicle and said something to me.

"What?" I couldn't hear him above the dull roar of traffic from the FDR beside us and the bridge up above.

"You made good time!" he shouted.

"Oh." It hadn't felt like it.

Looking understandably surprised to see us, Lopez approached where we stood. He wasn't wearing a hat, and his black, wind-tossed hair was damp and heavily flecked with snowflakes.

"What are you two doing here?" he shouted. "How did you find me?"

I started to explain, but this spot was just too noisy. Lopez gestured for us to follow him, and we walked about fifty yards, leaving the two cars behind as we moved away from the road and into the quieter park. I heard the roar of a motorcycle nearby, then the engine seemed to go dead. I looked over my shoulder at the highway, and traffic was moving very slowly, with people honking and engines idling.

The wind whipped up underneath my heavy coat, and I gasped at how cold it was. That was when I realized I was still wearing my hooker costume for *D30*. I had left the C&P building in such desperate haste earlier, I hadn't changed back into my own clothes—hadn't even realized until this moment that I was still wearing Jilly C-Note's costume. And that tiny skirt was a big mistake in weather like this.

Quinn and I both started talking, interrupting each

other and stepping on each other's sentences. We explained about Danny Teng.

"Seriously?" Lopez tugged his collar up higher around his neck. "I'm going to *sue* that goddamn lawyer. This is all his fault! Killing me is the first idea Danny Teng's ever had in his life, and it was put there by that sleazy shyster."

"God, that is *so* like you," I said in exasperation. "I think you're kind of missing the point here! Which is that your life is in danger!"

"Mostly, I'm in danger of freezing to death," he said crankily, "because I've been stuck out here for almost two hours in *another* broken-down car."

"Oh, and I don't think your phone is working," I said.

"I *know* it's not working! Of *course*, it's not working! I'm out here alone in the dark with a dead car, so why in the world would I have a *functioning phone* with me? That would just be *crazy!*"

"All right," said Quinn, "let's make an effort to compose ourselves and figure out—"

"*Don't* tell me to compose myself," Lopez snapped. "That's what her jackass friend kept saying!"

"Nolan's not my friend, he's a colleague," I said automatically.

"My *God*, do you ever owe us an apology for that guy," Lopez said, rubbing his red nose. "In fact, two hours ago, breaking down here seemed like a blessing, because he finally *left*. If I had known that would do that trick, I would have sabotaged the car yesterday morning."

"Yeah, well, he's how we found you, buddy," said Quinn. "Esther called him to find out where you were, since he was the only person in the Greater New York area who knew. Otherwise you'd probably be stuck here until the spring thaw."

"Let's go," said Lopez. "I'm abandoning the car. I don't care anymore. I've lost count by now of how many cars . . . how many phones . . . how much *crap* is going wrong. I don't get it. What the hell is going on?"

I looked at Quinn, who by now knew as well as I did what was going on. He gave me a cold glare and shook his head slightly, indicating we would *not* talk about it. Lopez, who was busy glaring at the broken-down car in the distance, didn't see.

"We should go back to the squad and talk to the lieutenant," said Quinn. "I'm worried about this Danny Teng thing. He seems crazy enough to whack a cop."

"Where does this information come from?" Lopez asked.

I never had a chance to prevaricate. Suddenly there were three *really loud* bursts of gunfire right by us. Once you've heard the sound, it's not easy to mistake for anything else. Plus, a bullet ricocheted off a lamppost and flew right past my head, so that was another clue.

"*Get down!*" Lopez shouted, shoving me to the

ground as he and Quinn crouched low and pulled out their guns.

I didn't have to be told twice. I was already in a huddle on the cold, slushy pavement, my head down.

When the next two bullets exploded in our direction, the two cops figured out roughly where the shooter was, which was a lot more than I could do, and took cover. Lopez dragged me with him behind a fat tree trunk. My feet moved as he pulled me across the snow and ice by my arm, but I didn't lift my head.

Once we were behind cover, he shifted me a little, then whispered, "Get down all the way. On your stomach. And stay there."

I did as I was told.

But when I felt him start to move away from me, I lifted my head. "Where are you going?"

"Stay here," he ordered softly. "Don't move, don't speak."

Quinn was huddled behind a garbage can nearby, peering over the top of it. He looked at Lopez and made a gesture that was not self-explanatory to me, but which apparently meant something to him. To my horror, the two of them left the marginal safety of cover and ran off in separate directions.

Danny, I thought.

It had to be him. But how had he found Lopez? Nolan, Quinn, and I were the only people who knew . . . Then I remembered.

"Shit. I've been looking for Danny all day!" Quinn had said.

And Danny had known.

A cop asking around Chinatown for him? Of *course* Danny knew.

He was an idiot, but he was an experienced criminal. To find Lopez, he realized that all he had to do was follow the cop who was searching for *him*. I recalled the motorcycle engine that had caught my attention minutes ago, and I suspected Danny had been riding it, tailing Quinn—to a dark, deserted park beside a traffic-snarled highway on a snowy night.

Well, this was just *great*.

I lay there, flat on the ground, for long, dark, silent minutes, shivering with cold, hearing nothing but traffic noises. What the hell was happening? Were Quinn and Lopez closing in on Danny? Was he about to ambush them? Did he realize he'd lost the element of surprise and decide to run away?

The tension was killing me. I was listening so hard that I tried not even to breathe, straining to detect any faint sound besides traffic and wind.

Finally, when I felt like I must have been lying there for half an hour, I heard footsteps, a shot, a shout, and then a whole volley of thunderous shots from multiple guns. Followed by silence.

Then Quinn's voice. "He's down!"

Adrenaline surged through me, and I tried to pop

up—but I was so cold and stiff, I could only crawl laboriously to my feet, moving slowly.

I could see Quinn, his red hair gleaming under the streetlamps, about forty yards away. The body of a man was on the ground in front of him. Quinn used his foot to shove something away from it—Danny's gun, I assumed—then bent over and put his hand on the neck, checking for a pulse.

"DOA!" he called over his shoulder.

I looked around, panicking for a moment when I couldn't find Lopez. Where was he? But then I saw the faint gleam of his black hair in a stray beam of light. He was standing in the shadows, a dark figure in a dark setting, about twenty feet away from Quinn and the body.

"Lopez!" I ran to him, slipping and tripping as I went. "Are you all right?"

When I got to him, he was breathing very hard, as if he'd been running through the park all this time, chasing his would-be assassin through the night. His gun was in his hand, his arm dangling at his side.

I threw my arms around him. He staggered a little under the enthusiasm of my embrace.

"Sorry! Sorry." I laughed a little, helping him get his balance. "I'm just so glad you're alive."

"Yeah." He nodded, breathing harder. "Me, too."

He opened his coat and tried to holster his gun, but his movements were clumsy and uncoordinated.

"Are you all right?" I asked with concern, my hand on his shoulder.

He shook his head, not as if answering me, but as if trying to clear his vision. "I feel a little . . ." His breathing, already fast, suddenly doubled its speed. "A little . . ."

"Lopez?" I said in alarm.

He looked at me, an expression of amazement on his face, as if just now discovering I was there. "Esther?"

And then he collapsed, sinking to the ground so fast I didn't have time to catch him. As he rolled over into a dim pool of light, his coat flapped open and I saw the crimson stain spreading across his chest.

"Lopez!" I fell to my knees and screamed his name again.

His eyes were half-closed. He was looking up at me, his expression sad now, as if wishing I would stop screaming.

I heard footsteps and then saw running feet. On the other side of Lopez's body, Quinn dropped to his knees while tearing off his down jacket. He wadded it up, smooshed it against Lopez's chest, and put my hands on top of this mass.

"Pressure!" Quinn shouted at me. "Put pressure on it!"

I nodded and did as he ordered, though this made Lopez groan.

Then Quinn was on his feet and on his cell phone,

shouting numbers and words into it. The only phrase I really understood was, "Officer down! Officer down!"

"No, no, no!" I pleaded, tears streaming down my face.

He couldn't be taken from me. Not now, not like this.

"No!" I wailed, pressing down harder on the wound, willing him to survive.

In the faint glow of the overhead light, I could see that Lopez's eyes were still open, but he looked dazed and confused. He also looked alarmingly pale.

Officer down! Officer down!

Quinn dropped to his knees again and leaned over to speak loudly into his partner's face. "They're coming. They'll be here right away. Hang in there! Don't you die on me."

I glared at him, angry he had used that word.

Ignoring my look, Quinn took over the task of keeping pressure on the wound and said, "Give him your coat. Try to keep him warm. He's losing a lot of blood."

I rose to my feet, tore open my coat, and as I lifted my chin to remove the garment, I looked straight ahead—and saw Danny Teng's fresh corpse rise from the dead and turn toward me, its eyes glowing with demonic green fire, its lips curled back in a snarl, and its bloody hands reaching for me like claws as it came staggering toward us.

16

I didn't manage to scream, but my horrified stare, inarticulate gagging, and rigidly pointing arm were enough clues to warn Quinn to look over his shoulder.

"Holy shit!" Like me, he was so shocked he just stared for a moment.

The thing was gaining speed as it adjusted to Danny's body. In a few more steps, it would be able to touch us.

And so I screamed, needing to break Quinn's paralysis, as well as my own.

His arm shot forward, gun in hand, and he pumped bullet after bullet into the reanimated corpse as it came toward us. Explosive shot after shot, the thing kept coming. When the body fell down, rather than give up, it *crawled* toward us.

Barely conscious now, Lopez turned his head sideways—and his dazed eyes widened as he saw Danny Teng's dead body, eyes glowing green and bright yellow drool pouring from its mouth, crawling toward him, its cackling laughter echoing through the night. Lopez made a faint, startled sound, but he couldn't move.

Quinn dropped the empty magazine out of his gun, reloaded, and fired again. Two, three, four times.

And finally the animated cadaver stopped coming toward us. It quivered, froze for a moment, then collapsed onto the ground as the demonic entity abandoned it, leaving behind only Danny Teng's bloody, mangled corpse.

I grunted out inarticulate sounds of revulsion and fear while tears streamed down my face. Feeling as if it took a great effort to move, I retrieved my fallen coat, knelt by Lopez, and tried to wrap it around his head and shoulders and arms.

Quinn was pale and shaking as he returned to Lopez's side and again applied pressure to his partner's blood-soaked chest. After a few moments during which I heard only our agitated, panting breaths, Quinn looked at Lopez's face and said, "He's unconscious."

"What else do we do?" I asked. "I don't know what else to do."

"Shh." Quinn lifted his head, listening for a moment, then said, "Oh, thank God."

I listened, too, finding nothing reassuring for a long moment—and then I heard it, too.

Sirens.

I was shivering and crying, kneeling in the snow next to the bloody, unconscious body of my dying lover when the ambulances and squad cars pulled up. I saw and heard everything that was happening through a dazed fog as uniformed men and women rushed toward us, carrying heavy equipment, all high energy and loud voices and rapid movement.

I was roughly shoved aside, then hauled to my feet. I stared numbly down at Lopez, noticing how black his hair looked against the snow and the ice. There were four strangers crouching around him now. I didn't know where Quinn was. Someone put something warm around me, but I couldn't take my eyes off Lopez, lying in the snow, so pale and still that he seemed unfamiliar to me.

"His heart's stopped!" shouted one of the crouching men.

And then I felt I'd been plunged into the East River, shockingly icy cold all over my body, a brutal awakening.

"No!" I choked out. *"No."*

Suddenly everything was noise and color, sound and stench, light and blurred movement. Sharp, hard edges and sensations that scraped along my nerves.

"He's dropped a lung!"

"Lopez!" I couldn't move. Someone was holding me back and shouting in my ear. I didn't hear any of the words.

I struggled and stared in horror as someone ripped open his shirt in the cold, cold night and then plunged an enormous needle straight into his chest.

"What are you *doing?*"

"It's all right," someone said loudly in my ear. "They're helping him breathe."

When they pulled the needle out of his lung, though, he didn't look like he was breathing.

When they stuck other needles into him, covered his chest wound, wrapped him up, and put a ventilator mask on his face, it still didn't look like he was breathing.

And when they rolled him past me on a gurney, taking him to the ambulance, it didn't look to *me* as if his heart was beating again.

As I emerged from my shock, they had to tell me a dozen times that Lopez was alive. I had trouble believing it, remembering it.

I remained at the scene after he was taken away in a flashing, wailing ambulance. I wanted to go with him, wanted to know where he was going—but I was confused and inarticulate, and *so cold.*

A paramedic wrapped me in some sort of weird blanket that warmed me up quickly. She gave me hot tea, and she made sure that none of the blood that covered me was my own. It wasn't—all of it had belonged to Lopez.

When my breathing, heart rate, and temperature were all declared normal, I borrowed a spare EMT jacket, since my coat was now bloody and lying in the snow, and looked for Quinn.

He was reviewing the crime scene with a bunch of cops, some in suits, some in uniforms. I realized after standing there for a couple of minutes that this was going to be very complicated and take a long time. The cops weren't just interested in where Lopez fell, which was all I could remember now. They wanted to know about every shot that was fired that night, every movement taken, every single beat of the whole hideous event.

I looked at Danny Teng's mangled corpse, which I wasn't allowed to go near now—as if I would want to. Uniformed cops were keeping the area secure while CSU officers prepared to go to work on the scene. More police vehicles were arriving.

A detective told me he wanted to get a statement from me. I said I wanted to see Lopez. I had to make sure he was alive.

Quinn noticed us talking and intervened. "She's his girlfriend," he told the detective. "Someone should take her to the hospital."

That worked, and the detective agreed. I was bundled into a squad car, still wearing my hooker costume and my borrowed EMT coat. My purse had been returned to me; I had left it lying somewhere in the park during the shooting, though I had no idea where. A couple of patrolmen took me to the trauma center where Lopez was being treated, got me some hot coffee, and told the staff there that I was with Lopez, the detective who'd just been brought in.

Doctors spent much of the night operating on him. The waiting room filled up with grim-faced cops, some of whom kept each other company by telling detailed stories of terrible wounds that other cops had survived. Some of them knew the nurses here well, so we got detailed information as the surgery progressed.

I was puzzled at first that his parents weren't there, but then I remembered that they were in the Galapagos Islands, on a trip they had dreamed about for years.

When I thought of them getting this news under those circumstances, it made me want to cry again.

Twice more that night, while he was on the operating table, his heart stopped. Both times I heard this news, I thought mine stopped, too.

"They finished surgery about two hours ago," I told Quinn when he arrived at the hospital a little before dawn. "He's in critical condition."

I hadn't slept. I felt like I would never sleep again.

Danny's bullet had traveled far, damaging multiple organs and nicking the heart. Most of the blood had come from an artery in the chest. Lopez might need a second surgery.

"He's in the ICU, and I can't see him," I concluded.

This had been the most hellacious night of my life. I felt at moments as if none of this was really happening—and at other moments as if it had been happening for so long that I couldn't remember anything I'd ever done before sitting in this relentlessly beige waiting room, unable to breathe or eat or think, unable to do anything but cling to hope and shrink from my worst fears.

"They've very good here," Quinn said quietly. "They handle a lot of wounded cops. If I were shot, this is where I'd want . . . I mean, he's in good hands here."

After a while, I asked, "Where have you been all night?"

"Some problems at the crime scene," he said grimly.

"What problems?" I asked, not interested, just trying to find something to think about besides the man who was lying in a hospital bed and trying not to die. "You were attacked by a murderous thug, you dealt with him, he's dead, and Lopez is . . . is here."

Quinn looked around the room. There were a lot of cops there. "Can I talk to you somewhere else?"

"I don't want to leave. If something happens, I . . . I don't want to leave."

"It's important," said Quinn. "Five minutes, okay?"

I thought about it. "Okay," I said after a moment. Maybe if I left, he'd wake up and I'd come back to good news.

Quinn took me into the chapel down the hall, which was empty.

"The problem," he said, now that we were alone, "is that they found Danny's body pumped full of a bunch of slugs from my gun, fired at close range, about six feet from where Lopez went down."

That was how I remembered it happening. "So?"

"But they found Danny's gun about twenty feet away from there. Near some of his blood, where he went down—the first time."

I didn't understand. "So what?"

"So it looks to Homicide and Internal Affairs like I fired repeatedly, at close range, at a wounded suspect who had dropped his weapon and was coming toward me, surrendering and pleading for his life."

I frowned. "No, he wasn't surrendering or pleading. He was . . ." Then I realized the problem. "*Oh.*"

"Yeah," he said. "We can't exactly say that he was dead but his body was reanimated by an ancient demon who looked like it intended to eat our eyeballs if it got any closer."

No, that didn't really seem like a story that the NYPD was going to accept from either of us.

"So what have you told them?" I asked.

"As close to the truth as I could get," he said. "In the revised version of last night, I didn't secure the scene and make sure Danny was dead, because Lopez collapsed before I could do that. So when you stood up to take off your coat, and you pointed and screamed, I assumed Danny had been playing possum, and was armed and attacking again, and I emptied most of a clip into him to put him down before he finished off my unconscious partner."

It sounded reasonable to me. "Will it fly?"

"Well, it would if Lopez was the one telling this story and I was the one lying in a hospital bed." He ran a tired hand over his face. "But like I told you at Antonelli's, I had some bad incidents on my record last year. Nothing as bad as shooting an unarmed suspect, but sketchy enough that I'm getting some fishy looks now." He shrugged. "Extenuating circumstances, though. Danny Teng was an aspiring cop killer who had just ambushed and gunned down my partner, and he took me by surprise while I was trying to keep Lopez from bleeding to death."

I didn't like the use of that word, and I went back to the waiting room.

Lucky phoned during the day, deeply apologetic that he had not solved this problem before Lopez got hurt. He also let me know that, due to the role that Alan Goldman's rhetoric had played in convincing Danny Teng to gun down a decorated police officer, the lawyer had just lost all interest in the Ning matter and was moving on.

I sensed the fine Italian hand of Victor Gambello in that decision, but I didn't ask any questions.

I had washed off the blood in the ladies room, but I hadn't slept. I was still dressed like a hooker, and I was probably on my tenth cup of coffee. My stomach lining felt like I'd need to replace it if I drank one more cup.

"Anyhow, I'm sorry about what Danny did, kid," said Lucky. "I should have stopped him in time."

"He acted so fast, Lucky. You didn't have a chance to stop him."

I didn't blame the old hit man. I didn't even blame Quinn, a cop who'd let that thug tail him to find Lopez.

I blamed Danny, and I was glad he was dead.

He was ignorant, violent, stupid, and vicious, and so we had all underestimated what an opportunistic predator he was. He had paid for his predation with his life.

I just didn't want Lopez to pay for it with his.

John heard what happened, and he brought me some Chinese food, herbal tea, and a change of clothes that he'd picked up on Canal Street—making a pretty accurate guess about the right sizes.

I hugged him tightly, grateful for all of these things, for his friendship, and for his sitting with me for a couple of hours to keep me company.

It was a relief to change into trousers, sneakers, and a sweater. Finally the cops who entered the waiting room stopped asking each other why there was a hooker waiting on news of Lopez.

Max and I spoke several times by phone throughout the day. I discouraged him from coming to the hospital to keep me company, though, because I wanted him to stick with his research.

The one thing I wanted most in the world right now was for Lopez to wake up and start arguing with me about something stupid. And the *next* most important thing after that was for us to vanquish the demon that had attached to Quinn. This thing was too dangerous for us to let it linger here any longer. And it was getting stronger with every passing hour. It had taken too many bullets for Quinn to put it down last night. What was going to happen next time?

I didn't want there to *be* a next time.

Approximately twenty-four hours after the shooting, a couple of detectives questioned me about it. I had watched enough episodes of *Crime & Punishment* to know that my story shouldn't mesh too closely with Quinn's—that would look like collusion. Since fear, shock, and confusion ensured that my memories of the night were pretty jumbled and vague, I played on that, contradicting myself a few times but never saying anything that would undermine Quinn's version.

And then, thirty-six hours after the shooting, Lopez was finally downgraded from critical condition and listed as "serious but stable." Which were, ironically, words I knew he'd never use to describe me.

He still wasn't conscious, and I still wasn't allowed to see him. A lingering dread of something going terribly wrong kept me in the waiting room for a few more hours after his condition stabilized. But finally, I went home, showered, and went to bed.

When I woke up, it was evening, forty-eight hours after the shooting, and Lopez was still stable.

He was also, we finally realized, demonically possessed.

Max, Quinn, Lucky, and I entered the hospital in the wee hours of the morning, in the dead of night, the time when people are quiet and spirits are restless.

We had not brought Nelli with us, because there was no way she would fail to attract attention, and our plan required discretion.

We had also not told the Chens what we were doing. This whole business had already caused considerable stress, trouble, damage, and expense to their family business. Since there was a possibility we'd get arrested for what we were about to do here, we decided not to involve any of them in this.

"I'm just not very comfortable with this," said Quinn. "I really think we should take a little more time to *plan*—"

"We haven't got more time," I snapped. "We've got

to exorcise this thing now, before it gets any more of a foothold in Lopez's body!"

While I had gone home to sleep after Lopez was declared out of danger, Quinn had gone to Max's place to ask for help getting rid of his attached demon before any more people got hurt—or any more corpses walked and drooled and cackled. In his sleep-deprived stress over his partner's shooting, he had forgotten about Nelli—until he entered the bookstore and saw her trotting toward him.

But rather than attack him, or even growl and snarl a little for form's sake at the demon that haunted him, Nelli had greeted him like a long lost friend, fawned on him, and asked him for a belly rub—something she only requested of her favorite people.

Max followed up with some experiments that quickly confirmed his hypothesis that Nelli's behavior indicated that Quinn was now demon-free.

Which led to an obvious, inescapable conclusion.

"That entity was too strong to just give up or get lost when it abandoned Danny's body," I said as we made our way along hospital corridors now, heading toward Lopez's room. "If it didn't reattach to you, then where did it go? To the fresh body lying *right there*. Someone who was dead, but just barely."

"Someone who could be revived," said Max.

"Who *was* revived," I said. "Lopez died at the scene. His heart stopped. For a couple of minutes, probably.

Long enough for a strong demon to enter that 'empty house.' "

"So *that's* how it intended to 'live again' even though it can only possess a dead body," Lucky said, impressed by the circle of life and death.

"Well, it's not taking over Lopez's life," I said firmly. "We're banishing this thing tonight."

When we reached the unit where Lopez was being treated, Quinn flashed his badge and informed the desk staff that he was Detective Lopez's partner, and we were an undercover unit assigned to protect the wounded cop. "We have reliable information that an associate of the dead shooter has made threats to 'finish the job.' I hope to receive confirmation by morning that the would-be assailant has been taken into custody. Until then, I am in charge of security for Detective Lopez."

As we went down the corridor to Lopez's room, I said to Quinn, "You're sweating. Try not to sweat."

"This is not a very good plan," he said unhappily.

Precisely because a gang leader had tried to murder Lopez two nights ago, there were two cops on guard outside his door. They knew Quinn and had no problem with his asking them to let three "specialists" into his partner's room for a while. He didn't explain what that meant, and they didn't ask.

Once Max, Lucky, and I were inside the hospital room, Max used a veiling spell on the door. From the corridor, this room would appear perfectly normal, even if exorcising a strong and opportunistic demon got a little messy.

Based on the ancient accounts Max had found of a demon that possessed the dead in search of one who could live again, we had brought a variety of supplies. Christian symbolism had not worked during the previous exorcism, so now we had a whole collection of traditional ancient amulets and lucky charms with us. The key weapon in our arsenal, though, was the enormous water pistol I had smuggled into the hospital. I removed it from my daypack while Max completed the veiling spell on the door.

Quinn stayed outside the room, partly to discourage people from entering while we were here, but mostly because there was a risk that the demon would reattach to him if he were present during the ritual.

When I looked at Lopez lying on his hospital bed, my heart contracted. He looked much better than the last time I had seen him, but far from well. He lay perfectly still, unaware of our presence, with many tubes and devices keeping him stable. It would be a long time, I could see, before he was really whole and well again.

And then? What about us?

Well, we would see. What was important now was that he was alive—and that he *must* be freed of the demon which had quietly slid into his body when he briefly vacated it two nights ago.

"Are we ready?" Max asked.

"Ready as I'll ever be," I said, hoisting my water pistol. We had practiced this a dozen times at the bookstore tonight, to make sure I knew exactly what to do. Precision would be important here.

"Let's get this done," said Lucky. "The boss sent a text saying he wants to see me before the night is over."

"Very well," said Max. "You know what to do."

Max gingerly unrolled an ancient scroll, cleared his throat, and started chanting a three-thousand-year-old exorcism ritual—the one which, he believed based on his research, had last worked effectively on this entity.

While Max did that, Lucky started placing various ancient charms all around Lopez on the bed, creating a circle of positive energy.

I raised my water pistol, took aim at a blank wall, and pressed the trigger to start painting a steady stream of archaic Aramaic symbols high above our heads. Rather than holy water, we were using an elixir recommended by the ancients, made of two parts red wine blessed by a wizard and one part . . . the blood of a mystical familiar. (Nelli had been squeamish but cooperative.)

If this worked, the amulets and chanting would draw the demon out of Lopez, and the enchanted red symbols on the wall would suck the demon out of this dimension and send it back to one where it could do less damage. It might well venture into our dimension again, but hopefully not in our lifetime—nor even Max's.

As Max's chanting rose in volume, tension filled the room—that age-old, never-ending tension between Good and Evil, a battle in which Max had long played a central role and in which I try to play my part. I became aware of heat coming from the bed, and I sensed a golden glow. I paused in my water pistol painting long enough to turn my head and glance at Lopez. To my astonishment, his unconscious body was floating about six inches above the mattress, and he was covered in glowing flames.

"Madre di Dio . . ." Lucky crossed himself. "Were you expecting this?"

A putrescent green fog rose from Lopez's body, writhing up through the flames that covered his flesh, and we heard a bitter, angry, wailing protest. The demonic entity which had briefly possessed him now twisted, fought, and clung, trying to stay with Lopez . . . but the mysterious power which was hidden so deeply inside him that even *he* didn't seem to know about it pushed the entity back out again, aided by Max's chanting. It fought to keep this foul thing from taking over his body, his mind, his life—and this fiery power which did not want to be ruled by anyone else.

After one last howl of rage over its thwarted ambitions, the foggy green entity floated up toward the wine- and blood-red symbols I had pistol-painted on the wall. It writhed like a ball of battling snakes for a few moments, and then it was sucked into the ancient lettering in a hissing, bubbling mist of spattering green and yellow and red—and disappeared.

I turned to the burning bed, wondering what to do about the patient. Before I could ask, though, the flames subsided and sank back into his skin, and his body floated back down to the mattress. He looked better, I thought—healthier, more like a guy who was definitely going to live. But I was worried that all this activity might have jostled or dislodged the bewildering profusion of tubes that seemed to be keeping him stable.

"We should get out of here and let the medical staff tend to him," I said.

Lucky nodded. "Sickrooms always kind of give me the willies, you know?"

Max made a few gestures, spoke some words, and blew some sparkling lavender-colored powder at the doorway, and the veiling spell was lifted. I was about to put my pistol back into my daypack when a woman's voice made me freeze in my tracks.

"What in the name of God is going on here?"

I looked up to see a woman standing in the doorway next to Quinn, who was grimacing at me. She was in her sixties and still beautiful, with long-lashed blue eyes, neatly coiffed red hair, and a trim figure.

"Mrs. Lopez," I said weakly. "How were the Galapagos Islands?"

"Heaven help us," she said, recognizing me. "It's the deranged elf."

"Oh, you remember me?" We had met before.

She entered the hospital room, saw the messy red graffiti high up on the wall that I had painted with my water pistol, and turned to look at me. "I don't even want to know," she said. "Just leave. Leave now. Leave without speaking."

I glanced at Max and Lucky, and I decided that this was an occasion where swift retreat was the best strategy.

So I turned and walked rapidly down the corridor, intending to exit the hospital before anyone had time to start asking questions about what we'd been doing.

Trotting behind me, Quinn said, "I don't think his mother likes you."

"No wonder they made you a detective," I said.

It remained to be seen whether or not Mrs. Lopez's opinion of me was even relevant. After all, right before dying, being possessed, coming back to life, and being exorcised, her son had broken up with me. *Again.*

I supposed we'd just have to wait and see how well it stuck this time . . .

Author's Note

When Max's canine familiar Nelli decided to lunge for Detective Quinn in *The Misfortune Cookie*, I was as surprised as Esther. Quinn seemed like such a normal guy to me. *Damn*. Now I was going to have to rethink the character and plant little hints that something was Not Right about him . . .

Until I realized, no, that was what made Nelli's reaction surprising and made me interested in pursuing the matter: Quinn's apparent normalcy.

Not every unexpected twist or detour works out well when I'm writing. In fact, I wind up deleting most of them. But in Nelli's unexpected reaction to Quinn, I realized that I had the start of my next book.

On the other hand, I was as clueless as Esther about what caused Nelli's behavior. And since I'm nominally in charge here, I have to figure out these things or the book doesn't get written. So after finishing *The Misfortune Cookie*, I cast around for a while, testing and discarding various theories about why Quinn offended Nelli's keen mystical instincts.

By chance, I also happened to be researching paranormal phenomena and ghost hunting at the time. I participated in several investigations, one of them in a particularly notorious location—Bobby Mackey's Music World, a honky-tonk in Kentucky that's considered one of the most haunted places in the country and which has appeared on numerous TV programs.

It was during the investigation at Bobby Mackey's that I first heard about demon attachment and oppression. Although I am a confirmed skeptic, despite being a fantasy writer, some of the accounts related to me in that shadowy, atmospheric place during the dead of night made a strong enough impression on me that I kept jumping out of my skin in my own (cheery, *unat*mospheric) home for the next few nights.

So I pulled all the demonology tomes off the shelves in the "Max and Esther" section of my personal research library and started reading. By the time I had gotten through several volumes, I'd finally figured out what was "wrong" about Quinn.

So here's a shout-out to Dan Smith, author of *Ghosts of Bobby Mackey's Music World*. He's the paranormal investigator who first introduced me to the concept of demon attachment.

I'm also grateful to the various people who took time to answer my questions for this novel about inflicting, treating, and recovering from gunshot wounds. Thanks to my fellow writers with medical backgrounds: Laurie Grant, Victoria Houseman, Scarlet Wilson, and Dianne Drake. And many thanks to Howard R. Bromley, MD, who was very generous with his time and thorough in his answers.

Special thanks to Dr. Ginger Bell, the medical director for the Cincinnati SWAT team, who was a valuable resource and patiently answered my many questions. I was introduced to her by Captain Douglas Wiesman, Training Section Commander of the Cincinnati Police Department.

I met Captain Wiesman when I enrolled in my local Citizens Police Academy in an attempt to learn more about the world that Lopez and Quinn inhabit. It was an excellent course with many eye-opening lectures and some exciting hands-on experience, and I encourage anyone who's interested in learning more about police work to look for a Citizens Police Academy in their region.

It goes without saying (so now witness me saying it) that any mistakes, inaccuracies, embellishments, liberties, or double negatives in the text are strictly my own.

As usual, I offer thanks and praise to the team at DAW Books, still the best publishing house I've ever worked with. In particular, my thanks to editor and publisher Betsy Wollheim, and to managing editor Joshua Starr, who is indeed a star. I hail the genius of Dan Dos Santos, the artist who's created yet another fabulous book cover for this series.

With this particular demon vanquished, Esther Diamond, her friends, and her nemeses will return soon for their next mystical misadventure when they enter a place of unmatched, unbounded, unmitigated Evil: Wall Street.

—Laura Resnick

Sherwood Smith

CORONETS AND STEEL
978-0-7564-0685-1

BLOOD SPIRITS
978-0-7564-0747-6

And now available in paperback:

REVENANT EVE
978-0-7564-0807-7

To Order Call: 1-800-788-6262
www.dawbooks.com

Diana Rowland

To Order Call: 1-800-788-6262
www.dawbooks.com